ENEMY TERRITORY

BOOK 3

ALASKAN SECURITY-TEAM ROGUE

Jemma WESTBROOK

CHAPTER 1

"I'M IN *YOUR* bed?"

Harlow rolled her eyes from side to side, taking in the space around her. The room was about as boring and sparse as it could possibly be.

"Don't look so unimpressed, Mowry."

Harlow lifted one shoulder and let it fall. "I just expected it would be more exciting to be in your bed."

Dutch's gaze never swayed from her face, even as the hazel color of his eyes barely darkened. He shoved one pointed finger out the still-open door and into the hall behind him. "Out."

Harlow grabbed the covers, tossing them off, doing her damndest to make sure they hit the floor in the process. "Fine." She dropped both feet over the side of the bed and jumped out, stomping her way toward the most irritating man in the world. She stopped just in front of him, craning her neck so she could glare up into his too-handsome-for-his-own-good face. "I never wanted to be in it anyway."

Dutch's lips barely twitched.

Did he look like he wanted to smirk at her?

It would be the last fucking thing he did because—

"You're a liar, Mowry." He leaned down, bringing the fresh but almost spicy scent of his skin closer. "And I wasn't talking to you." Dutch's lake-water eyes slowly lifted over her head to where Eli was still standing in the room.

"Got it." Eli rounded the bed and skirted past them, not even glancing at where Harlow still stood, scowl focused on Dutch.

Her '*boss*'.

More like her enemy. The man she had to continually fight every second, of every hour of every day.

For her own well-being.

Eli barely cleared the door frame before Dutch started barking orders at her. "Get your ass back in bed."

"No." She stood a little straighter, glared a little harder. Clearly she hadn't made her position clear.

No man told her what to do.

Not ever again.

"No?" Dutch finally straightened from the relaxed pose he'd been in since his unwanted arrival, pushing off of the spot where he leaned to come to his full height. "I carried you a half mile in the snow last night, watching your fucking lips turn bluer by the second, Harlow. I'll be damned if you're not going to get back in that bed until Eli clears you to get out of it."

"He just did." She smoothed one hand down the front of her shirt.

Nope.

Not her shirt.

"Goddammit, Dutch." Harlow grabbed the fabric of the long-sleeved t-shirt and pulled it away from her body. "What in the hell am I wearing?"

"That's mine too, Mowry." He did smirk at her this time, and hell if it just made him more attractive. The dimple in his left cheek barely peeked out, daring her to look.

Notice one more thing about the man whose very existence threatened her way of life.

Her sanity.

Her safety.

"This is stupid." Harlow tried to sidestep him. Running wasn't her style. Never had been. Even when it was probably the wisest choice.

But Dutch made her want to run. Hide.

Pretend he didn't exist. Find a way to convince herself he was as awful as she had to believe he was.

"Nope." Dutch moved with her, blocking the escape she desperately needed. "I'm not kidding, Harlow. You could have died last night. Might have if—" Dutch cleared his throat. "Here." He shoved one of the cups in his hand her way. "Go get in bed. Drink some coffee. I'll bring you breakfast."

It sounded so good.

Which was exactly why it could not happen.

Because everything sounded good at the beginning.

"I'm not hungry." She pulled away from the coffee he offered. "And I don't want coffee."

"You keep saying shit like that and I'll have Eli come back to check you out again." The smile he gave her this time was different.

Teasing.

She wasn't laughing.

The Dutch-shaped clench in her stomach tightened until it hurt, twisting with an ugliness she'd learned to live with.

Used as fuel to rise above.

A way to be sure she would never again make the mistakes that brought it into her life.

Into her soul.

"Fuck you, Dutch." Harlow shoved him in the center of his chest and ran, her bare feet still a little numb as they hit the industrial carpet of the main hall of the first floor in the rooming building at Alaskan Security.

She sped along the glassed-in connecting hall that led to the main offices.

This was not a time to be caught without backup.

Harlow didn't slow down until she reached the door to the office for Alaskan Security's newest team.

One very few people knew existed.

She flung open the door and stumbled inside, only to find herself staring down a handful of surprised faces.

Pierce stood from where he'd been perched on Mona's desk, looking as unflappable as ever.

It's what made her want to try to prove he was human. Capable of something besides the non-emotion he did his best to convey.

"Is something wrong, Ms. Mowry?" The owner of Alaskan Security came her way. "Is there something you need?"

"Not from you." Harlow kept her eyes on him as she strode to her new work spot, grabbing her laptop and deftly yanking all the cords free before turning back toward the door. "I just wanted my computer." She dropped one hand on her hip and tried to strike a nonchalant pose.

One that made it seem like she wasn't still wearing Dutch's shirt.

Harlow glanced down.

"Oh for fuck's sake."

She needed to get into her own room, strip off the shirt and pajama bottoms that most definitely did not need to be anywhere near her skin, and shower the smell of Dutch off her body.

Eva was up from her desk and rushing Harlow's way. "Are you feeling okay?" She rested both hands on Harlow's shoulders. "You scared the shit out of me last night." She pulled Harlow into a tight hug. "The look on Dutch's face when he saw you had me so freaking worried."

Imagining the look on Dutch's face was not anything she wanted to do. It didn't matter.

The whole incident was cloudy, thank God.

Because it didn't matter how she got out of the woods anymore than it mattered how she got there.

Didn't matter if Dutch gave one shit or two about her condition.

None of it mattered.

All that mattered was that she had a job to do and time was passing her by.

Harlow backed out of Eva's embrace. "I'm going to go grab a shower then I'll come back so we can get started."

"You want me to come with you?" Eva's eyes were still on her, filled with concern and worry.

"N—" A movement in the hall caught Harlow's attention, dragging it to where Dutch's eyes rested square on her as he strode right past his office, heading her way. "Yup." Harlow turned her attention to Eva, doing her best to ignore the weight of his gaze. "I would definitely like for you to come with me."

"Okay." Eva slung one arm around Harlow's shoulders and directed her out of the room and straight toward Dutch. Her face lit up when she saw him. "Is that for Harlow?" Eva snagged the second cup in Dutch's hand. "You are so sweet. Thank you." She passed the cup to Harlow, not even noticing that Dutch didn't look her way for so much as a second.

Harlow eyed him over the lid of her coffee as they moved past and back toward the rooming building.

"How are your toes?" Eva peered down at Harlow's bare feet. "Why don't you have socks on?"

Lots of reasons. "Eli was checking my toes out when I realized I needed my computer."

"So you just sprinted away without putting anything on the feet that almost froze off your body last night?"

Yeah. Pretty much.

"I was in a hurry." Harlow pressed her toes into the floor as they continued walking. "And they're still a little numbish so…"

"Pretty sure that's an even better reason to put some damn socks on." Eva stopped right outside Harlow's door, waiting as she typed in her code, then following her in. She frowned down at the perfectly-made bed.

One of the few parts of her old life Harlow hadn't been able to make herself shake.

"And you made your bed before you ran to get your computer?"

"Yup." It would have been true anyway, so that made it less of a lie, right?

"I don't think I've ever made my bed in my life." Eva dropped down to sit on the corner of the mattress. "Maybe right after I washed my sheets, but that's it."

"That's cool." Harlow grabbed some clothes from her closet and drawer. "I'll be right back."

She didn't wait for Eva's response before ducking into the bathroom attached to her single, hotel-style room, and started shucking clothing, dropping it to the floor as she switched on the water.

Ten minutes later her skin was pink, her hair was dripping wet, and she no longer caught the occasional whiff of Dutch's distractingly manly scent when she moved.

But she still didn't feel better.

Even taking her frustration out on the long mass of dark hair she fought every day didn't help. Today the comb went through easily, raking out the tangles left from being abducted, hauled upside down through the woods, and nearly frozen, with no problem.

There was a light knock at the bathroom door. A second later Eva's head poked in. "You okay?"

"Yup." Harlow snapped on a smile like she had a thousand times in the past two years, before repeating the same lie that always followed. "Fine."

"That's about the fakest smile I've ever seen." Eva bumped the door fully open and came in, dragging the chair from the small corner desk along with her. She spun it Harlow's way. "Sit down. I'll dry your hair for you."

"No thanks."

She'd wanted other women here. Wanted some sort of a buffer between her and all the testosterone swarming Alaskan Security.

But the specific women who showed up were turning out to be almost as big of a problem as Dutch.

"Wasn't asking." Eva shoved the chair closer, knocking the edge of the seat into the backs of

Harlow's knees in a move that sent her butt straight down.

Eva smiled. "There." She snagged the blow dryer from the counter and switched it on. The loud sound of the motor echoing around the small room made it impossible to carry on a conversation, which was perfect.

Talking led to questions and questions led to people trying to get to know her. Wondering about her life before Alaskan Security. But keeping the person she used to be a secret from everyone here was imperative. For her own sanity more than anything else.

It made it easier to pretend the past never happened.

That she was never weak.

Broken.

A shadow of a person who allowed someone else to control every aspect of her life.

Eva's hands were gentle as they wrestled the length of Harlow's dark hair. "I didn't realize how thick your hair was."

Harlow let out the air that seemed to be getting trapped in her lungs more often than not lately. "That's why it's always down."

"It's really pretty." Eva grabbed a brush from the counter and swiped it through as she continued to dry. "I wish my hair was this nice."

Thankfully Eva went quiet again, the action of blow drying seeming to lull her into a trance. By the time she finished, Harlow was itching to get up and get away.

13

Talking about other people's problems made it easy to deflect. Most people loved to talk about themselves. Preferred it actually. Unfortunately, the longer Harlow knew Eva, the clearer it was becoming that Eva wasn't like most people.

Harlow jumped up from the chair. "Thanks." She hurried out of the bathroom, nearly toppling over the man sitting on the edge of the bed in her haste to get away from a potentially invasive moment. Harlow pressed back, trying to put some space between her and the sexy smirk shot her way. "What in the hell are you doing here?"

"We weren't done talking." Dutch sipped at the lidded cup in his hand like breaking into her room was the most normal thing in the world.

"How did you get in here?" She shoved one finger his way. "And why are you on my bed?"

Dutch's eyes flicked to the bathroom doorway before coming back to rest squarely on hers. "Only seems fair since you've been in mine."

"So, I'm gonna go." Eva quick-stepped across the room, headed straight for the door.

"No!" Harlow started to run after her, but Dutch stood up, blocking her path with his broad body.

"We'll see you later." Dutch's tone was smooth and easy, carrying the smile she would consider smacking off his face if he didn't have his back to her.

Dutch didn't face her until the door clicked shut behind Eva.

When it did, the turn of his body was torturously slow. The line of his lips barely turned down in a frown.

Which made him slightly less devastatingly attractive.

But only slightly.

And attractive men were the devil. Sometimes literally.

"You can't keep running from me, Harlow."

"Stop calling me that." It was too familiar. Too close.

"It's your name." He moved in. "But I'm happy to call you something else if it makes you happy."

"You do have something else to call me." She crossed her arms over her chest, a knee-jerk reaction to being so close to a man she wasn't in control of. "Mowry works just fine."

Dutch studied her for a minute, his eyes sharp as they moved over her face, never venturing below her neck to the baggy, shapeless sweater she layered over a binding sports bra and long-sleeved t-shirt. He barely shook his head. "Everyone else can call you that, Harlow. Not me. Not anymore."

"This isn't a negotiation." She sucked in a breath, straightening to her full height, which was still not much. "And I don't want you calling me Harlow."

There was a split second where his expression almost changed, his features almost softened, but it was gone before she could decide what it meant.

"Fine." Dutch reached down to grab the cup Eva stole from him earlier, holding it out to her.

Harlow barely glanced at the forgotten drink. "It's cold."

"It's not." He pressed it closer, his mouth turning up in a wicked smile. "I freshened it up for you, Darling."

Harlow blinked up at him.

Did he just say—

"What did you just call me?" The best thing in the world she could do right now was snap the lid off that damn cup and chuck it in his face. Make her feelings for him as clear as possible.

Dutch eased a little closer, closing a tiny bit more of the space between them. "You said I couldn't call you by your name and I agreed to your terms, Darling."

That one word eased down her spine slow and warm.

Darling.

It wasn't some casually tossed out false endearment like sugar or sweetheart.

Darling.

It was almost intimate, and that was something she could never be with Dutch Mackey.

"Why would you call me that?" She worked hard to be forceful. Abrasive. Aggravating. But the words still sounded more like the woman she used to be.

The woman who was too naïve to see what was right in front of her face and then waited too long to do something about it.

Dutch was even closer now, making Harlow's arms twist tighter into place.

She wasn't scared of him. Wasn't worried Dutch would try to hurt her.

That was most of the problem.

Dutch took a long, slow breath she could almost feel in her own lungs. Probably because hers were screaming for air since she hadn't inhaled since he came close. His hold on the cup tightened as he studied her.

"Don't look at me like that." Harlow backed up, trying to put more space between them.

Dutch stayed where he was, feet fused to the floor, lips pressed into a thin line as she pressed tighter to the wall.

He took a step back.

Then another, before sitting down on her bed in the same spot he occupied minutes ago. His body took on a relaxed-looking pose, knees spread, arms draped across them, but the clench of his jaw made it clear he was anything but relaxed.

"Let's start again." Dutch set his cup on the nightstand next to hers before leaning forward, hands clasped together loosely. "How are you feeling?"

The wrap of her arms over her chest loosened just a bit. "What?"

"You could have died last night. I need to know you're okay."

"Oh." The tension in her sternum eased a little. Maybe all of this was just Dutch being a pain in the ass. Maybe this was simply about him being concerned she wouldn't be able to pull her weight. "I'm going back to work today."

"That's not what I asked." His tone was low and calm. "How are you feeling?"

"I can still do my job if that's what you're worried about." This was easier. This was comfortable. The banter. The bickering. It was safe.

Distant.

"That's not what I'm concerned with at all." Dutch worked his jaw from side to side. "I don't want you to run yourself down. I want to be sure you get the rest you need."

Harlow rolled her eyes. "Don't worry your pretty little head about me, Dutch. I'm a big girl. I've handled worse than this."

She clamped her mouth shut, eyes snapping to the man in front of her, hoping he missed the last bit of what she said.

He had not.

Dutch teeth were clenched so tightly together he might not have any left in the next five seconds, and chances were good the twitching in his eye might rupture a blood vessel.

"Good to know." He suddenly stood, immediately turning for the door.

The breath of relief was barely out of her lungs when he turned and stalked back her way, stopping right in front of her. He pointed at her, moving the single finger down her frame and around the cross of her arms. "I don't know what the fuck this is about, but I do know one thing."

Harlow waited, forcing air to move in and out of her lungs for what felt like forever.

But Dutch didn't continue.

And she needed him gone.

"What is it you know, Pretty Boy?"

18

His pointer turned, the pad of it pressing just under her chin. "If I find whoever hurt you, I will bury him in a deep fucking hole."

CHAPTER 2

DUTCH DIDN'T BOTHER knocking on Shawn's door before going in. "What the fuck happened to Harlow?"

Pierce was sitting in one of the chairs across from Team Rogue's mission coordinator, looking as relaxed as ever.

Dutch's fingers curled with the need to punch something. Mostly Pierce.

How in the hell he could be relaxed at a time like this bothered the shit out of him.

Shawn's grey eyes shifted to Pierce before coming back to Dutch. "I thought Eli checked her out and said she was fine?"

"I'm not fucking talking about that." Dutch crossed to the desk, leaning both hands against the surface. "I mean before she came here."

Shawn leaned back in his seat. "You know damn well I couldn't tell you if I knew anything."

"Really? You're going to play the confidentiality card right now?"

"I'm unwilling to compromise the security and future of Alaskan Security to appease your curiosity, Dutch."

He snapped a glare Pierce's way. "I'm not talking to you."

"You should be. I'm the one who makes the rules."

Dutch slowly turned to face the owner of Alaskan Security. "If you know what happened to her—"

"If I knew what happened to Ms. Mowry I wouldn't be at liberty to disclose it." Pierce stood, buttoning the jacket of his expensive-as-shit suit. "But I would assume you know what Ms. Mowry is capable of hiding. If she didn't want us to see something in her past I can assure you, we wouldn't."

Dutch looked from Pierce to Shawn. His team lead sat silently, expression unreadable.

"If there is something you wish to know about Ms. Mowry, then I would suggest figuring out how to obtain the information from her." Pierce moved toward the door, pausing at Dutch's side. "Because that's the only way you will find it."

Dutch stared at Shawn as Pierce left, the nearly-silent click of the door as it closed pissing him off even more.

How could they be calm right now?

"Harlow's business is her own, Dutch." Shawn leaned back in his seat, steepling his fingers together. "Do you want her knowing about yours?"

The comment stalled the anger.

But only for a second.

"My past didn't leave me fucking scared of people who are just trying to help me." He'd seen the flicker of fear in her eyes when he got too close. Saw the involuntary way she tried to protect herself. Preparing for something he didn't want to imagine.

"Is that what you're trying to do, Dutch? Help her?"

His focus zeroed in on Shawn. Dutch snapped one hand out, swiping across Shawn's desk to knock a cup holding pens across the room. "Fuck you."

Shawn didn't react. "Feel better?"

No he didn't feel fucking better.

She shouldn't be scared of him.

Harlow shouldn't be scared of anyone.

But especially him.

The sight of her last night, lying in the snow, no coat, no shoes, body convulsing from hypothermia.

It fucking broke him.

Torched the lines he tried to draw between them.

And once they were gone there was nothing to hold him back.

At least he didn't think there was. Not until this morning.

"Something happened to her." Dutch dropped into one of the chairs across from

Shawn's desk, catching his head in his hands. "Something fucked-up."

"Does it affect her ability to do her job?"

Why did everyone think his concern had anything to do with her job? "I don't give a shit about that."

"You should. You need her to be able to pull her weight. You were struggling to keep up before everything went to hell. There's no way you could handle it all now."

"Is that all you care about? The weight she can pull?"

"She's part of our team. A team that is only as good as its weakest member. Her ability to do her job should matter to all of us." Shawn eyed Dutch. "If you want to worry about more it's your problem."

Problem?

Harlow would never be a problem.

"Fine." Dutch stood, the sudden move aggravating the ache throbbing in his leg. He went for the door, working hard to keep the limp out of his step.

"Dutch."

He almost didn't stop. So far Shawn had done nothing but piss him off more.

Dutch pulled the door open and turned. "What?"

"Go see Eli. Have him make sure you didn't hurt yourself last night."

"I'm fine." Dutch yanked the door closed and stalked to his office, digging into the top desk drawer for the bottle he was after, knocking back a couple of pills with a coffee chaser just as Brock poked his head in the door.

His eyes lingered on the bottle still sitting on the desk. "How ya feeling?

"Fine."

Brock lifted a brow.

"Just a little stiff." Dutch grabbed the bottle and stashed it away.

"Probably because you carried Mowry all the way back to headquarters through three feet of snow." Brock came in, settling into a chair. "She remember what happened?"

Dutch shrugged.

Harlow was in shock by the time he got to her. She barely gave him any shit when he found her and then was quiet the whole way back.

He'd assumed her silence was due to the shock of what just happened.

Now he wasn't so sure.

"How's she doing this morning?" Brock stretched his legs out in an easy move Dutch could barely remember being able to make.

"Eli said she's fine." It was the easiest answer to give Brock.

And it was the only one he really had.

Harlow wasn't fine. He could see it in her eyes. What happened last night bothered her on a level he didn't know enough to be able to understand.

But he wanted to.

Would if it killed him.

"Eva said you were in Mowry's room this morning, so I assumed you'd gone to check on her." Brock's eyes were too focused.

Looking too close.

"I figured she'd need some coffee." It was the easiest excuse. One he'd used hundreds of times as a reason to see her.

And as a way to cut down on the excessive amounts of caffeine the woman consumed. She was going to stop her heart with the stuff. Might already have if he hadn't started sneaking her decaf.

"Harlow always needs coffee." Brock chuckled. "I swear it makes up half her bodyweight."

That probably wasn't as much as Brock thought it was.

He'd been surprised by how light she was last night. With the baggy clothes Harlow always wore it was impossible to tell how tiny she really was. The curves he'd imagined hiding under the bulky knit of her sweaters and loose-cut jeans were not as present in reality, making her seem so much more delicate.

Breakable.

The sound of her voice carried through the open door, sending Dutch to his feet and the burning ache he lived with flaring to life.

"I'm fine." Harlow marched past his office, not even glancing his way, computer tucked under one arm and the coffee he gave her clutched in her free hand. Eli trailed along beside her. "Pierce just wants to be sure you aren't having any problems."

Harlow stopped suddenly, turning to face Eli. "You tell Pierce to mind his own fucking business."

Eli's shoulders dropped. "I'm just trying to do my job, Mowry."

"Then go do your job somewhere else." Her attention snapped to where Dutch stood in the doorway to his office. Her pale blue eyes barely raked down him before snapping away. "Fuck!"

Harlow screeched out a frustrated-sounding wail as she marched down the hall to the space Pierce dedicated to Alaskan Security's most valuable asset.

Brock and Eli stared at her as she left.

Finally Brock leaned in close to Dutch's side. "I think you did something to piss her off, man."

"I got that." Dutch wiped one hand down his face, trying to work up the gumption to go back to his office. Take his place in the world and be happy with it.

But this office wasn't his place. Not anymore.

There was only one place he should be.

"I'm gonna go talk to Pierce."

****

"WHAT THE FUCK is going on?" Harlow jumped up from behind the desk at the front of the large room, eyes wide. "What are you doing?"

Pierce strode into the room as soon as the desk Dutch and Brock were carrying in cleared the doorway. "Dutch made a good argument for moving his workspace." Pierce's gaze moved

27

over Harlow's area. "And for structuring things a little differently than I originally planned."

Harlow's head slowly turned his way. "Did he now?"

"He's been the main technical support for Alaskan Security until now, and I believe you will find him to be an asset to your team, Ms. Mowry." Pierce pointed to the wall behind Harlow's desk, turning his attention to where one of the facility management staff stood. "Clear this wall for the monitor bank."

Harlow stared at Pierce as he continued to bark out orders to the men scrambling to do his bidding. "Wait." She blinked a few times. Her eyes barely flicked Dutch's way. "Did you say *our* team?"

Pierce held his arms out wide, fingers stretching toward the corners of the room. "This is your team, correct?"

Harlow's eyes came Dutch's way once more. "So his team will work with our team?"

Dutch set the desk he'd been sitting at for the past five years beside Harlow's, bumping it until they were in line, sitting side by side. "Not my team." He took a few slow steps toward the woman watching him with wary eyes. "Just me."

"He's part of your team now, Ms. Mowry." Pierce unbuttoned the jacket he was never without before sliding out of it and draping it across Mona's desk. "It doesn't make sense for him to be in a separate part of the building when you can each benefit from the other's abilities." Pierce unbuttoned one cuff, rolling the fabric of his sleeve up his forearm. "I need you to be close. Time is something we don't have the luxury of wasting any longer." He repeated the process on the other sleeve. Once it was in place, Pierce climbed on top of Dutch's bare desktop and slid one of the ceiling tiles to the side, reaching up to feel around for a second before gripping the hidden joists and pulling himself up and into the ceiling.

"What is he doing?" Mona stood from her desk, eyes wide as she stared at the ceiling.

"Dropping down cables." One of the maintenance men stood watching, one hand resting on his sizable gut. "I can't get my ass up there."

A second later one of the tiles near the wall lifted up before sliding away. A tangle of lines dropped down. Pierce leaned out of the opening, his attention on Dutch. "Check and make sure I got them all."

Dutch quickly sorted the mess. "We're good."

"Excellent." Pierce disappeared as the tile slid into place. A few heartbeats later his feet came into view, hanging for a second before his whole body dropped down, landing perfectly upright on the desk.

"Thanks." Dutch stood back as Pierce jumped down. "I could have gotten them."

Pierce's gaze barely shifted. "Of course." His eyes drifted to where Mona stood. "Next time."

"I don't like this." Harlow finally managed to find the fight Dutch expected from the very start. He knew this would piss her off. Knew Harlow would want nothing to do with him being so close.

She was going to have to get over it.

This made sense. He needed her, and whether she wanted to admit it or not, she needed him. And Pierce was right. When things went bad there wasn't time to run down the hall for help.

They should be close.

"I think it's a good idea." Eva leaned back against her desk, arms crossed as she eyed the setup being assembled. "We need all the help we can get right now."

Pierce's gaze slowly moved to Mona. "What do you think, Ms. Ayers. Do you believe Dutch will be a worthwhile addition to your team?"

Mona's skin paled the tiniest bit.

Pierce was a lot by anyone's standards, let alone a woman like Mona.

Eva's friend was quiet and definitely used to blending into the world. Going with the flow to avoid confrontation or disagreement.

That wasn't going to fly around here.

Mona's lips rolled in, pressing tight together as her eyes bounced from Pierce to Eva to Dutch to Harlow. "Well." She cleared her throat, shifting on her feet.

"There's no wrong answer, Ms. Ayers." Pierce's tone was softer than normal. "Just the truth as you see it."

Mona's gaze landed on Dutch, sizing him up. "I think he should stay. We will be stronger if we work as a single team."

"Very good." Pierce's agreement carried a note of praise. "Thank you for your opinion, Ms. Ayers."

"Her opinion is wrong." Harlow tipped her chin up a little as Pierce faced her.

"That's not how opinions work, Ms. Mowry." Pierce stepped closer to Harlow as he rolled the cuffs of his sleeves into place. "Everyone is entitled to have, and should feel comfortable voicing, theirs." Pierce continued to move in Harlow's direction. "And I will respect and honor her opinion the same way I do yours."

"Well my opinion is she's wrong." Harlow barely shifted back. "We don't need Dutch in here."

"While I appreciate hearing your opinion, Ms. Mowry, you are outnumbered." Pierce snagged his jacket from Mona's desk, pulling it on as he continued to close in on Harlow.

Her arms suddenly came up, curling around her middle in an almost cross.

Almost.

Dutch stepped between them, blocking Pierce, stopping him in his tracks. He barely had time to plant his feet before a hard shove knocked him forward and into Pierce.

Harlow darted out from behind him. "I don't need you to protect me, asshole."

Before Dutch could blink she was gone, bolting from the room to race away from him for the third time today.

"Damn it." Dutch glared at Pierce as he went for the still-open door. "Don't come at her like that."

Pierce's dark brows shot up in surprise.

It made sense. Everyone at Alaskan Security saw Harlow as unbreakable.

So did he until this morning.

Harlow's dark head disappeared around the corner leading to the rooming building, putting her a good clip ahead of him. By the time Dutch got to her door there was no sign of the woman who took up more and more of his thoughts with each passing day.

From the second she walked into his life, Harlow had done her best to shove him far away. Make sure he disliked her as much as she claimed to dislike him.

But it would take so much more than she had to dish out for him to dislike Harlow.

Dutch knocked. "Open the door, Darling."

"Don't fucking call me that." Something hit the other side of the steel.

"Does that mean I can call you Harlow?"

"No. It means you can go the hell away."

"Not going away, Harlow." Dutch rested his head against the cool metal, breathing deep. Seeing her like this made him antsy. Agitated.

And that was the last thing she needed from him.

"I just want to talk to you, Harlow." He inhaled slow and steady, trying to calm the tone of his voice. "Please open the door."

"Not happening." Her voice was louder now. Like she was right on the other side.

"What happened?"

"You just moved all your shit into my office. What do you think happened?"

"I'm not talking about that and you know it." Dutch eased a little closer, wishing there was no door making it impossible to see her face.

He needed to know she was okay. That was part of the reason he convinced Pierce to move him.

He'd only recently admitted to himself how much the dark-haired spitfire mattered, and then someone attempted to snatch her away.

Tried to steal the first bit of hope he'd had in so long he couldn't remember.

It's why he couldn't just let this go. Bide his time a little longer.

The silence dragged out. Seconds turned to minutes.

Harlow really didn't think she would have to talk to him.

She might not have to talk to him, but hell if she was going to be alone when she was clearly struggling. He knew what that was like. Had done it to himself when he was young and proud.

Dutch turned his back to the door and slowly lowered his ass to the floor, resting back as he tried to straighten his aching leg.

Carrying Harlow had sent the mangled muscles into a fit, and they were cramping and tight, making the normally steady drone of pain he'd learned to live with an almost unbearable stab.

Eli had muscle relaxers that would knock him out and give the leg time to recover, but that would mean leaving Harlow to deal with whatever this was by herself.

And that wasn't going to happen.

CHAPTER 3

HARLOW STARED DOWN at her sneakers and the man sprawled across them. "You're really starting to piss me off, Dutch."

One dark brow cocked as he watched her from his spot half inside her room, half in the hall. "Just now?"

She was tired and it had nothing to do with not getting enough sleep. "What are you doing?"

"I'm making sure you're okay." He slowly pushed up to a sitting position, keeping his tall frame partly in her room.

"I'm fine." Why was it so difficult to understand? "Eli said so. You heard it yourself."

Dutch eased up from the floor, taking longer than Harlow expected to get both feet under him. Even when he did, his stance favored one leg.

"Did your leg fall asleep sitting there?" The thought that he'd been sitting on the floor outside her room for the three hours she'd spent on her personal computer made guilt tug at her gut.

It shouldn't. If he was stupid enough to park his ass there, then it was his own damn fault.

"I'm fine." Dutch shifted, putting weight on both legs. The move made the line of his jaw a little tighter.

"Good. That makes two of us then." Harlow smirked at him.

"You know what?" Dutch stepped past her, not even asking to come in. He dropped to her bed, giving her a visual she definitely didn't need burned into her brain yet again. "I'm not fine, actually." He reached down to grab the leg of his well-cut pants, yanking up the hem.

Harlow took a step back, eyes locked on the bit of his body revealed as all the air rushed from her lungs. "Your leg."

His eyes were on her, unwavering.

But Dutch didn't say a word.

What was left of the flesh on his shin and calf was mangled and scarred. The skin was puckered and discolored. Twisted.

Angry.

Ruined.

The arms across her chest tightened as if they could shield her from the sight.

The pain it brought.

The sadness.

Harlow bit her lip, pinching off the urge to ask what happened.

Dutch was offering her his own story in exchange for hers.

But this wasn't something she would bargain with.

Could bargain with.

What she needed to do was ignore it. Shove it all back where it belonged.

The memories.

The fear.

The embarrassment.

If she could ignore it long enough, it would go back where it was supposed to be, buried deep enough it didn't affect her. She put it there once, she could do it again.

"I was in the military. A Marine."

Harlow backed up a little more, shaking her head. "I don't need to know this."

"You do." Dutch dropped the tapered leg of his pants back into place, giving her heart a blessed break from the assault the sight waged on it. "It's how we met. Me. Pierce. Shawn. Brock and Wade."

Harlow squeezed herself tighter. This was not a good story. She could see it in his eyes. In the set of his jaw. The slight slump of his shoulders.

"And Jack."

Harlow's attention jumped to Dutch's face. "Who's Jack?"

"He was our friend." Dutch's tone softened. "Our brother."

Was.

She didn't want to know what happened to this man.

This Jack.

"Please stop."

"No." Dutch didn't come any closer, but his presence almost seemed to wrap around her, filling the small room she called home. Where she was safe.

Protected.

Hidden.

But Dutch being in this sacred space didn't feel intrusive.

Even though it was.

"We were sent out on a secret mission in the Middle East." Dutch's eyes grew distant. "They were bombing all around us—"

"Stop." Harlow put her hands out. This couldn't happen. It was too painful.

But not for her.

"Please." She rushed at him, her palms pressing against his face, covering his mouth. "Just stop."

Dutch held perfectly still, eyes locked onto hers.

His skin was barely raspy, rough with the day's growth of the dark hair across his jaw and chin.

But his lips were soft where they pressed her palm.

Harlow yanked her hands away, this time using them to cover her own mouth.

She shouldn't have touched him. She'd been successfully avoiding it for almost two months.

"Jack was hit."

She closed her eyes, squeezing them tight against the reality of Dutch's life.

His past.

"I went back for him." Dutch's voice was so low. So soft. "We almost made it out."

Harlow's throat clogged, tightening so much she couldn't swallow. Couldn't speak.

Could barely breathe.

A barely-there touch swept across her cheek. "I'm not telling you this to make you upset, Harlow."

Her eyes snapped open. "Then why in the hell are you telling me?"

What Dutch was doing wasn't fair, and it sure as hell wasn't nice. If he only knew—

"Everyone has a past, Harlow. One that affects them." The finger that touched her cheek moved to snag a strand of hair caught in the dampness on her skin, pulling it free with a gentle touch. "I work in the office because I can't go out in the field. Sometimes I lock up and I can't move. My brain shuts down."

But he was out there last night. Running through the snow like there was nothing wrong with him.

But there was. She'd seen it with her own eyes.

"I came out last night because you were out there, Harlow." Dutch barely eased closer. "The thought of you being hurt and afraid—"

She straightened. "I wasn't afraid."

Dutch's lips barely lifted. "No. You weren't." His gentle touch brushed her skin again. "I need to be honest with you about something, Harlow."

She should fight with him. Tell him he couldn't call her that.

But it sounded so good on his lips.

"I've been alone a long damn time, trying to get my shit together." The careful glide of his finger moved along the line of her jaw. "And I've decided I'm done being alone."

"Good for you." She tried to make the words snap out. To be the bitch she'd worked so hard to show the world.

But it just wasn't in her right now.

Maybe because of the devastating sadness Dutch's story brought.

Or maybe it was because the soft way he touched her made it impossible to hurl the bad attitude she wore like armor his way.

"Not just for me, Harlow." The finger on her skin paused at the tip of her chin. "I plan for you to be a part of it."

"No, thank you."

"I'm going to wear you down."

"I doubt it."

The smile teasing his lips widened until the white line of his teeth flashed out at her along with the tiny dimple in his cheek. "I plan to prove you wrong."

"That doesn't even make any sense." She'd worked so hard to be undesirable. She hid her body. Acted like a bitch.

She was abrasive. Irritating. Insulting.

"Then you're clearly not paying attention." Dutch's head barely tipped to one side. "You might have everyone else here believing the line of shit you're feeding them." He leaned a tiny bit closer, bringing along the smell she worked so hard to scrub from her skin. "Not me."

Wanting a man in more than just the physical sense was something she decided never to do, and had been quite successful at.

Men were threatened by her. By what she was capable of.

This one should be no different.

Yet here they fucking were.

Suddenly Dutch straightened. "Come on."

"No." Harlow snapped her spine as straight as the thing would go, tipping her head back to glare right into his handsome face. "You come on." She marched past him.

He wasn't the boss of her.

No one was.

"I'll happily go wherever you tell me to go, Harlow."

He was trying to be charming and it grated on the thick hide she'd grown. "How about hell then?"

Dutch stopped. "I've already been there, Darling. Didn't enjoy it."

41

She should just keep going. Get the hell away from this man and this whole situation.

Unfortunately, she'd already tried that. More than once just this morning.

Instead Harlow turned to face him, ready to go to battle in the kind of fight that kept people at bay.

But the haunted look in his eyes stopped the words from coming, stole the desire and replaced it with a pain that sometimes seemed never-ending.

"You've been there too. I can see it." Dutch came toward her, moving slower than normal, gaze sharp where it rested on her face. "It won't go away, Harlow. Stuffing it down will only make it worse."

"You're wrong."

"I'm not. Not about any of it." He stood in front of her now, nearly a head taller than she was. Wide shoulders and long arms cut with the kind of muscle that usually made her stomach turn. "But I wish I was."

The single statement hit her harder than anything else he'd said. The emotion it carried was clear and unhindered.

"I thought I could go about this a different way, Harlow." Dutch took a long breath. "I thought I knew how to chase you." His eyes snagged hers. "But I was wrong."

"I don't want to be chased."

"Then stop running." Dutch leaned down, bringing his eyes level with hers. "Because that's the only way it's not going to happen."

Why did he have to be like this? Why couldn't Dutch see her like everyone else did? It was always right there in front of his face. She made sure to remind him regularly.

"I think right now the truth is the most important thing I can give you, Mowry." Dutch straightened, tucking one hand into the pocket of his pants. "I am coming for you, and you should realize I'm not the kind of man who does something like this without being absolutely positive it's what I want."

"What about what I want?"

She expected the question to deflate him a little, knock his certainty down a peg.

At least make him pause.

"You're not willing to admit what you want, Harlow." He smirked at her. "Yet."

She glared at him a second longer. "I'm going to work."

"I'll see you in there, Darling."

If he called her that in the office she'd kill him. String his fine ass up from the ceiling now that she knew it could hold a man's weight.

Harlow was still cursing him when she plopped down at her desk. By now it was well into the afternoon. She'd wasted most of the day because of Dutch.

Not necessarily wasted. The time in her room was well-spent making sure the reason she was more than a little happy to come to Alaska was still right where she left him.

"You okay?" Eva studied Harlow from where she sat, eyes narrowed over the monitor on her desk.

"Yup." Harlow reached into the drawer of her desk and pulled out the giant cup she filled about this time every day. "I'll be back." She unscrewed the lid as she walked into the large space that was more of a rec room than a break room. It had both a ping pong and pool table, along with ample seating in the form of couches and comfy chairs. The kitchen at one end was state-of-the-art with a commercial grade fridge and freezer, along with a gas range and an island large enough to seat twelve around the back side. This time of day the space was usually empty, which meant she could enjoy her afternoon ritual in peace.

Today was not one of those days.

"Sit down." His tone wasn't sweet like it was before. This time it was sharper. Almost irritated.

"What in the hell, Dutch?" Both her arms dropped to her sides. "Just leave me alone."

"Nope." He slid a plate across the island. "I've been with you since you got up this morning and you haven't eaten anything." He tipped his head to the chair behind the plate stacked with the biggest sandwich she'd ever seen. "Sit your ass down and stop being a pain in mine."

The shift in his attitude made the offer tempting. It was easier to fight with him. Safer. "It better not taste like shit."

"Do I look like I make a shitty sandwich, Mowry?"

Her eyes moved over his body more than they should have. What the man looked like he was capable of accomplishing shouldn't matter.

Dutch bumped the plate closer then turned to start packing the items lined across the counter back into the fridge.

She eyed the hunk of carbs and cheese. It looked freaking fantastic. The scent of smoked turkey made her empty stomach growl so hard it ached.

It was just a sandwich. And he called her a pain in the ass.

So that was something.

Harlow walked silently to the island and slid onto the stool. Dutch continued what he was doing, back to her as she picked up one half of the monstrous thing and tried to get her mouth around it. The sub bun it was built on was soft with the tiniest bit of brown crust on the outside. Piles of lettuce, tomato, cheese and turkey were topped with pickles and some sort of brown mustard.

Dutch didn't look at her as he snagged a bag of chips and two bottles of water and rounded the island. When he sat on the stool right next to hers the pace of her heart picked up, but not for the usual reason.

He grabbed the other half of the sandwich and took a bite.

Harlow scoffed around the bite filling her mouth. "I thought this was mine."

"You know damn well you can't eat this whole thing. It's as big as you are." He shook the opened bag of chips at her, bouncing them around inside as he lifted his brows. The scent of vinegar barely burned her nose.

She leaned to peek at the label.

"They're your favorites." He shook the bag of salt and vinegar chips again, tempting her.

She snatched the biggest one she could see. "Lots of people like these. They're always here."

Dutch shook his head. "No one likes these but you, Harlow."

Her eyes snapped to the matching bag sitting on the counter.

Dutch scooted the bag closer to her and went back to eating his half of their sandwich. Harlow stared straight ahead, fighting to keep her eyes from trying to peek at the man beside her.

There had been men since—

But they were easy to keep in line. Capable of being controlled by her snark and honestly, well-timed sex.

When they tried to get too close, she cut them loose, making sure the break stung enough they'd never try to come back.

But Dutch wasn't like that.

At least he didn't seem like that.

At first she thought maybe they could work some sort of arrangement out. She'd even tried a few times at the very beginning. But after being at Alaskan Security for a few months, it was obvious there would be no way to have a clean cut if something went wrong.

"What are you two doing?" Shawn went straight for the fridge, pulling out a bottle of water before turning to lean against the row of cabinets as he tipped it back and guzzled half.

"Just grabbing a late lunch." Dutch shoved in the last of his half of the sandwich before washing it down with his own water.

Shawn nodded to the bag of chips in front of her, his attention still on Dutch. "You want me to put a bag of those on our next order?"

Harlow's head snapped Dutch's way, but he didn't even give her a glance. "How about two?"

"Got it." Shawn nodded as he straightened. "I've got a meeting with the other team leads. I'll let you know if I hear anything interesting."

"Thanks." Dutch scooted the plate Harlow's way. "Finish up, Mowry. We've got work to do."

At least he was back to calling her Mowry. "Don't tell me what to do."

Dutch leaned close, resting one arm across the back of her chair. "Someone has to, otherwise you'll run your ass into the ground."

And then he was gone, up and away before the pang of fear had a chance to dig into her gut, leaving her to finish her sandwich while he wiped down the counter and rinsed off the knife he used.

By the time Dutch was done, so was she. He snagged the empty plate, adding it to the dishwasher before setting it to run.

Harlow rolled up the bag of chips and pinched on a bag clip.

"Thank you, Harlow." Dutch took them from her hand, the tips of his fingers barely brushing hers. The barely-there graze sent a ripple of warmth across her chest and down her arms.

Dutch slid the chips into the spot she always found them when the craving hit.

His eyes were soft and warm as they rested on hers. "You ready, Mowry?"

CHAPTER 4

HE'D SPENT THE whole damn day chasing her, and based on the look on Harlow's face, he might be about to chase her again.

"You look like you're considering being a pain in the ass."

The stiffness in her spine barely relaxed. "I'm always a pain in the ass. I would have expected you to realize that by now."

From day one she'd been about the most stubborn, hard-headed, mouthy woman he'd ever met. "I've definitely realized that, Harlow." Dutch slowly stepped closer, giving her time to see him coming.

What happened last night had her jumpy as hell. At least before, he could get close without having to see fear in her eyes.

"Have you done any work today?" Dutch gave her the verbal jab as he rested one hand against her back.

Harlow jumped away, blue eyes snapping to the palm hovering in the air.

"Too soon?" He gave her a wink. "It's okay, Mowry. I can be patient."

He wanted to have with her what Wade had with Bess. What Eva and Brock had.

It went so fast for them. In a matter of days they were in deep. Crazy about each other. Inseparable.

It didn't appear his path would be the same.

Which was fine. He learned a long time ago the value of patience. Especially when trauma was involved.

And Harlow definitely had trauma somewhere in her past.

"You think." She snarked it out at him as she spun away to march toward their shared work space. When she barged into the office Dutch was right behind her, close enough he nearly collided with Harlow's back when she stopped short.

"You've got to be fucking kidding me." Harlow's palms both came up to rest at each side of her face as she stared at the front of the room.

It was a mess. Wires everywhere. Three of the guys from maintenance were punching holes in the wall, dragging down additional wire to make room for the added power needs their new setup would involve.

Harlow's arms dropped to her sides as she slow-walked toward the bank of monitors that reached the ceiling. They sat ten wide and ten tall. "There's a hundred monitors here." She turned to Dutch. "Why are there a hundred monitors?"

"Last night someone came to our front door and tried to take something very valuable." He stayed put, wishing he could go be closer to her. Find a way to ease the worry pinching her brow. "They will come back, Harlow. We have to be ready."

She stared at the flat screens lined across the room. "What will they display?"

"Depends on what we need to be watching." Dutch dared to take a few steps her way. "We have a rotating schedule of men from each team keeping an eye on things around here, but now we have to be everywhere." He looked to the bank of monitors. "We have to watch it all."

Pierce had been in the process of recruiting individuals to fill his position on Alpha, Beta, and Shadow. Until recently Dutch ran the tech for them all. The past year it had been consuming, but still doable.

After this it was impossible.

"I work for Rogue exclusively now. We will add three more tech coordinators, eventually making them part of our team. One for Alpha, one for Beta, and one for Shadow."

"Why in here? She glanced to where Mona and Eva sat at their workspaces. "I thought this was just our room."

"It was going to be." Dutch glanced toward the other women. "But until we find out what the hell is going on, we have to do everything possible to keep our teams safe." He turned back to the woman at his side. "That means we have to have as many eyes on this as possible."

Eva stood to join them. "Mona and I were able to get in touch with part of our team from Cincinnati." She slid her butt onto Dutch's desk. "I didn't sugarcoat anything." Her eyes moved to Mona. "There were fifteen people we thought would be a good fit for this job. Of those, nine agreed to come here."

"Nine?" That number seemed high. "You think they'll stay?"

Eva shrugged. "I made the circumstances really clear."

"When are they coming up?" Training nine people in a time like this wasn't ideal, but their options were nonexistent. They had to have more help even before the shit hit the fan. Now it was critical.

"Rico said he can fly down and get them in three days."

Dutch looked to Harlow. "Can we be ready to train by then?"

Harlow's eyes shifted from him to Eva. She gave him a tiny nod. "I guess we have to be."

Eva's brows came together as she studied Harlow. "Are you sure you're okay today?"

"I'm fine." Harlow turned, going to her desk and flopping into her seat.

Eva glanced Dutch's way. "I think Mona and I are going to head out. There's not much else we can do until they have everything set up here."

"It will be up and running when you get here in the morning. We've got a team going out at four." Dutch checked his watch. That gave him eleven hours to finish hooking up all the shit he needed to be sure his men stayed safe.

"Where are they going?" Mona's tone was soft and curious as she finally joined in the conversation.

"There's a warehouse at the other end of Fairbanks that has had some unusual activity going on." Rogue was set to take this one since Shadow was still dealing with the mess from last night.

Mona shifted on her feet a little. "We will be here too."

"Good." Pierce strode into the room, his eyes never leaving Mona. "As will I." His attention slowly turned Dutch's way. "For now though, I need to steal Dutch. We have an interview to conduct."

Harlow let out an almost silent breath.

She wanted to be away from him. The realization stung more than it should. It was what he should expect.

But damn it was painful.

"Who are you interviewing?" Harlow's question wasn't directed at Pierce.

It was for him.

"We have someone who might be a good fit as Alpha's tech coordinator." Dutch waited, hoping she might have more questions.

Harlow nodded. "Don't hire a dick."

He smiled. "I will do my best not to hire a dick."

She nodded, her eyes moving away. "Thank you."

"You're welcome, Harlow."

Her eyes snapped back to his, narrowing.

He gave her a wink. "I'll be back."

Pierce kept pace with Dutch as they made their way down the hall. "I'm cautiously optimistic this candidate could be useful as more than just a tech coordinator. Apparently, he is also a quite capable hacker. It could be beneficial for Harlow to have someone to help carry the load."

"I still say Roman would be the best fit for Alpha. He's been part of the team since the beginning, and has the skills the position requires." Dutch had been gunning to have Roman work at his side since it became clear he needed help, and while this guy's resume was impressive, he was missing one very important thing.

Military experience.

"Unfortunately, Alpha's technical needs make it the simplest to hire in for, and his lack of a military background won't have as great of an impact in that position." Pierce paused outside his office. "But if his skills are even close to Harlow's then it's possible Alpha will still be in need of a technical coordinator."

The potential addition to Alaskan Security was already waiting in Pierce's office when they walked in. He didn't bother getting up, just gave them a nod. "Hey."

Pierce stopped, sliding one hand into the pocket of his pants. "Hey."

Dutch swallowed the snort of laughter that tried to jump free at the informal word coming from his friend's mouth. He'd known Pierce since they were eighteen. Both enrolled in the military before they were even out of high school.

But for very different reasons.

Never once had he heard Pierce say 'hey' to anyone.

Which was not a good sign for the dude sitting in the expensive leather chair, looking more relaxed than he should.

Dutch sized the man up. He was tall and clearly worked out. Probably caught his fair share of women between the body and the face.

Pierce's sweeping gaze said he was doing the same. "Tod Talbot?"

"That's me. Tod Talbot, hacker extraordinaire." The guy still didn't get his ass out of the chair. "You Pierce?"

Pierce rocked back onto his heels, dark eyes assessing the man in front of them. "I can say with complete certainty that is irrelevant information at this point." He reached back to open the door. "I'm afraid this is clearly not a good fit."

Tod Talbot didn't budge. "You're not even going to interview me?"

"Don't need to, Mr. Talbot. It is quite apparent you will not be compatible with Alaskan Security." Pierce stared the other man down.

"Because I didn't come in here and kiss your ass?" Tod leaned back in his seat, stretching his legs out in front of him. "I'm here because I'm the best at what I fuckin' do, and you said you wanted the best."

"I have the best." Pierce barely smirked. "You're not even close to her."

Tod's eyes narrowed. "Her?"

"Of course." Pierce stepped back, clearing a path for Tod Talbot to get the hell out.

It was in the prick's best interest that he do exactly that.

"Who in the hell is this 'her' you seem to think is better than me?"

"Also completely irrelevant information to you, Mr. Talbot."

Dutch stepped in beside Pierce. "I think it's time for you to go." He didn't like this fucking guy to start with, but now that he was asking questions about Harlow, Dutch wanted him as far from Alaskan Security as possible.

And as far away from Harlow.

"I can't believe this bullshit." Tod pushed up from the chair he sat in like he owned it. "Fuckin' waste of my damn time."

"Wasted *your* time?" Making it to the interview point at Alaskan Security took weeks. They'd been vetting applicants for twice as long, with Dutch barely treading water as he tried to keep up with all four teams' tech needs.

Pierce rested one palm on Dutch's chest as he tried to step forward.

He'd been itching for a fight since this morning. Some way to take out the shit he felt about—

"It's not Harlow Mowry is it?" The way Tod said her name made it seem like he knew her more than just in passing.

"I'm unfamiliar with that name." Pierce gave him a smile. "But I will be sure to look her up since I still have a position to fill."

"Right." Tod smirked at Dutch as he passed, shoulders back. "Well, when you talk to her tell her I said hi."

"Definitely won't be fucking doing that." Dutch stepped in close. It was time for this prick to get the fuck out of here and far away from Harlow.

"What's your problem?" Tod stood straighter, rocking from foot to foot as he held his hands out. "You wanna go, motherfucker?"

It had been years since he'd been in a fight, and right now this dick had no clue how bad he wanted one.

"Yup." Dutch smirked at the surprised look on his face.

He'd bet money this ass was all mouth. The kind of amped-up meathead who liked to pretend he was ready to fight, banking on the other guy's unwillingness to go up against arms that clearly spent time in a gym.

But that didn't mean shit.

Tod reached out and planted both hands on Dutch's chest, shoving.

It was all he'd been waiting for.

A second later Dutch had the front of Tod's shirt clenched in his fists, and was dragging him toward the main hall.

"What the fuck, man?" Tod scrambled to keep up with him, trying to twist free of his hold. After a few bungled flails Dutch let him go, watching as Tod nearly toppled back.

Which seemed to piss him off a little.

Tod lunged at him. While Dutch might not spend much time in the field, years of hand to hand combat training meant he was just as dangerous as the men he worked with.

Especially considering this bastard knew Harlow. Tod needed to realize coming here was almost as big of a mistake as thinking he had the right to say her fucking name.

Dutch grabbed him as soon as he was close enough, immediately taking them to the ground. Tod managed to get a couple of swings in, opening up an old scar in his eyebrow. The pain was welcome. It was the distraction he'd been seeking.

By the time Tod was screaming from the pain of his shoulder being strained just to the point of dislocation, a crowd had formed. Brock, Shawn, and Tyson joined Pierce, staring down at him and Tod.

"Let him go." Tyson squinted down at Tod's face. "Whatever he did he looks real sorry for."

"He's gonna break my fucking arm." Tod's protest was a high-pitched squeal.

"He's not gonna break your arm." Brock crossed his arms over his chest. "He's gonna dislocate your shoulder."

Tod yelped as Dutch tightened his hold.

Pierce had both hands in his pockets. "I'd rather not deal with that mess if you don't mind, Dutch." He shrugged. "But I'm willing to make an exception if you think it's warranted."

He really wanted to send this dick to the hospital. Leave him with something to remember what happens when you don't know how to fucking act right.

When you think you can claim something that doesn't belong to you.

But it wasn't worth the fallout. Dutch dropped Tod's arm and shoved him off, rolling away.

Tyson held out a hand, hefting Dutch to his feet. He pointed to the bleeding slice in his brow. "You probably need a couple butterflies."

"It's fine." Dutch stared down Tod as the other man fought his way to his feet. Two members of Alpha, dressed in full tactical gear, came through the front doors, one grabbing each arm.

"I'm fine." Tod tried to pull away.

"They're not concerned about your condition, Mr. Talbot. They are escorting you from the premises." Pierce nodded to Bobby and Micah. "Please be sure Mr. Talbot makes it home safe."

The geared-up men half-dragged Tod out to a blacked-out Jeep in the lot, hefting him inside.

Pierce turned to Dutch. "Feel better?"

"Yup." Dutch reached up to press one hand to the seeping cut on his head as he glared at Shawn. "How the fuck did he make it all the way to this?"

Shawn was still watching the lot. Micah stood at the open driver's door to Tod's Jeep. Based on his stance alone, the eviction was not going well. "I'm honestly shocked as hell at this." Shawn shook his head as Micah dragged Tod back out of the Jeep and Bobby climbed in. Another member of Alpha Team came to Micah's aid, helping him stuff Tod into the backseat of the Alaskan Security Rover idling beside the scene. In a few seconds they were pulling away. "I talked to that guy on the phone more than once." He frowned at the bumpers of the two vehicles as they drove toward the front gate. "He was fine."

"Well he sure as hell wasn't fine today." Dutch blinked as a trickle of blood ran close to the corner of his eye. "And now we have one more fucking thing to worry about." He spun away, intending to go straight to Harlow.

Find out who in the fuck Tod Talbot was.

"Dutch." The sharpness in Pierce's voice made him stop and turn.

"I don't believe Ms. Mowry is in a position to handle this right now." Pierce was many things. Controlling. A little arrogant. Driven.

But he was also very protective of the people he allowed into his world.

"What if he's a problem?"

"He's definitely a problem, which is exactly why I believe we should be cautious with how much we allow Ms. Mowry to know of what just transpired." Pierce came closer. "She has been through quite an ordeal in the past twenty-four hours." He glanced down the hall toward the office where Harlow was still working. "If she's struggling now, this will only make it worse."

Holding more information back from Harlow was not something he wanted to do. "She needs to know."

"I don't disagree." Pierce pulled the pocket square from his jacket and passed it to Dutch. "But I think she will benefit from a day or two to process what happened last night before we burden her with this as well."

Shawn tapped his earpiece. "Alpha got Talbot out of the gate and is lined up to follow him."

"Good." Pierce stepped back. "We will keep a team on him until Ms. Mowry is in a place where she is willing to aid our investigation."

"Who's with him?" Alpha's normal focus was business-based. Companies having personnel problems. White collar sorts of issues that required visibility more than anything.

Which meant they were not as practiced at being invisible.

Pierce studied Dutch for a minute. "I will have Shadow step in."

Dutch nodded. "Good."

"I wish I could say we can give Ms. Mowry all the time she needs, but you know that isn't the case." Pierce tipped his head to the spot where Dutch held the pocket square to the split. "Go have Eli tape you up then check on Ms. Mowry. The faster she is recovered from last night, the faster we will get to the bottom of Talbot's appearance."

The men glanced at each other, the reality of the situation sitting heavy between them.

Tod Talbot didn't come from nowhere.

He had a reason for doing what he did.

And the fact that he named Harlow meant she tied into it somehow.

"I think we should tag her." Dutch looked to Brock. He was the most likely to understand where he was coming from. "Make sure we can find her no matter what."

Pierce lifted one brow. "If she discovers it and asks why, you have to be prepared for the potential ramifications."

"If it means keeping her safe I'll take full responsibility. She can come after me for it."

Pierce smiled. "I'll be sure to send her your way."

CHAPTER 5

"WHERE IN THE hell are my glasses?" Harlow shoved through the files on her desk, trying to find the black-frames that were the difference between seeing two feet in front of her face and twenty.

She'd taken them off for a second. Just long enough to try to rub the burning from her eyeballs.

"Right here, Mowry." Dutch's voice sent her sitting up straight.

He was already at her side.

"How did you get in here without me hearing you?" She snatched her glasses away, shoving them back on her face.

"Just because I'm not out in the field doesn't mean I'm not as capable as the men who are."

Harlow worked to keep her focus on his face instead of letting it drop to his leg.

She'd assumed the slight sway of his walk had more to do with swagger than missing a huge chunk of the muscle required to walk without a limp.

A limp that was more pronounced today than normal. Maybe it was because she simply knew it was there.

But it really did seem worse.

She squinted up at him through her much clearer lenses. "Did you clean my glasses?"

"Maybe." Dutch dropped the soft cloth in his hand onto her desk. "I grabbed one of these for you when I was in Eli's office."

Guilt tugged at her insides.

His leg must really hurt. Probably because he went and did something stupid, like carrying her through the snow.

She leaned a little closer. "What's wrong with your eyebrow?"

"Old scar split open." Dutch turned so she couldn't see the tiny bandages across the pink, slightly swollen skin of his brow bone. "What are you doing still here?"

Mona and Eva left two hours ago, leaving to get dinner and some sleep before coming back at the ungodly hour Pierce was sending Team Rogue out. "Just working."

It was the best way to get through the kind of shit life seemed to enjoy hurling her way.

Work. Powering through until she passed out.

Then she'd get up and do it again.

"What are you working on?" Dutch pulled one of the rolling office chairs close to hers, settling into it as his eyes focused on her computer screen.

Harlow couldn't resist peeking his way. "Just trying to see if I can figure out how Howard got into Eva and Mona's system." She fought the urge to pull away as Dutch leaned in, peering at the code across her screen. "Were any client documents compromised?"

"It's hard to tell." Harlow scrolled through the lines. "It looks like he was primarily digging around employee data."

"Is it possible he left a trail to make it appear he was after employee data when he was actually after client data?" Dutch still didn't look her way as he took the mouse from her, using it to flip through the screens.

"What good would client data do him if he's trying to recruit their employees?" Harlow watched as Dutch moved through the same information she'd been scrutinizing for the past three hours.

"Maybe he was trying to recruit." Dutch's eyes moved her way, his head barely turning with them. "But maybe he also knew the right information about the right person could be very beneficial."

"Like blackmail?" This was what she loved about what she did. Digging out the evil hiding behind a computer screen and cutting it off at its knees. Taking it down before it knew what happened.

"Maybe." Dutch leaned back in his chair. "Maybe there's someone out there who could help further the agenda of the people Howard was working for."

"But what is their agenda?" She'd been trying to work through what was going on since her first day in Alaska. Digging into all the possibilities.

She always came up empty.

"Drugs? Maybe filtering arms to the cartel? Whatever it is, these are not the kind of people who dick around."

"No shit." Harlow stared at the screen, willing something to stand out. Some sort of hint about what was going on.

"I should have found you sooner last night." The regret in Dutch's voice was palpable.

"I don't want to talk about it." She'd been able to function just fine for almost two years by not talking about this kind of bullshit. Ignoring it until it went away.

Until it barely affected her at all.

"I know." Dutch's eyes moved over her face, serious and steady in her peripheral vision. "But whatever happened isn't going away, Harlow. You can try to ignore it, but shit will keep happening to bring it up, and every time it gets stronger. Meaner."

Usually advice like this was dished out by some sweet, well-intentioned person without a fucking clue how horrible things could be.

How horrible people could be.

But Dutch knew. He'd seen the worst of the world firsthand. It made his comments harder to brush off.

But she never quit something because it was hard.

"I'm fine." Harlow grabbed the cup Dutch distracted her from filling earlier, standing up to go back to the kitchen.

"Is that why you drink every day?" He stood beside her. "Because you're fine?"

"I drink every day because you stress me the fuck out." If Dutch came in here ready to stage an intervention then he could save his breath.

Regardless of how he saw things, she was fine. In her own, screwed up, functionally dysfunctional way.

"You drink every day because you're self-medicating." He stayed right behind her as she tried to escape him, catching the door as she tried to pull it open, slamming it closed with one wide palm. "You drink because you want to forget shit that happened. I know. I've done it."

"You don't know what you're talking about." The fight she normally brought wasn't there right now. Instead of sounding like the woman she tried to be, it sounded weak.

Broken.

And she wasn't fucking broken. Not anymore.

"I may not know why you're doing it, but I sure as hell know what it looks like, Harlow."

"It? You know what *it* looks like? What the hell is this *it*?" The fire was blessedly back. Burning hotter than it had all day.

"PTSD. It's what I've got." He pointed her way. "And it's what you've got."

She laughed. Not because anything about this was funny.

It was ridiculous. "I'm sorry to tell you, but you're wrong as shit."

She wasn't sorry. Dutch being wrong was a relief. Proof he wasn't seeing what she worked so hard to hide from everyone around her. "I've never been in combat, Pretty Boy."

"You've obviously also never looked up the actual definition of PTSD either." His voice was low and even. "It's got nothing to do with combat. Not in the sense you're talking."

Just as his closeness was getting uncomfortably comfortable, Dutch straightened. "Come on, Mowry. I think you've worked long enough today." He stood, holding one hand out to her. "Let's go do something else."

She eyed his outstretched hand, looking from it to his face. "I like working."

"You like working for the same reason you drink every afternoon. It keeps you from thinking about it."

She threw her arms out. "About *what*?"

"Whatever brought you to Alaska."

Her eyes jumped to meet his.

"No one comes to Alaska without a good reason, Harlow."

"Even you?" It was meant as a challenge. A way to drag this conversation back into territory she could handle.

"I came here because I needed help. I couldn't find a way to go forward after what happened to me. Pierce offered me a way to move past it with people who understood where I'd been."

She snorted. "Is that why you're being like this now? You think I need you because you understand?"

"No, Darling." Dutch leaned down, bringing that hand closer. Within reach. "I'm here because you are everything I've been waiting for." His lips pulled into a devastating smile. "And I'm here because I'm stubborn enough not to fall for your shit."

"It's not shit." She didn't like how he put that. Didn't like the way it made her life sound.

Like it was all bullshit.

"Isn't it?" He looked amused now. Like he was calling her bluff.

"I'm just as big of a bitch as it seems like I am."

"Good." His smile didn't slip at all. "I like you just the way you are, Harlow." His hand still hadn't moved. "I don't want you to change." His lips finally fell into a soft line that wasn't quite a frown. "I just want you to feel safe. Here. With me."

"I'm not afraid of you." Saying it made it true. Had to.

It was the only way she'd been able to move forward. To live in a way that kept her from feeling the fear that once ruled her life.

"Unfortunately, you will be." Dutch didn't seem put off at all that she still hadn't budged from her seat.

Harlow shook her head. "No. I won't."

"I'm not here for some quick fuck, Harlow." He moved in closer as her skin heated at his words. "I'm not here to have you in my bed once."

She swallowed hard as he closed in, bracing both hands on the arms of her chair. "I'm here because I plan to make my bed yours permanently, and that is what scares the shit out of you."

Her throat went dry. Partly from the fear that came anytime a man was too close. And Dutch was sure as hell too close, and it had nothing to do with his location.

Unfortunately, the other reason her throat was dry had to do with the smell of his skin. The heat she could already feel easing from his body to hers.

The look in his hazel eyes.

"I don't do relationships, Dutch." She tried to sit straighter, but it wasn't as easy as normal. "I'm only interested in the quick fuck you mentioned."

"I'm not offering you a quick fuck, Darling." His lips twisted into something between a smirk and a grin. "Like I said, I'm not really a quick fuck sort of man."

Why did that make all this worse?

She could not…

Not…

NOT…

Have sex with Dutch. No matter how quick.

No matter how detached she wanted to believe it could be.

That man might as well be covered in fucking Velcro.

"Well I'm not a relationship sort of woman."

"Right now."

She hadn't even gotten her full statement out before he qualified it.

"Ever." She tipped her head in a nod like it would make it more final.

Two years ago, lying in a hospital bed, she'd made the decision.

No more.

And it had been easy. Dressing like she did helped weed out the complete pricks, giving her time to filter through any prospects before offering up the only thing she was interested in. "If you're looking for a mutually beneficial situation then I might consid—"

"No." It was sharp and loud, making Harlow bounce back a little.

Dutch barely flinched. "I'm sorry. I didn't mean to yell."

Harlow laughed, snorting a little. She'd been yelled at, and this was nothing like that. It shouldn't be funny, but if she couldn't laugh at what she'd been through then she'd be stuck doing something else, and that wasn't going to happen.

Dutch took a long, slow breath. "How about a movie and some popcorn?"

"I don't like popcorn."

He stared at her for a minute. "I feel like you're lying because you think it will get you out of this."

"I'm serious." For some reason she'd given him the truth. "I just never really liked it."

"That's because you've never had my popcorn." He stepped back. "I'm not trying to brag, but I've been told my popcorn is better than theater popcorn."

"I would hope so." She stood, not intending to do anything other than go to her room for some much-needed space. "Theater popcorn sits for days and they just keep mixing fresh in with the old shit."

"That would explain why mine's better." Dutch wasn't deterred at all. It was one more reason she'd tried to piss him off from the start.

"I'm going to take your word for it." Harlow packed up her computer. Dutch might have interrupted her for now, but she had a whole night ahead of her to fill. "Enjoy your movie."

"What about cookies?" Dutch followed behind her. "Fresh-baked chocolate chip cookies? Would those convince you to watch a movie with me?"

She glanced at him over one shoulder. "You clearly don't realize how unfun I am to watch movies with."

"I don't believe you." He grabbed her computer bag as she tried to heft it up, snagging it away and swinging it over his own shoulder.

"You should." Harlow tried to grab her bag back from him, but Dutch dodged her, blocking her with his body in a way that meant if she missed the bag she would end up with a handful of whatever was hiding under his perfectly pressed button-up shirt.

And what lurked beneath the pale yellow fabric was not something she should be thinking about.

If he wanted to carry the damn thing she'd let him. Not like it made any difference.

"One movie. Any movie you want."

"Any movie I want?" Maybe she'd been going about this all the wrong way. Maybe Dutch just needed a reality check. "Fine."

"Good." He led her across the glassed-in walkway into the rooming building, but instead of turning to head down the long hall leading to the single rooms, Dutch continued on through the kitchen and common area, past the recliners and sofas where she'd been expecting to stop, and through a set of doors. Another long hall ran down the length of this side of the building. At the end of it Dutch swiped his badge across the small monitor fixed to the wall beside a single door. The lock clicked open and he pushed it wide, waiting for her to pass inside.

She leaned to peek into the dark room. "What is this?"

"This is the theater room." He reached in to hit a switch. Dim uplighting illuminated the room in a cool blue-tinted glow. Rows of reclining sofas sat in front of a wide screen set into the wall.

"I didn't even know this was here." Harlow stepped into the space, rubbing her arms at the cool air inside.

Dutch pointed toward the black buttery-soft seating. "Go get comfortable. I'll be right back." He backed out the door, letting it click shut behind him.

Harlow glanced back at the sofas, then toward the closed door.

Did he just lock her in here?

She walked over and tried the handle. "That son of a—"

Suddenly the screen at the front of the room flicked on and Dutch's giant face smiled out at her. "Don't get your panties in a bunch, Mowry. It's a security feature I set up last night. All the doors in the building stay locked now." He held his phone in one hand and dug around the pantry of the kitchen with the other. "We will have badge stations set up inside within the next couple of days, but for now it means if a door closes behind you there's a good chance you're stuck wherever you are."

She walked closer to the screen. "Why didn't anyone tell me about this?" Harlow pushed up on her toes, peeking around the edge of the screen.

Could he even see her?

"I thought you were going to go sit down and relax?" Dutch stood up from a crouched position and moved to the fridge, pulling out a couple bottles of water before stacking them onto a tray next to a pack of Chips Ahoy.

"I thought you were making me fresh-baked cookies?"

"I asked if fresh-baked cookies would convince you to watch a movie with me. Didn't say I was going to actually make them." He grinned at the screen. "If you wanted a man who could cook you missed your chance with Brock."

Harlow wrinkled her nose. "Brock's not my type."

"That's good news." Dutch was walking now, passing through the same hall they just came down. "Because I'm not much like him."

"What are you like?"

"That's a complicated answer." His steps slowed dramatically. "I'm not charming."

She snorted. "No shit."

His grin widened. "I like how you aren't scared to give me a hard time."

That was exactly why she *did* give him shit. Because she was scared not to.

"You deserve it." Harlow backed to the front sofa and sat on it. "You're a pain in my ass."

Even that comment didn't damper Dutch's smile. It flashed out at her from the giant screen, along with the barely-there dimple she could never ignore.

"Why is it taking you so long to get back here?" She eased back on the sofa. "I know it's not because you're bringing me the cookies you promised."

Dutch's face was suddenly serious. "If I promise you something I will always come through, Harlow." His eyes seemed to fix onto her through the screen. "You really want to know what I'm like?"

She couldn't look away from his face where it filled the front of the room. She'd done everything possible not to know this man.

To shove him as far away as possible.

Because from day one it was clear Dutch was nothing like the men she'd known.

The man who'd broken her in so many pieces they never fit back together just right. Figuratively.

And literally.

But the way he looked at her last night. The way he held her so close and so carefully.

It was the first time she'd felt safe since the night she broke free from a level of control most people couldn't imagine or understand.

Harlow swallowed hard as a tiny truth slipped out.

"Maybe."

CHAPTER 6

DUTCH LEANED AGAINST the wall outside the theater room door.

He never expected one degree of separation would make such a difference.

"That's not very convincing, Mowry." He pushed her a little.

It was what kept her comfortable. The occasional jab that helped her not feel the closeness as it grew between them.

She scowled at the screen. "Good. Because I'm not very convinced you're worth knowing."

He laughed. "You're not the first one."

Brock's steps carried down the hall behind him.

"I'll be inside in just a second." He shut the video off just before Brock came into view.

"Did you lock her in there?" Brock held out the plate of cookies he and Eva threw together. Brock always had the stuff to make cookies on hand, so it was an offer Dutch knew he'd be able to follow through on.

"Technically." He was the one who set up the new security measure. "She's got her computer in there. If she wanted out she would have already overridden the system."

Brock chuckled. "She's something." His smile faded. "How's she doing?"

Dutch shrugged. "That's what I've been trying to figure out all day."

"Good luck with that." Brock eyed the cookies. "I did my part to help."

"I appreciate it." Dutch added the still-warm cookies to the tray in his hands.

Brock lifted a brow at the pack of Chips Ahoy. "What in the hell are those for?"

Dutch pulled his badge from the spot where it was clipped to his waistband, stretching the extendable string. "Those are in case the lady eats all the good cookies." He shot Brock a grin as he unlocked the door and pulled it open. "Thanks."

Harlow was sitting cross-legged on the front sofa, her computer on her lap. The screen at the front displayed the hall directly outside the theater room. "You bribed Brock into baking cookies?"

"Didn't have to bribe him." Dutch went to the front of the room, setting the tray on the floor in front of Harlow so he could pull the plush blanket his sister sent him for his birthday off his shoulder. "Lift your computer."

Harlow didn't look up. "No thanks."

And just like that any warmth she'd shown him was gone. She'd shut him out in the time it took Brock to drop off a plate of cookies.

"You're cold. I saw you rub your arms when we came in."

"I'm fine." She continued tapping on her keyboard. "Did you mean to set all of the offices to auto lock too?"

"I was in a hurry. Didn't have time to pick and choose." He moved closer, laying the blanket across the arm of the sofa at Harlow's side.

For some reason she was resistant to letting him take care of her in any way. The nicer he was to her, the more distant she became.

"I thought you'd be more interesting than this, Mowry." Dutch dropped to the spot just beside her, sitting close but not touching.

She shot him a glance from behind the thick rim of her black-framed glasses. "Sorry to disappoint you."

"Not disappointed." He bent over and picked up the plate of chocolate chip cookies Brock brought. "Not even a little."

Harlow's eyes stayed locked on the screen as she continued working her way through the security measures he'd rushed through putting in place last night, hurrying to get the building as locked down as possible before he went to check on Harlow where she slept.

In his room.

In his bed.

"You have a movie you want to watch?" Dutch pulled out the iPad connected to the screen and tabbed through the apps until he found the one he wanted, pulling up a list of movie options. "You like romantic stuff?"

"Nope." She didn't miss a beat.

"Drama?"

Harlow shook her head as she chewed a cookie and scanned the screen in front of her.

"What kind of movies do you watch then?"

"Musicals." Her eyes slid his way.

"Like Seven Brides for Seven Brothers musicals?" Dutch tapped the search bar.

Harlow's head spun his way, one side of her nose crinkled up. "What?"

He smiled. Harlow wasn't the only one with a few surprises up their sleeve. "Didn't expect me to know what a musical was?"

"Didn't expect you to know the name of one." She turned back to the screen, but her fingers weren't moving nearly as quickly across the keys.

"I know the name of more than one." Dutch leaned a little closer as he scrolled through the musicals offered. "I've been in more than one."

Harlow's chewing stopped.

"You said you wanted to get to know me, Harlow." Dutch selected the musical he was most familiar with. "I was the lead in my high school's musicals." The screen went black for a second, then the opening credits of a movie he'd watched at least once a year for as long as he could remember lit up the room.

Harlow's eyes locked onto the scene, wide and guileless. She sat perfectly still as Danny Kaye and Bing Crosby pretended to be soldiers in a combat zone attempting to put on a musical production while bombings happen around them.

As the scene came to an end, Harlow turned to him. "You don't mind watching that?"

He shook his head. "No."

"Even with your—" Her eyes dropped to his leg. "Even though…"

"I've gone through a lot of therapy, Harlow. It didn't just happen." He leaned down to grab a bottle of milk from the tray. "You want this now or should I put it in the fridge?"

She blinked a couple of times before finally focusing on the bottle. "Oh. Um." She cleared her throat. "I'm lactose intolerant."

"Good to know." He grabbed both the milk bottles and took them to the back of the room, stashing them in the mini fridge sitting under the coffee maker.

Harlow slid her computer off her lap and onto the arm of the sofa. "What is this room for?"

"We use it for lots of things. Sometimes we watch videos of ops we've carried out. Sort of the way sports teams watch games." He eased back into the seat beside her as Rosemary Clooney and Vera Ellen performed his mother's favorite song of the film. "But most of the time we use it for this."

"Oh." Harlow's dark brows pressed together as she chewed her lip.

"What's wrong, Mowry? You look distressed."

"I'm not distressed." She snapped it out at him. "I just didn't realize there were enough women around here for you to be locking them in a room until they watch a movie with you."

He pressed his lips together until the urge to smile passed. "You might actually be the first woman to ever grace this room, Mowry." Dutch settled back into the plush cushions. "What I meant was we use this to watch movies and relax after a shit week."

He barely caught the pink tint of her cheeks before Harlow's head jerked toward the screen and she slouched down, crossing her arms over her chest.

The next hour passed in silence as they watched the movie his mother played every Thanksgiving. It was barely ten o'clock, but Harlow was blinking slower and slower with each passing minute.

Dutch leaned closer, reaching around her to slide the computer onto the next sofa over before flipping the armrest up to reveal the controls for the recliners. He pressed down the button, taking Harlow's seat back and the footrest up. She was silent as the furniture repositioned. When the whirr of the motor stopped she peeked his way.

"Thank you."

He nodded, reclining his own seat.

Harlow scooted down a little more, letting out a soft sigh as her lids got heavy again.

In five more minutes she was out.

Dutch grabbed the blanket she refused and stretched it over her small frame, tucking it under her chin before easing back into his own recliner and closing his eyes.

It wasn't the way he imagined their first night together would go, but nothing good in life came easy. Not healing. Not growth. Not peace.

He had all of those. He'd worked for them and waited for them.

He could sure as hell work and wait for the woman beside him.

****

"NO!" HARLOW SAT straight up, both hands grabbing around as her breath came in raspy bursts.

Dutch reached for her, blinking away the cloud of deep sleep. The second his hand met her arm she recoiled, scrambling over the end of the footrest, toppling to the floor in her haste to get away.

"Harlow." Dutch scooted after her. "Harlow. It's me."

"Leave me alone!" Her hands covered her face as she curled into a ball.

He dropped to his knees at her side. "Harlow." Dutch rested one hand on her shoulder.

She yelped like he hit her, knees curling tighter to her belly.

Her body trembled under his palm.

"Harlow." Dutch went to the floor beside her, lying down and pulling her close. "It's okay, Mowry. Everything is okay."

She went still.

"You're in the theater room at Alaskan Security." He kept his voice soft and calm. "We watched White Christmas until you fell asleep." Dutch smoothed one hand over her dark hair, pushing it back from her face so she could see what was around her. "Brock made you cookies and I confessed my love of musicals."

Her head barely tipped toward his, blue eyes wide as they found his face. She sniffed. "You didn't do that."

"Maybe that was you then." Dutch continued running his fingers down the length of her dark hair, easing out the mess it tangled into during her night terror. "I know it was one of us." She hadn't moved away from him, a fact that settled something deep inside him. An unrest he didn't know was there until this moment. "How in the hell do you deal with all this hair, Mowry?"

"I like having it. It makes me feel—" Her lips pressed together and her eyes dropped from his.

"My mom has hair almost the same color as yours." Dutch finished smoothing one section of the mass and moved onto the next. "Not this much of it, though."

"Your mom's hair is this dark?" Her blue eyes tentatively came back his direction, moving over his own, less-dark brown hair.

"Surprised?"

"I guess I would have pictured her looking more like you."

"I look like my dad. The only way to tell pictures of us apart is to look at the clothes." It brought his dad no small amount of joy when people mistook them for brothers instead of father and son.

Harlow sniffed again. She slowly started to sit up, her attention moving around the room. "Sorry about," she pulled the front of her sweater away from her body, "that."

"There's nothing to be sorry for, Harlow." Dutch sat up but didn't stand, instead pulling his knees up and draping both arms over them. "It happens to lots of us."

It was the thing that tied them together from the beginning, he just didn't know it. A shared pain.

One he'd worked hard to overcome.

"It shouldn't." She stood, grabbing her computer and packing it into her bag. "I need to go."

"What if it happens again?"

"It won't." Harlow zipped her bag.

"You have to sleep sometime, Harlow. You can't avoid it forever."

"I can." She straightened. "And I will."

"It doesn't work that way."

"How would you—" She huffed out a breath. "Shit."

He smiled. "You might be able to slide this right past everyone else." Dutch eased up from the floor, being careful not to immediately put weight on his bad leg. "Not me. I know it because I've seen it in the mirror, Mowry."

"I am fine." She slung the bag over her shoulder and marched toward the door.

"You're not fine. Not even close."

"I guess we'll find out." She grabbed the door and yanked it open, turning to give him a smug smile.

Like he didn't already know she'd unlocked the door to the theater room.

It was probably the first thing she did after hacking into the security camera in the hall. And she'd stayed with him anyway.

Because she wanted to.

"We definitely will."

She scowled at him.

It was sexy as hell. Everything about her was, and eventually he'd tell her that.

"Go brush your teeth. You have milk breath." The door slammed shut behind her.

Dutch chuckled as he started to clean up their mess. After folding the blanket and tossing it over his shoulder, he went to his own room to shower and get a few hours of sleep before picking another fight with Harlow.

****

"WHAT THE FUCK?"

Harlow snarled at him as he opened the door to her room.

"I told you all the doors were set to lock when they closed."

"The private rooms were not on that list last night when I checked."

86

"Are you sure?" Dutch stepped back to let Harlow stomp out past him. "I'm positive they were."

She stopped short and spun to face him. "Then how did you get out of your room?"

"Good point." He took a sip of his coffee. "Must just be your door that's locking then." He held out the cup of half-caf he'd made for her before going to find Harlow wiggling the knob to her room as she banged on the backside, trying to get out.

"What if there was a fire?" She ignored the coffee. "I would have burned to death."

"There's a failsafe connected to the smoke alarms." He pushed the coffee closer. "And I would have come for you."

She snatched the cup away. "How noble."

"I saved you once, Harlow. I'll do it again."

She turned away. "You didn't have to save me."

"I did." He fell into step beside her. Being completely honest with her right now might be a good idea.

It might also blow up in his face, but nothing with Harlow was ever going to be easy.

That was part of the appeal.

She stood up for herself. For the people around her.

"Do you know I'd almost convinced myself wanting you was a bad idea?"

"Too bad it was only almost." She didn't seem flattered at all by his admission of wanting her.

"When we found out you were gone I realized it didn't matter if it was a bad idea or not." Dutch reached out to open the door to the walkway, standing back as she went first. "Knowing someone had you. Could hurt you, it made me lose my fucking mind."

"You've definitely lost your mind." Harlow snapped a glance his way. "You could have hurt yourself hauling my ass back like you did."

"I don't care." He opened the next door, but Harlow didn't go through. She let out a breath, dropping her eyes to the floor between them. "This isn't going to go the way you think it will, Dutch."

"How do you know what I think?" Harlow clearly had expectations when it came to him.

To men in general.

It was time for her to realize those expectations were wrong.

"You think what all men think. That if you just tell me what I want to hear enough, I'll suddenly be all sweet and agreeable."

"I don't expect you to ever be agreeable, Mowry." He'd known from the start she was different from most women.

But similar to the ones he knew and loved.

She scoffed. "That's—" She blinked. "You just—" Harlow heaved out a sigh that ended with a frustrated-sounding groan.

"Sounds like you're the one with expectations, Mowry." He rested one palm on her back, putting a little pressure there to get her feet moving again. "Put a wiggle in it. We've got shit to do today."

Eva and Brock stepped out of Shawn's office as they passed. Eva's eyes lit up when she saw Harlow. "Hey! How were the cookies last night?"

Harlow scooted away a little, eyes resting on Eva for a second before moving farther away. "Fine."

"Just fine?" She bumped her way to Harlow's side, knocking Dutch back with the giant leopard-print bag slung over one shoulder. "Those are the best cookies I've ever had." She smiled. "If you know of a better recipe then I'm going to need it."

"I don't cook." Harlow pulled her own bag tighter to her body, using it as a barrier between her and Eva.

Dutch slowed down, letting the women move farther in front of him so he could watch the interaction better.

Harlow's body language looked familiar as hell. The closed-off stance. The way she avoided eye-contact.

Looked like it wasn't just him she was trying to keep out.

It was everyone.

CHAPTER 7

HARLOW SHOVED PIERCE'S door open without knocking. "I need my office back."

At first the idea of being in a room with the other girls sounded fun.

Then she realized they weren't interested in idle chat and afternoon cocktail hour. These chicks wanted to be actual friends. They wanted to discuss how they felt and what they thought and all the bullshit that went with that.

Pierce sat at his desk, perfectly unaffected by her surprise visit.

If only she could figure out how to be as emotionally untouchable.

It used to be easy. Keep things light and easy. Be unapproachable enough people didn't quite know how to navigate around you. It meant she controlled the conversations. Where they began.

Where they ended.

But the women at Alaskan Security didn't seem to realize she was not friend material.

"Your old office is otherwise occupied."

"By what?" Harlow crossed her arms, calling his bluff. No way did they fill that spot already.

"I've decided the team leads should all be located in the same hall as your new office to ease interaction." Pierce leaned back in his leather chair, crossing one leg over the other, the ankle just above his expensive shoe resting on one knee. "May I ask why you wish to be alone again?"

Alone.

That was the whole crux of this issue. She wanted to be left alone.

But not feel alone.

Before it was perfect. She could work in her office, going find someone to bicker with when the isolation started to leave her too much time to think.

Now there was always someone asking her questions she didn't want to answer.

"It's distracting in there. I can't focus."

Pierce was silent for a minute, his eyes staying on her. "What is it you would like to be focusing on, Ms. Mowry?"

"My work." It was the only thing she wanted to focus on.

"Your work now involves being part of a team set up to keep all of Alaskan Security safe from men like the ones you met two nights ago. Is that the work you're struggling to focus on?"

A tightness in her chest suddenly squeezed to the point she couldn't breathe.

"There you are." Dutch stepped through the open office door. "I came up missing you." He wrapped one arm around her shoulders. "I need your help."

She couldn't answer. Couldn't form words around the need to fight oxygen into her lungs.

Dutch moved fast down the hall, pushing open the door to Shawn's office. Shawn glanced up from his desk as they rushed in.

"Get out." Dutch's tone was sharp and loud. He ushered her to a chair as Shawn stepped around them, closing the door as he left.

Dutch crouched down in front of her. "You've gotta breathe, Mowry." He rested both hands on the side of her face. "Close your eyes."

She blinked as the room got fuzzy.

"Please, Harlow. Just trust me." His thumbs stroked over the numbing skin of her cheeks. "It will help. I promise."

She squeezed her eyes shut.

"Now. Imagine you're outside. The sun is warm on your skin as you sit on a beach listening to the water as it moves." His voice was soft and even. "A breeze moves around you. You can smell the ocean and feel the sand under your toes."

He was quiet for a minute. "Are you there with me, Harlow?"

She nodded.

"Good." His hands still held her face.

Harlow slowly opened her eyes, expecting to find Dutch staring at her.

But he wasn't.

Dutch's eyes were closed, his brows pressed together in concentration.

"Why are you doing it too?" She didn't mean to whisper.

"Because I still need it sometimes." His lids slowly lifted. "Better?"

The next inhale was shaky as her lungs adjusted to the influx of air. "Better."

"Good." Dutch still held her cheeks in his hands. His eyes moved over her face for a second. "Why do you want to have your own office again, really?"

"I don't like people being in my space."

"You don't like people getting close."

"That's not what I said." She managed another shaky breath. "If I can't focus, I can't do my job."

"I watched you focus during a movie while you ate a plate full of cookies last night, Mowry." Dutch was close enough his stomach rested against her knees.

And it was not soft.

Even through the crisp fabric of his shirt and her baggy jeans, the tightness of the muscle there was unmistakable.

Her hands rested on the tops of her thighs, so close to where his body touched hers.

Part of his body.

The warmth of his palms still pressed into her face, holding it with a solid presence that she wasn't quite ready to shove away.

"I don't like being close to all of you."

"All of us?" Dutch's gaze moved over hers. "Or just me?"

If only Dutch was the primary issue. Him alone she might have been able to deal with.

But Eva and Mona took everything to another level.

There were too many people coming closer and closer.

Maybe if they hadn't been taken two nights ago it would have been fine.

Maybe she would have been able to continue on like she had. Keeping everyone and everything where it belonged. Instead she was stuck with Mona and Eva thinking they had some sort of camaraderie.

"I just can't work when people are around." Harlow rubbed her palms down her pants, trying to wipe away the clamminess collecting there. "I just want to be left alone."

"That's not happening, Harlow." Dutch leaned down to catch her eyes. "You only want to be alone so you can try to pretend you're fine. Find a way to muffle the shit eating you up inside."

She stared at him, unwilling to give him anything else to use against her.

"Whatever this is, even you can't make it go away."

"What's that mean, even I can't make it go away?"

Dutch barely smiled. "I've known you long enough to realize you can do almost anything, Mowry." His hands finally slipped free of her face as he stood up. "Almost."

Harlow reached up to press one hand to the lingering warmth he left behind.

"Let's go get breakfast. I'm starving." He held one hand out her way.

"I'm not hungry."

"You sure? Because Brock brought over some biscuits and gravy for us." He wiggled his brows at her. "He used lactose-free milk."

"Why is Brock making all this stuff?" She eyed the hand he offered.

"Because Eva is making him." Dutch wiggled his fingers. "Come on, Mowry. You can do it."

"Fine." She slapped her hand into his, letting Dutch pull her to her feet, assuming he would let go once she was up and moving.

Instead, his long fingers laced with hers, clasping her palm flush against his as he lead her out of Shawn's office and down the hall toward the break room. Shawn was sitting at the island, scrolling through his phone. He glanced their way. "Looks like we might have another spot to check out." He flipped the screen around, pointing it right at Dutch.

"Is it connected to the place we hit this morning?" Dutch pulled out a chair and waited, nodding to the seat when Harlow didn't immediately move.

"Eva found a trail that might be plausible." Shawn scooted out of his seat. "I'll go check and see when we can move on this."

They'd all sat and watched this morning, hoping the warehouse Rogue staked out might be the break they were looking for.

But after two hours it was clear that if the building had been used by the people threatening Alaskan Security, they'd abandoned it and moved on.

Dutch pulled out a plate and broke open a biscuit from a Ziploc bag sitting on the counter. "I'm disappointed we didn't find anything this morning."

"Me too." She'd barely been able to breathe watching the screen as the five-man-team moved through the snow with agonizingly slow steps.

"You like lots of gravy, or just a little?" Dutch glanced up as the plastic container of sausage and milky gravy hovered over the plate.

"Lots." Usually when she was struggling, the last thing she wanted to do was eat, but for some reason biscuits and gravy sounded really good.

Dutch smiled. "A girl after my own heart." He dumped on half the gravy before dropping the other half on the other plate of biscuit. "What's your favorite breakfast food?"

"Coffee." She eyed the coffee maker on the counter. It was half-full and calling her name. Harlow eased off the stool and pulled two mugs from the cabinet, filling them before adding sugar into one and just cream into the other.

Dutch's eyes followed her as she moved back to her seat.

"What?" Harlow sat her cup and his in place.

"Thank you." He pulled one plate from the microwave and sat it in front of her before sliding the other in and setting the timer.

"Whatever." She took the fork he offered. "Don't read anything into it."

"I'm going to." Dutch smiled at her as he picked up the coffee she made him and took a sip. "Perfect."

"You're making me regret being nice." Harlow shoved in a chunk of biscuit. The second it hit her tongue she looked up at Dutch. "Holy shit. This is really good."

"He's had lots of practice." Dutch pulled out his plate and came to sit beside her.

"What's that mean?"

"Means Brock has made his share of ladies breakfast." Dutch forked in half a biscuit.

Harlow chewed her food a little more slowly as she peeked at the man beside her. "Are you jealous?"

Dutch's head barely tipped her way. "I used to be."

Her gaze slid down his body. No doubt the man could snag any woman with eyes. "Why?"

Dutch pulled in a long, slow breath then let it out. "I changed a lot after—" He angled his injured leg her way. "Temporary situations made me real anxious."

"Do they still?" It shouldn't matter.

Dutch nodded. "They do. I like consistency. Feeling safe. Knowing that tomorrow will be like today."

"Then how do you work here?" It seemed like the danger, the potential issues that come out of nowhere, would send someone like Dutch into a tailspin.

"That's a complicated answer, Mowry." Dutch wiped a napkin across his mouth before leaning back in his chair and draping one arm across the back of hers. "These men are my friends. The thought of them being out there without me makes it hard to breathe." His thumb stroked across her back. "I'm with all of them, all the time. Keeping them safe."

"Harlow." Eva poked her head into the doorway of the break room. "We need you. Mona and I have hit a dead end on this second location."

"Yup. I'm coming." Harlow went to grab her plate, intending to take it to the sink to rinse.

"I've got it." Dutch took the plate from her hands as he tipped his head toward Eva. "Go do what only you can do."

Harlow turned away, pressing down the smile trying to lift her lips.

Of course Dutch knew what she could do. He'd seen it firsthand. She shouldn't feel any sort of way that he acknowledged it.

Eva waited for Harlow at the door. The minute Harlow was at her side, Eva started talking. "I think we found a connection, but it's about three times removed.

"Probably not." Harlow fell into step beside Eva, her mind already working its way through what Eva was saying. "So far it seems like there's only a handful of players at the top. They use aliases and different bank accounts and addresses to cover their tracks, but they don't catch them all." She tried to give Eva a snarky grin, but it ended up being more of a genuine smile. "Men in a pissing contest aren't always as careful or smart as they should be."

"Probably why they tried to kidnap us." Eva strolled through the door to their group space and went straight to Harlow's desk. All three women's computers were hooked up to the monitors on the wall, displaying on three different screens. Harlow dropped into her seat and scanned the data, following along with the connections Mona and Eva made as they explained them.

"This is definitely something." Pulling Eva's computer closer she pointed to two names. "You two dig into these. Find anything you can." Harlow rolled her head from side to side. "I'll get this one." She typed the final name into her own self-built program.

The rest of the day passed in a blur. Dutch came and went as she worked, head down, mind finally occupied with something besides her past and the lingering effects still rearing their ugly head.

"This is an alias." Eva came up to the front, plugging her computer in. "There's nothing until six months ago." She stood beside Harlow as the three women studied what she'd found.

"We'll add it to the list." Harlow shot Eva a smile. "Good job."

An hour later Mona was in the same place, staring down a faceless name born less than a year ago in Alaska who was the owner of three buildings across the state plus two more on the lower California border.

"Have you found anything?" Eva bent to peek over Harlow's shoulder at the screen.

She'd taken the most difficult of the three. The one Eva and Mona had struggled to find anything on, knowing if she couldn't find who this was, then they were fucked.

So far it seemed like they might be fucked. Anything she'd been able to dig up went nowhere, leading her to one dead-end after another.

"I'll find him." Harlow reached for her coffee cup, but the spot it always sat was empty.

"Right here, Mowry." Dutch walked into the room, her cup in hand. "You went through a whole pot already."

"Really?" She reached out to take the cup. Usually after a pot she was shaking at least a little.

"How's it going?" Dutch moved in at her side as Mona and Eva went back to their desks to organize and compile all the data they'd collected.

Harlow shook her head as she stared at the screen. "This guy." She moved through the list of potential leads her program found, clicking on the next one in line.

Her screen went black.

Harlow looked up at the ceiling where Pierce went crawling around yesterday. "Shit." She was just about to stand up to go give him hell when her screen flashed back to life.

Displaying a familiar face. One that sent the coffee she'd just consumed racing back up her esophagus.

"Hey there, Harls."

The smile shining out at her was the same one she saw at night. Wide. Bright.

And fake. Nothing about it was real. It was a mask.

Most masks were scary, and this one was no different.

"Harlow?" Eva stood up from her desk, brows pulled together. Mona was on her feet a heartbeat later, eyes locked onto the screens at the front of the room as they each lit up, one after the other.

Each showing his face.

Harlow stared at the eyes she once thought were warm.

The nose she should have broken.

The man she should have walked away from long before she did.

"I told you I'd find you." Tod's smile sharpened. "Did you think I'd just let you go?"

"Turn him off." Eva rushed to the front of the room, reaching for the line of cords still dangling from the ceiling and walls.

"No." Harlow pushed up from her seat, eyes lifting to the screens on the wall. "We can't."

Tod laid a trail for her and she'd fallen right into his trap.

"This could have all been so easy, Harls." Tod's smile faded. "You should have taken my call. Then you would have been on the right side of this whole thing." The iciness she remembered well crept into his gaze. "You can thank your friend for keeping me from seeing you today." Tod worked his jaw from side to side.

Harlow stepped around her desk, eyes glued to the biggest of the screens on the wall. Large enough she could get a good look at Tod's face. The tone of the skin across his cheek and jaw.

The colors just beginning to bloom under the surface.

"I came to save you, Harls. I was going to protect you. Keep them from stopping you however they have to." His nostrils barely flared. "But the man you replaced me with kept it from happening." Tod's lips were twisting into a snarl, the same one he wore the last time she saw him. "You should be sure to thank him for signing your death certificate."

Harlow jumped back as the screens all went black.

Then the lights switched off.

The echo of locks clicking open and closed rang down the hall, making the silence in the room even more deafening.

She slowly turned to face the eyes staring at her.

Eva's face was pink, the flush rapidly spreading down her neck and over her collarbone. "Who the fuck was that?"

Harlow swallowed hard. This wasn't supposed to happen.

She was unfindable. A ghost of a person.

Her eyes found Dutch.

"Who is he, Harlow?"

She blinked a few times. There was no way out of this.

No way away from him.

Again.

"My ex."

CHAPTER 8

HARLOW HADN'T TAKEN a breath in too long.

Her skin went pale as she swayed a little.

Dutch moved in, scooping her up just as she went down. He was barely to the door when Pierce rushed in with Shawn on his heels. Pierce went straight past him into the room, eyes snapping from Eva to Mona. "Are you okay?"

Mona's attention went from Eva to Pierce before jumping to the line of windows overlooking the property outside. "Is everything unlocked?"

Pierce turned to Shawn.

Shawn had his phone against his ear. "Everyone is on the move. We can hold it down until the system is back up and running."

Pierce's gaze fixed on Dutch. "We need her awake."

"We need to give her a goddamn minute." Dutch pulled Harlow closer. "Do you have any idea what the fuck just happened?"

Pierce glanced at Shawn. "It broadcast everywhere, Dutch. The televisions. The computers, everything."

"And you still want to use her?" Dutch turned. "Fuck you, Pierce."

"Yeah. Fuck you, Pierce."

His eyes dropped to the woman in his arms. Her blue gaze held his. "You're going to hurt your leg again."

"I'm fine." He took a step, intending to take her somewhere no one could bother her.

"Me too, then." Harlow kicked her legs. "Put me down."

"No. You just passed out. You need to lie down." Dutch took another step.

"Pierce is an ass, but he's right." Harlow tried to squirm out of his grip again. "I'm the only one who can override whatever he's done." She huffed out a breath. "Put me down."

Her skin was pink again. The glassiness of her eyes was gone. For all intents and purposes, Harlow looked fine.

But looking fine and being fine were two different things.

Dutch slowly lowered her to the ground. "Don't make me regret this, Mowry."

She smiled at him. "I plan to make you regret everything."

Harlow booped him on the end of the nose before spinning away to go back to her desk, false facade firmly in place.

She was good at putting up enough smoke and mirrors so most people didn't see the fire burning just out of sight, threatening to incinerate everything at any second.

She plopped into her chair, took a swig of the decaf coffee he'd just brought her and pulled another computer from her bag, setting it on her desk and flipping the lid open.

"Ms. Mowry." Pierce eyed Harlow as her fingers danced across the keys.

Harlow didn't answer him. Didn't even acknowledge his existence.

"Ms. Mowry?" Pierce stepped closer.

Still Harlow didn't make any move to indicate she'd heard him.

"Harlow." This time Pierce said it louder.

Harlow turned to face him, her dark brows high on her head. "Do you want me to fix this, or not?"

Pierce stared at her a second, lips parted. "I do, in fact, want you to fix this, but I believe there is more to it than you simply doing," he waved around her desk, "this."

"There's not." She turned away, leaving Pierce to stare at the back of her head.

Pierce looked toward Dutch, one hand out in question.

"Mr. Pierce, I believe what Harlow is trying to tell you is that she could use some peace and quiet while she works." Mona stepped toward

Pierce, her face serious. "Maybe you and your men could go be sure the perimeter is still secure."

Pierce's expression barely softened as he studied Mona. "That is a very good suggestion, Ms. Ayers." Pierce gave Harlow one last glance before leaning into Dutch, dropping his voice. "I trust you can contain any issues here?"

"I can." Dutch didn't miss the last place Pierce's gaze swept before he left the room.

"What do you need us to do?" Eva stepped in beside Harlow. "Is there something we're capable of handling?"

"How much do you understand code?" Harlow didn't look away from her screen. Her eyes barely narrowed as she hit a key.

The locks on the hall doors stopped flicking open and closed.

"Some. Not a lot." Eva leaned in close, watching over Harlow's shoulder. "I have a girl on my team who's really good at it and tried to teach me some things."

"Is she one of the ones willing to come here?" Harlow's fingers were on the move again.

"She is." Eva went to her own desk and pulled out her personal computer. "But that won't be for days. Maybe weeks at this point."

"I don't need her here." Harlow's head turned as Eva sat her computer on Harlow's desk. "Give me just a second and I'll have our internet back up. Get her on a video chat as soon as you can."

"You can fix all this that fast?" Mona's eyes were wide as she watched Harlow work.

"Not all of it, but I can at least get us back up and running. Dick face has learned a few new tricks, but not as many as I have." Harlow's eyes lifted to Dutch, holding his gaze a second before dropping back to her laptop. "He's cleared out all the connections I set up to the government cameras around town and I need someone else to help me, otherwise it will take days." She let out a breath. "There. Internet is connecting."

Harlow leaned back in her chair, staring at the screen of her work computer. "I can't fucking believe this."

"At least I'm not the only one with a crazy dude following me." Eva snorted.

Harlow didn't look amused. "He's not crazy."

"Ya sure? Because he seemed pretty fucking crazy." Eva's lip curled. "If he called you Harls one more time I was going to scream."

"Why?" Harlow's eyes stayed on her screen.

"I didn't like the way he said it." Eva shook her head. "Like it's still okay for him to have a pet name for you."

The screens across the front of the room flashed to life.

Harlow turned to Eva. "Call her."

Eva pulled up a chair and a handful of minutes later a woman popped up on the screen. She was sitting on a couch, blonde hair in a wad at the top of her head, wearing an oversized sweatshirt eating Cheetos. "What's up girls?" Her smile dimmed. "You look like you did the day we caught twat face cheating on Mona."

Eva's eyes slid toward her friend.

"Oh shit. She's there, isn't she?" The woman's smile went tight as she waved at the screen. "Hi, Mona."

Mona stepped into the camera's view. "Hi, Heidi."

"Fuck that guy." Heidi shoved in a few bright orange puffs, talking around the mouthful. "He had a little dick anyway."

Mona frowned. "How did you know that?"

"Little dick energy." Heidi leaned in, peering at her screen. "Who's hot stuff over there?"

"That's Dutch." Eva scooted her chair a little closer.

Heidi gave him a slow nod. "They don't all look like that, do they?"

Eva turned to size him up before looking back at her friend. "Yeah. They all pretty much look like that."

"Holy shit." Heidi's grin widened. "When are you guys coming to get me?"

"Tomorrow." Dutch thumbed across the screen of his phone.

The women all turned to look at him.

But there was only one set of eyes he was focused on. "You said you need her, right?"

Harlow glanced. "If she can help, but I don't need her here right away."

"Will it be better if she is here?"

Harlow shrugged. "Possibly."

110

"Then Rico will go get her tomorrow and bring her here." Dutch leaned down, looking directly at the woman on the screen. "Can you be ready to come here tomorrow, Heidi?"

"Sure thing, handsome." She winked. "Will you be on the plane?"

Dutch wrapped one arm around Harlow's chair as he crouched down. "I'm unavailable, but I'm sure I can come up with someone who is."

Heidi's gaze skimmed over where his arm rested around Harlow. "Works for me." She reached out to pull her computer closer. "What do you want me to do until I get there?"

"Eva says you understand code." Harlow barely leaned closer to him.

Heidi slowly smiled. "I might know a thing or two."

"Can you find a breach?"

Heidi's eyes widened. "Holy shit. Did someone break into your system?"

"Not someone." Harlow's mouth pressed into a frown. "If I send you the information can you start helping me isolate the infecting code?"

Heidi nodded. "Hell yeah, I can." She rattled off her email.

"Is it secure?" Harlow glanced her way.

Heidi smirked. "Very."

"Good." Harlow's focus was back on her computer. "I'm sending this your way right now. Get through as much as you can."

"Will do, boss lady." Heidi blew Eva a kiss as she disconnected the call.

"I like her." Harlow didn't look away from the email she was crafting.

"She's cool as hell." Eva glanced at Mona. "Sorry about that."

"It's fine." Mona straightened a little. "Shit happens."

Dutch paced the room as Harlow worked. She and Heidi chatted a few times by phone, working through the breach together. By the end of the night the gates were locked. The security codes were all updated, and the internal communications system was back.

Pierce and Shawn came in just before midnight. Dutch stared at the owner of Alaskan Security. "Haven't seen you geared up in years."

Pierce was wearing head-to-toe black. A vest wrapped across his chest and an earpiece was tucked into one ear.

His gaze snagged on where Mona was stretched across two chairs, eyes glazed as she watched Harlow work. "I'm willing to do what has to be done to keep the people here safe." He stepped to Harlow's desk. "You've done well, Ms. Mowry."

Harlow barely glanced up at him, eyes dropping to her computer before immediately bouncing back up. "What in the hell are you wearing?"

Pierce looked down at the tactical gear. "I would think it was fairly obvious."

Harlow's eyes went back to her screen. "It looks stupid on you."

Eva snorted from her spot on Harlow's other side. "It does seem weird to see you in something besides a suit."

"I wear things besides suits." Pierce sounded a little defensive.

"It is a little strange." Mona's eyes dragged down the front of Pierce's frame. "Not bad, though."

Pierce's head tipped in a nod. "I will take that as a compliment, Ms. Ayers."

"I wouldn't ." Harlow's snark was back in full force, but Dutch could see that the day was wearing on her. She was blinking more, each one moving slower than the last. "I think it's time to call it a night." He moved to stand behind Harlow's chair. "You will have a long day tomorrow and you need some rest."

"What I need is to get this motherfucker out of here." Harlow's tone was cold and flat.

Dutch turned, moving to the doorway where Pierce stood, keeping his voice low. "Where is he?"

Pierce didn't even pretend not to understand the question. "We don't know."

"How the fuck do you not know? Shadow followed him out of here. Where did he go?" Knowing Shadow was on Tod was the only thing keeping him from losing his mind.

Pierce's gaze moved away. "Shadow lost him about ten miles out."

Dutch stared at Pierce. "You've got to be kidding me."

Brock came through the door, outfitted in the same gear as Shawn and Pierce. "You ready, Sunshine?"

Eva glanced Harlow's way. "I'm not going until Harlow does."

Mona straightened. "Me either." She shrank back a little. "Not that anyone asked."

"Go." Harlow waved one hand at them. "I'll be fine."

"Of course you'll be fine." Eva reached out to shove at Harlow with one foot. "But we're a team. We're staying until you're done."

"That's stupid." Harlow continued working.

"You're stupid." Eva nudged her again. "Go to bed. Tomorrow Heidi will be here and then you two can take that son of a bitch to his digital knees."

Harlow's head dropped back and she huffed out a sigh. "Fine."

"Oh, thank God." Mona stood up, leaning from one side to the other. "That chair was starting to get to me."

Eva stood and grabbed the back of Harlow's chair. "Come on. Time to take a break from the bullshit."

Harlow didn't even try to hide her irritation. "You are all perfectly capable of going to bed without me."

"Yeah, but we don't wanna deal with your ass tomorrow when you haven't had any sleep." Eva grabbed her bag, loading in her personal laptop. "I'll keep my computer with me in case Heidi needs anything."

"I set us up a direct line." Harlow grabbed both her computers and shoved them into her own bag. "When is Rico going to get her?"

"We fly out at zero four hundred hours." Shawn stood somber and straight at the door, watching the women collect their things.

"You're going to go with Rico to get Heidi?" Eva snorted as she tucked into Brock's side.

"Is there a problem with that?" Shawn's eyes snapped Dutch's way before moving back to Eva.

"Nope." Eva shook her head. "I think you'll have a perfectly wonderful time."

Mona followed Eva and Brock out with Pierce close behind her. Dutch waited for Harlow, watching as she finished packing her bag.

"You don't have to wait for me. I'm fine." She shoved in her phone and the bag of chips she'd been nursing all afternoon.

"Unfortunately, until this is resolved you will have a guard at your side at all times." Shawn backed out the door as Harlow's eyes widened his way.

"What?"

"It's not safe right now, Harlow." Dutch took her bag, the agitation he'd been fighting all day threatening to shut him down now that he knew Tod was loose. "A direct threat was made to your life and Talbot's shown us he can override our security."

"Once. He did it once." Harlow grabbed her mug from the top of her desk and started to tip it back.

Dutch caught it before she could drink anymore of what she thought was regular coffee. "How in the hell do you think you're going to sleep if you keep chugging that shit?"

"I hardly even feel it anymore." She held one hand out between them. "See? Steady as shit."

"You can have tea." Dutch wrapped one arm around her, leading Harlow toward the door. "Or chocolate almond milk or something. No more coffee."

"You're the one who brought it to me all day." Her feet stopped moving and her eyes scanned him. "You bring it to me all the time, actually." One finger shoved toward his face. "So, technically, it's your fault I drink so much."

"You got me." Dutch pulled her a little more. "I'm your coffee dealer." He led her down the hall toward the glassed-in walkway leading to their rooms.

Harlow reached to grab the door, but Dutch held her tight as the prickle of awareness crept along the skin of his neck.

Something was wrong.

"What's—"

Dutch dropped her coffee cup, wrapping the newly freed hand over Harlow's mouth as he dragged her back toward the closest open door, pulling her into the storage room and silently closing the door behind them. He grabbed the door stop from the floor and held it out to her. "When I go out, shove this under the door so no one can open it."

"What?" Harlow whisper-yelled at him. "No."

"Yes." Dutch shoved it into her palm. "Shove it as far in as you can get it. No one will get through. Don't open the door for anyone you don't know."

"What is going on?" She pulled her hand away, dropping the stop to the floor.

"I don't know and I can't find out until I go out there." Dutch grabbed it and tried again to make her take the pie-shaped piece of rubber.

"I don't want you going out there if someone's out there."

Dutch stopped, unable to stifle the smile her admission brought on. "I think that's the nicest thing you've ever said to me, Mowry."

"Stop being an ass." She pulled her hands away again, refusing to take the stop. "Shove it under the door now." Harlow grabbed her bag and pulled out her personal computer, flipping it open. She set it on one of the shelves and laid her finger across the pad. In a few seconds the feeds from various cameras set up around the property displayed across the screen. Dutch leaned in close, scanning the frames.

"There." Harlow pointed to the lower left-hand corner. "Something moved."

Dutch zeroed in on the spot as he touched the piece in his ear. "We've got movement in the southwest corner. Anyone out there?"

"Negative." Shawn's tired voice came through the line. "Got two on their way to check it out."

Harlow gasped, one hand coming to cover her mouth as a pinpoint of light flashed in the same spot they saw movement. She hit a few keys and another set of feeds filled the screen.

A body laid motionless on the floor of the walkway they just almost passed through.

No. Not one body.

Two.

CHAPTER 9

HARLOW YANKED OPEN the door and ran out with Dutch yelling for her to stop as he chased her down the hall toward the walk way.

This was her fault. There wasn't a doubt in her mind she was the one that bullet was meant for.

She ran into the enclosed hall and went straight for the pile at the center of the space.

Pierce rolled to his back, groaning. "Holy hell that hurts more than I remembered." One hand came to rest over his eyes as he huffed through the pain.

"Are you okay?" Harlow reached for Mona who was still lying motionless on the floor.

Mona's eyes rolled to one side, resting on where Pierce's body was stretched out next to her. "Yeah. I'm fine."

All the air rushed from Harlow's lungs as she grabbed Mona's hands and pulled her up, helping her to her feet as the walkway clogged with men from the different teams, all shouting.

All angry.

Their voices bounced around the confined space, making it so loud her head hurt.

Harlow pressed her hands to her ears, trying to drown out the overwhelming sounds. Unfortunately it did nothing to block out the looks on their faces. The rage making their skin red and their jaws tight.

A hand wrapped tight around her arm, pulling her down the hall, toward the rooms and away from the scene. She tripped along, struggling to walk with feet that wouldn't move right as the soles of her sneakers skidded across the low pile of the industrial carpet.

"Hold on, Mowry." Dutch's voice barely made it through the buffer of her palms, but something about the low timbre of it settled the biting tightness in her stomach. "I got you."

The next second her feet were off the ground and once again she was tucked tight to Dutch's chest.

"Damn it."

"Sorry to keep disappointing you, Mowry." He managed to scan his badge, bumping open a door. "But I'm not going to stand there and watch you suffer just because it makes you uncomfortable to be close to me."

"It doesn't make me uncomfortable to be close to you." She yelped as he set her down abruptly, but didn't move away.

"Prove it."

Harlow swallowed. He was so close. Only a few inches of air separated them.

That and about a hundred different excuses.

No. Not excuses. Reasons.

Dutch eased a little closer.

If it were any other man she would be struggling to breathe. Finding some way to push him back. Deter him from the path he was on.

But after this shit show of a day, the desire to fight was barely existent. "I'm tired, Dutch."

"I know, Darling." His hands came up to rest on her arms, warm and heavy and strong. "I know."

She held her breath, knowing what was coming next. No doubt he had a million questions about Tod.

Questions she had no intention of answering.

Probably couldn't even if she wanted to.

"I think I just need to go to sleep." She tried to will her feet to move. Find their way to the door so she could open it and Dutch would leave.

"I think that's a good idea." Dutch's hands dropped from her arms. He tipped his head toward the bathroom. "You go get ready for bed. I'll make sure everything is okay."

Her eyes slid to the door to her room. "Someone was on the property."

"They were." Dutch reached out to slide one hand down the length of her hair. "No one will get to you, Harlow. I promise."

She snorted. "I think the last thing we need to worry about is them getting to me."

A sharp rap on her door made Harlow jump.

"It's Shawn." Dutch turned to the door.

Harlow jumped at him, grabbing one of his arms with both her hands, pulling him back. "How do you know? It could be someone else who got on the property."

Dutch stopped and turned to her, both hands coming to her face this time. His lips barely twisted into a pleased-looking smile. "Worried someone will get *me*?"

"I think that's a valid concern based on the past few days." She'd just watched someone shoot into the walkway. Two days ago a whole team managed to make their way onto campus and kidnap three people.

All of those men were dead now, but that wasn't the point.

The knock came again, but this time Harlow noticed the distinct pattern of the sound. "It's Shawn."

"Pretty sure that's what I said." Dutch backed away, keeping his eyes on her as he moved to the door. When he turned away, his big body blocked the tiny bit he opened it. He and Shawn's voices were hushed, staying low enough she couldn't make out anything they were saying.

Which meant it had to be about her.

Dutch closed the door, waiting a beat before turning around, a small duffel bag in his hands.

"What?" She crossed her arms.

"Pierce and Mona are fine." Dutch's eyes were too focused as they zeroed in on her. "But whoever shot at them is gone. It looks like it might have been a sniper on the other side of the fence."

"Okay." She tried to give him the level of indifference that carried her through life now, but it wasn't as easy as it used to be.

Coming to Alaska sounded like a good idea. A way to effectively disappear.

Go somewhere no one looking would be able to find her.

But it had happened anyway.

And that wasn't even the worst part.

"Okay." Dutch didn't push any further. Didn't fire off the questions that had to be there.

"Okay." Harlow dropped her arms and stood taller, knowing what was most certainly coming.

Who is Tod Talbot?

Why were you married to someone like him?

Why weren't you smart enough to see him for what he was?

"I thought you were getting ready for bed?" Dutch unhooked the badge clipped to his waistband and tossed it to the top of her dresser.

Harlow stared at it for a second before Dutch's next move dragged her eyes back his way. "What are you doing?"

He finished unhooking the buckle of his belt. "Getting ready to try to get a little sleep." He added the belt to her dresser, his lips barely lifting at the edges. "Don't look so panicked, Mowry. You don't get the pleasure of sharing a bed with me tonight."

"I'm not panicked." Her eyes burned as she stared at the fingers working the button of his khaki pants loose.

"Of course not." Dutch pulled the fly wide. "You planning to turn around, or are you gonna stand and watch me get naked and pretend like you don't care?"

"I *don't* care." Harlow tipped her chin up, willing the words to be true.

But she'd imagined this same scene unfolding in front of her more times than she could count, knowing full well it would never happen.

Because she wouldn't let it.

Showed what a liar she turned out to be.

"I think you do care." Dutch's hazel eyes barely darkened. "And you wish like hell you didn't."

Harlow's stomach squeezed at his scarily accurate assessment.

Most people only saw what she showed them.

All people. All people saw what she showed them. Knew her as the snarky, sometimes bitchy, workaholic she presented.

And at first, that seemed to be what Dutch saw her as too. It made things easier.

Unfortunately, at some point he started trying to see past the façade she built.

"I don't care what you think." Harlow kept her eyes fixed on his face as the sound of sliding fabric threatening to steal her gaze.

"Good." Dutch grabbed something from the bag on the bed between them, his gaze never leaving hers.

"What's that supposed to mean?"

"It means you shouldn't care what anyone else thinks. Including me." Dutch straightened, the pair of pajama pants covering his previously-exposed lower-half making it significantly easier to breathe.

But the reprieve was short-lived.

Dutch's fingers went to the buttons of his shirt, working them free with a deft touch. Before she could fully inhale he pulled the front open wide and tugged it down his arms.

"Holy shit." The response shouldn't have come out. It was only supposed to be a fleeting thought she allowed herself.

Like when you burp a soda bottle so it won't explode on you.

Dutch ran one hand over his left side, drawing her attention to a scattering of puckered discolorations peppering the skin covering his abdomen. "Shrapnel."

"Oh." It should be better that the scars were what he assumed she was looking at, but for some reason guilt settled into her stomach, making it twist in an uncomfortable way. "I hadn't noticed those."

Dutch lifted a brow at her.

"I mean..."

Dutch was silent for a minute, watching her. "I'm listening, Mowry. What did you mean?"

He was making her uncomfortable in a way she shouldn't want to continue. Pushing her to a place she hadn't been in…

Ever.

But there was something addicting about the discomfort. Something she couldn't help but want more of. "I mean I didn't expect you to be in such good shape considering you sit on your ass all day."

His immediate laughter filled the room. "Glad I could surprise you."

"Whatever." It was her go-to response when conversations got complicated, and it usually shut things right down.

"You've surprised me too." Dutch moved a little closer, bringing the tight plane of his bare chest closer. "I thought you were just hell on wheels when you first showed up here."

"I am."

"I know." He continued on, his mouth moving along with his feet as he closed in on the boundaries she kept around herself, literally and figuratively. "But that's not all you are, is it, Harlow?"

She wanted to tell him she was exactly that. A hard-headed woman he should leave be.

But the words wouldn't come out. Couldn't when a bare-chested Dutch was so close she could reach out and touch him if she wanted.

And fuck it all, she wanted to. To see if he was as warm as he felt every time he pulled her close. If he was as strong as he seemed.

As unyielding.

"You can touch me, Mowry. I don't mind." Now his voice was low. Barely a whisper of a rumble between them.

"I can't."

"Why not?"

Her eyes jumped to his. "Why not, what?"

"You said you can't touch me."

"No I didn't." That's not what she said. Was it?

"Good." He eased a little closer. "There's nothing stopping you then."

That was technically true. Not a damn thing was keeping her from reaching out to feel the tiny bit of sandy brown hair scattered over the wide plane of his chest.

And it was just a touch, right? Nothing more.

She'd touched plenty of chests.

This one was no different.

Before she could talk herself out of it, remember all the reasons this chest was not, in fact, like all the rest, Harlow reached up and pressed her palm square in the center of it.

If she hadn't heard the sharp intake of his breath, she sure as hell would have still felt it. It sent her lower lip between her teeth, pinned in place as she bit down.

"Mowry." Dutch's tone held a hint of warning. "I'd prefer it if you didn't look at me like that right now."

"Like what?" Her mouth was running on autopilot while her brain was otherwise occupied.

"Like you might be considering touching me with more than your hands."

"That's not how I'm looking at you." She widened her eyes, fighting them up to his face.

"Then what would you call it?"

"Disgust." She swallowed hard, unable to avoid looking down again. "I can barely stand to look at you."

He chuckled, low in his chest, one more thing she felt as much as she heard, only this time it went all the way to her toes, rippling through her body, slow and warm. "I can tell."

"Why do you look like this?" She stared at where her fingers were spread across his skin. "It's repulsive." Her other hand itched with the need to enjoy the same sensations as the first.

"I don't like feeling weak. Regaining as much strength as I could physically helped me mentally. Made me feel like I was still the same man as before."

"Are you?" Harlow finally gave in, resting her neglected palm next to the first as she stepped a little closer.

Dutch barely shook his head. "No. Not even close." His hands slowly lifted to rest on her hips. "Thank God."

That caught her attention. "What?"

"I was an ass before. Selfish. Conceited. All I cared about was myself."

"That doesn't make any sense." She accidentally moved his way a tiny bit more. "You risked your life to go get one of the men on your team."

"I wish I could say I did it for him." Dutch's fingers splayed across the thick knit of the sweater hanging past her butt. "But I didn't. I did it for me. For the attention it would get me."

Harlow blinked up at him. "But—"

"I want you to know that the man you see isn't always the man I've been, Harlow." His hands slowly eased around her body, sliding slow and steady up the center of her back. "It took something fucking awful for me to see what a miserable bastard I was."

"Why did you change?" Harlow stared up at him. The Dutch she'd known since her arrival at Alaskan Security was not a man anyone would call selfish or conceited.

She had called him an ass a few times.

Few hundred.

But that had more to do with her than it did with him.

"Because I had to. It was the only way for me to move forward." His body was pressed tight to hers now, his head tipped low.

Within reach.

"I had to be better. Do better. Deserve the life I didn't lose that day." His voice barely caught. "I had to find some way to get past the fact that I lived and Jack died."

"Did you ever wish you were the one who died?" The thought made her body ache deep inside.

"So many times I can't count."

She swallowed hard, trying to fight around the lump in her throat. "I'm glad you didn't die."

Dutch gave her a barely-there smile. "Good."

He leaned closer, moving so slowly it took a second to realize it was even happening. His nose ran alongside hers. "I'm glad I didn't die too." His lips barely brushed hers. "And I would go through all of it all over again to be right here, right now." Another pass of his lips. "With you."

"You make stupid decisions then." Her eyes dropped closed as his lips teased her again.

"We can agree to disagree on that one." One warm hand moved up her back and across her shoulder, easing in to cup the line of her jaw. His thumb pressed against the tip of her chin, parting her lips.

She sucked in a breath as Dutch's mouth came to hers, pressing slow and easy into place, sealing them together as his tongue slid between the lips he held open with the gentlest of touches. The man might be careful in his delivery, but nothing about the act was hesitant. He held her firmly, the hand from her face moving into her hair as his tongue swept through her mouth, rubbing hers before pulling back. His teeth scraped her lower lip as his palm curved against the back of her head, fingers tangled in the mass of her hair.

When his mouth once again covered hers Harlow couldn't help but lean into him, reaching up to wrap her arms around his neck and pulling him closer. A low growl moved from his mouth to hers as Dutch tugged her tight to him, the long, tight line of his body heating the front of hers.

A second later they went down, falling to the bed behind her, his weight pressing her into the mattress.

Pinning her in place.

Suffocating her.

"Stop." Harlow shoved at him, fighting for her next breath.

For her life.

Her stomach rolled and the skin of her face went numb. He was going to hurt her. Punish her for any list of perceived offenses.

Break her.

"Leave me alone." She kicked at the legs holding her down. "I can't breathe."

"Harlow." Dutch caught one of her swinging fists, blocking it from making contact with his face before immediately letting it go. "Mowry." This time his tone was sharp.

Loud.

Loud enough to open her eyes. He was off her now, laid out at her side.

Dutch pushed back the hair matting to her skin. The look in his eyes was cold and hard, but the touch of his hand was tender.

Careful.

"I'm going to fucking kill Tod Talbot, aren't I?"

CHAPTER 10

HARLOW STARED AT Dutch.

He was clearly waiting for an answer.

She took a slow breath, trying to calm her still-racing pulse. "Murder is illegal."

Dutch's lips twisted into a slow grin. "Only if you get caught." He rolled onto his side, tucking one arm beside his head. "And I can promise you I wouldn't get caught."

The idea was much more tempting than it should be. Maybe if Tod was dead all this would stop.

He would finally stop ruling her life.

That's what this was. Tod still controlled what she did. How she did it.

"You're thinking on that awfully hard, Mowry." Dutch wrapped one arm around her waist, pulling her closer.

"It's a tempting offer." It was an admission she wouldn't make to anyone else. Not even her parents.

No one knew the extent of what happened. The lingering damage it caused.

"I can imagine." Dutch sounded as if he completely understood, which couldn't be further from the truth. She'd worked hard to make sure no one knew the truth of the life she lived before coming to Alaska.

"He's an asshole."

"That he is." Dutch curled closer. "Are you in a place where you can handle some upsetting information?"

"I just freaked the fuck out when we made out, so obviously I'm perfectly fine." Harlow pressed down on the smile threatening to ease onto her lips.

"Obviously." Dutch nosed his way into her hair. "So you would call that making out?"

"I thought you had upsetting information for me?"

"I just want to be sure I understand what your definitions are, in case I decide to proposition you again." His voice held a smile she couldn't see.

"You are still in my bed. You're definitely planning to proposition me again."

"Not in the next five minutes."

She laughed a little in spite of the horrible turn her life took today. "You're a glutton for punishment."

"I'm definitely a glutton, but I wouldn't call what I'm looking for anything close to punishment." His lips barely skimmed over her ear. "I would suffer unbelievably to be close to you, Harlow."

He had. She'd noticed Dutch's limp was much more prominent these past few days. No doubt carrying her through the snow made his pain worse. "I don't want you to suffer for me."

She'd suffered for another person before, all to prove her love and devotion was real. It didn't turn out well.

Dutch took a slow, deep breath, his eyes serious on hers. "We've been looking for technical coordinators for the other teams. People to perform my job with Alpha, Beta, and Shadow."

"You told me that already." An uneasy feeling settled into her stomach. "I don't like where this is going."

"You're going to fucking hate it." He reached up to slide one hand through her hair, working his way down the long strands. "Shawn vetted the hell out of everyone. Talked to the options as we narrowed them down."

Harlow struggled to breathe.

That was how Dutch was so confident Tod was an asshole.

"One of them was Tod, wasn't it?"

Dutch barely nodded. "He made it all the way here for an interview with me and Pierce."

Bile climbed up her throat. "He was here?"

Dutch's jaw was tight and one of his eyes twitched the tiniest bit. "Not long."

Harlow's gaze moved just above his eyes to the tiny bandages taped across one brow. "What happened?"

"He was a dick from the second we walked in. Pierce told him it wasn't a good fit and he only got worse."

"He doesn't like not getting his way." She fought not to blink. Not to let her eyes close long enough to see the memory of Tod's face when he didn't get his way.

The uncontrollable rage that made his eyes almost unrecognizable.

"He got over it."

Harlow swallowed, trying to ease the threat of a gag fighting for control of her esophagus. "Why was his face bruised in the video?"

Dutch was silent as he stared at her.

"Please tell me." She shouldn't care. What happened to Tod should be completely irrelevant to her.

But damn she wanted to know if he ever suffered. Ever went through the same kind of pain he gave her.

"He asked if we were interviewing you, Harlow."

She couldn't breathe. Couldn't react.

"Pierce told him we didn't know who you were, but obviously he already knew the truth." Dutch's eyes stayed on hers as his hand continued to smooth down her hair. "Talk to me, Mowry."

She shook her head, blinking away the burning in her eyes.

If Dutch knew the truth he would judge her. Everyone did.

Hell, she judged herself.

Dutch took a deep breath, his bare chest lifting and falling in a slow, calming move. She focused on it, closing her eyes when they started to ache as much as her throat.

The covers of her unmade bed tucked up and around her body, making her heavy lids lift.

Dutch smiled at her. "Go to sleep, Mowry."

****

"WHY ARE YOU naked?" Brock eyed through the open doorway to the suite he shared with Eva.

"You're fucking kidding me, right?" Dutch pushed past him into the main living area of the space. "I've seen you start a shoot-out in the snow wearing just a pair of underwear and a set of boots."

Eva lifted one brow from her spot at the small peninsula lining one end of the tiny kitchen. "Where's Harlow?"

"She's asleep." He hadn't wanted to leave her, but the anger crawling across his skin was going to be impossible to hide if he didn't get up and find a way to get it under control.

And that started with making sure Tod Talbot would never get close enough to hurt Harlow again.

And he'd hurt her before. Dutch could see it in her eyes.

"I'm going out to find Tod Talbot and kill him. You wanna come?"

"Hell yes, I do." Eva was off the chair and across the room before he could react. She was already twisting her hair back off her face.

"What do you think you're doing?" Dutch stared at her, a little thrown off by Eva's immediate reaction.

Her nose curled up on one side. "Pulling my hair up so no one can grab it."

"You already want to go hand to hand with someone?" Dutch turned to Brock. "She can't come with us."

"Why the fuck not?" Eva moved closer to him, clearly not suffering from the same issues Harlow had with closeness. "Because I'm a fucking woman?"

"No. Because I'm worried you're going to make a fucking mess." Dutch inched away from Eva's hard glare. "I want to kill him without getting caught."

Eva huffed out a breath. "He should suffer." She turned to Brock. "How much does a severed penis bleed?"

Brock blinked a few times. "I don't think—"

"Ugh. Fine." Eva grabbed her phone. "Siri. How much does a severed penis bleed?"

Brock snagged her phone away, shutting the search down before Siri could give Eva any information that might work against them. "No one is killing Tod Talbot."

"Like hell we're not." Dutch dropped to the sofa. His leg was aching, but the pain was nothing compared to the knife twisting in his gut.

He was supposed to be able to help Harlow. Show her it was possible to get past awful things and move forward as a stronger, better person.

But after tonight he wasn't so confident that was an ability he had, which meant the best thing he could do to help Harlow was end the reason she was struggling.

And he was willing to bet his life that reason was Tod Talbot.

"He did something to her." Dutch met Brock's gaze. "Something bad."

"Have you tried figuring out what?" Brock came to sit across from him in one of the small armchairs in the tiny living room.

"There's nothing."

Both men turned to Eva, who was back in her seat at the counter, facing away from them.

"How do you know?"

Eva spun to face him. "Uh, because as soon as I realized this Tod person was an issue for her I hunted his ass down." She popped a chunk of cheese into her mouth, continuing to talk while she chewed. "He's never been to New York as far as I can tell. Lived his whole life in Texas. Worked for his father's business as a computer analyst."

"Harlow's from New York." Dutch leaned back in his seat, hands rubbing down his face. "Maybe they crossed paths in the hacking world."

"Harlow's not from New York."

Dutch immediately sat up. "Yes, she is. That's where we flew her in from. That's where all her references were from. Where all her past jobs were."

Eva stared at him blankly. "I'm disappointed in you, Dutch."

"What?" He glanced at Brock before looking back to the woman frowning his way. "Why?"

"I thought of everyone you would be the one most aware of what Harlow is capable of."

Dutch worked his jaw as he held Eva's glare. "Shit."

"Yeah, shit." She turned away, going back to her computer. "I've been looking up Todie boy all night since he's our best lead." She grinned at him over one shoulder. "Unless you want to ask sleeping beauty about her past because I can find even less of her shit."

"That's probably not a good idea."

"We can't help her if we don't understand what's going on." Brock's tone was understandably irritated.

"Not so sure she wants help." It was the most frustrating thing about all of this. Harlow very obviously needed help. Literally and figuratively.

She needed them to keep her physically safe.

And she deserved to feel safe. To know everyone around her would do anything to keep her that way.

"Sure she does." Eva was still eating chunks of cheese at the peninsula, now mixing in handfuls of pretzels here and there.

"Obviously you haven't discussed that with her." At least he wasn't the only one who thought he understood the woman he left sleeping a floor below, an armed guard outside her locked door.

"I don't have to." Eva tapped on the keyboard of her laptop. "If Harlow didn't want help she would have kicked you in the nuts days ago." She leaned into the screen, eyes narrowing. "Well this is interesting."

"What did you find?" Dutch stood, rounding the sofa to watch over Eva's shoulder.

"Looks like Tod-Tod had some charges filed against him."

"No way." Dutch scanned the screen. "We did a background check on him. It was clean as hell."

"It was clean." Eva tipped back a sip of wine. "Until today."

"Today?" Dutch found the date of the court filing. "Someone filed charges today?"

"Not someone." Eva pointed to the name at the top of the scanned forms. "That's the District Attorney of the county where he lived a year ago."

Dutch fell silent as he read the charges a DA in Texas filed against Tod Talbot. With each line his stomach turned more, until it squeezed so tight the chances were high he would lose anything it contained.

Eva downed the rest of her drink in one go. "Can I help kill him now?"

Dutch straightened, dragging his eyes from the screen. "Don't say anything to Harlow."

Eva glanced up at him. "She really hasn't told you about any of this?"

Shaking his head was almost painful as the information Eva just found carved its way through his brain, digging out a spot where it would stay forever.

Eva's eyes dropped. "I'm sure it's not you."

Of course it was him. It was everyone. Harlow didn't want to let anyone close.

Now he knew why.

"I'm going to go talk to Shawn." Dutch walked to the door, turning back to Eva. "Find everything you can on Talbot."

"Like I needed you to tell me that." Eva was pouring the last of her bottle of wine into a glass as the door closed behind him.

Dutch hobbled his way back downstairs, letting his gait be uneven, hoping to relieve some of the pain throbbing all the way to his hip. He nodded at Bobby, one of Alpha Team, as he passed where the other man was stationed outside Harlow's room. Dutch peeked inside, checking to be sure she was sleeping peacefully before going to find Shawn.

The coordinator for Team Rogue was at his desk, eyes lined with exhaustion.

"Any idea how Talbot is connected?"

Shawn sat silently for a minute. "I have guesses. You?"

"Just guesses." He sat in the chair across from Shawn. "Eva found charges filed against him today in Texas."

"Shit." Shawn rubbed his eyes. "I can't believe I didn't see that prick coming." He huffed out a long breath, setting his jaw. "Do I want to know?"

"Rape."

Shawn's gaze stayed steady. "And?"

"Domestic violence. Kidnapping. False Imprisonment."

"Do we know who it was against?" Shawn sat perfectly still except for the slow tap of his pen as he turned it, dropping each end to the top of his desk before flipping it again.

"Eva's working on it." Dutch shifted in his seat. "If I had to guess, I'd say it was a girlfriend."

Shawn dipped his head in a single nod. "Has Harlow said anything?"

"Not a fucking thing."

Shawn's finger went to his ear, tapping the device tucked into place. "He's with me." Shawn's eyes sharpened. "He's on his way." Shawn stood up. "Bobby says he can hear Harlow through the door. She's upset."

Dutch was up and running, bare feet eating up the hall and walkway, dodging the fully-geared men stationed throughout the area. Bobby was pacing when Dutch turned the corner. He swiped his pass and flung open the door.

The sight of her almost broke him.

"I'm here, Mowry." Dutch rushed in, crouching low, talking the whole time he moved. "Everything's okay." He went to his knees, crawling across the carpet toward the corner where she was curled into the fetal position. "Just breathe, Sweetheart." He slowly reached one hand out to her, barely managing not to pull it back when she shrunk away.

"Please don't hurt me. I didn't mean it."

"I will never hurt you, Harlow." Dutch crept closer, moving as slow as he could stand. Not pulling her close went against everything inside him.

But it would only make things worse right now.

He held her shoulder tight, using the touch to try to rouse her from the terror gripping her subconscious. "It's Dutch, Harlow."

"Dutch." His name rushed from her lips on a whisper. Her eyes opened, wide and filled with fear as they locked onto his face. "You're here."

"That's right." He dared to edge closer. "I'm here."

She blinked a few times. "I don't know what happened." Her lips pressed tight together as her eyes barely shimmered in the near darkness.

"Everything's okay." He repeated the mantra he used to get through his own night terrors. It was something he hadn't had to do in almost a year. Long enough he took a good night's sleep for granted.

Dutch rested his other hand on the side of her face. "Deep breaths." He inhaled, hoping she would go along with him, then the air out slow and steady.

On the second breath her shoulder relaxed just a little under his hand. "Good job."

"I'm not a child." She scowled at him around the barely-there O of her lips as she exhaled along with him. "I know how to breathe."

Dutch slowly eased his arms around her, making sure not to move too fast. "Let's get you up off the floor."

Harlow pulled away from his grip. "I can get up on my own. I don't want you to—" Her eyes dipped to his leg.

"Are you worried about me, Mowry?" He smiled as she pulled herself up.

"No." She flopped onto the mess of her bed. "I just can't handle watching you limp around trying to get my sympathy."

Dutch leaned closer, righting the sheets and blankets. "Don't fill this room with your lies, Darling. I know the truth." He eased onto the bed, pulling the covers over them both. "I worry about you too." He kept a little space between them, unsure how Harlow would handle being next to a man if another night terror grabbed hold of her.

"You're staying here?"

"I told you that already."

Harlow was quiet for a minute. "But you left."

Her voice was softer than normal. Almost fragile.

It dug into his hide, burning through to the deepest parts of him.

He'd let her down.

Already.

She needed him and he wasn't there. Had gone off, trying to soothe his own discomfort, and left her to fend for herself against an enemy he knew well.

The same one he was supposed to be helping her battle.

"I won't leave you again, Mowry. I promise."

CHAPTER 11

THE ROOM WAS still dark thanks to the blackout shades hanging on the single window, but it had to be morning. Past time to get out of bed.

But moving was not something he was remotely interested in doing.

Harlow was curled tight to him, one arm wrapped around his chest, her head resting on his shoulder, a thin dribble of her drool making his skin damp and sticky.

It was fucking amazing.

He could barely see the outline of her features in the shadowy space. The relaxed line of her jaw. The soft fan of her lashes. The smooth skin of her brow.

Harlow was sleeping peacefully, holding him tight, bits of her hair stuck to his face and in the crease of his neck. Her soft body was sprawled across the mattress, one leg slung over him, the other stretched in the opposite direction, her socked foot peeking out of the covers.

The woman was even a tornado in her sleep.

A light knock at the door forced him to attempt to unwrap his body from her grip, the act taking more strategic maneuvering than any op he'd ever been on. By the time he opened the door, Pierce was tapping one foot against the carpet.

Dutch leaned against the door frame, keeping the door open. It might disturb her deep sleep, but he wasn't letting her wake up without him again. He promised not to leave her and he meant it.

"How is Ms. Mowry this morning?" Pierce's gaze slid into the darkened room where Harlow still laid.

"She's still asleep." Dutch kept his voice low, hoping Pierce would follow suit.

"I understand she needs to rest, but we need to have a discussion, and we need to do it sooner rather than later." His lips pressed into a thin line. "Last night could have been devastating, and I'm unwilling to risk a similar occurrence."

Dutch glanced into the room. "I'll get her up and try to talk her into it."

"There's no talking her into it. Not anymore." Pierce took a step back. "This has moved beyond giving her time. I understand this is difficult for her, but there simply isn't an option at this point."

148

As much as Dutch hated Pierce for saying it, he was right. He carefully closed the door, the lock clicking silently into place.

"I was married to him."

Dutch turned.

Harlow sat in the center of bed, her hair mussed from sleep. She was perfectly still, watching him.

Waiting for a reaction.

"I don't think he's so happy about the *was* part of that statement."

Her gaze lingered on him a second longer before dropping to her lap. "I left one day while he was at work. Packed up what fit in a backpack and walked away."

"Why did you have to run?" Dutch walked to the bed, easing down to sit on the edge beside her.

Harlow barely shook her head. "I didn't say I ran."

There was clearly a difference to her. Walking away gave her the power. Running passed it to the man who continued to try to hurt her.

But Tod didn't stop at hurting Harlow.

"There were charges filed against him yesterday in Texas, Harlow." Dutch reached out to smooth down the mess of her hair. He tried to ease his fingers through the strands, but they were a matted tangle. He grabbed the hairbrush from the table beside her bed. "Come here."

Harlow's head lifted and she eyed him. "You want to brush my hair?"

"I want you to relax." He settled in behind her, one leg running down the length of her body. "The charges were pretty disturbing."

She was quiet as he started to carefully work the brush through her mass of almost-curly waves.

"Domestic violence." One slow, easy glide of the brush. "Kidnapping."

Harlow's back was stick straight as she sat, staring straight ahead, making it impossible for him to gauge her reaction to the information. "Rape."

Her head barely dipped toward her lap.

Dutch set the brush on the mattress beside him and wrapped both arms around her, pressing his nose into her soft hair. "Should there be more charges against him, Mowry?"

She sucked in a long breath. "That's information you probably don't want."

He pulled her closer, tucking her body back against his. "It doesn't change anything." He leaned back, taking Harlow with him as his back rested against the headboard. "I was going to kill him before. I'm still going to kill him now."

Harlow's weight rested against him, her body warm against his skin. "When am I meeting with Pierce?"

"We are meeting with Pierce whenever you want to meet with him." Dutch slowly stroked across the soft knit of the sweater she slept in.

"I should probably shower then." Harlow pulled out of his hold, scooting across the bed. She peeked back his way over one shoulder. "Are you staying here?"

Dutch wrapped one arm behind his head and eased down the mattress. "What do you think?"

Harlow rolled her eyes and turned away, but not before he saw the smile trying to find its way onto her lips. "Whatever."

He flipped on the television, watching half an episode of The Office while Harlow showered. After about fifteen minutes the shower shut off, signaling it was time for him to get dressed.

Dutch stood up, dropping the pants he slept in and pulling out the khakis he packed for today.

"I swear to God, Dutch."

He turned his head to look over one shoulder, finding her standing in the doorway to the small bathroom, eyes glued to his ass. "Something wrong, Mowry?"

"You're fucking naked again." Harlow still hadn't pulled her gaze from him.

Hadn't blinked either.

"You don't seem too upset about it." Dutch turned to face her, holding the pants strategically as he went.

Harlow's eyes narrowed in a glare that slowly worked up to his face. "You're doing this on purpose."

"Definitely."

"You're trying to prove I'm attracted to you."

"Not what I'm doing." He shook out the pants. "Not even close." He grinned. "It's nice to hear you're attracted to me, though."

Her eyes widened. "That's not what I said."

"That's what I heard." He bent a little, leaning down to step into the pants that had until this moment given Harlow ample time to close her eyes.

Dutch glanced up.

"Your eyes aren't closed, Mowry."

"Was I supposed to not look?" She crossed her arms. "Because I feel like if you just fling it around like that I'm supposed to look at it."

"Fling it ar—"

"You know what I meant." She wiggled one hand in the direction of his dick. "It's going everywhere."

Dutch straightened, giving her a grin. "I'm going to take that as a compliment.

****

SHE WAS GOING to have to leave Alaska.

Jump on a plane.

Rent a car.

Hitchhike.

Something.

Because whatever lurked outside the walls of headquarters was definitely less of a problem then the man standing in front of her, finally zipping his wiener into his pants.

"Why aren't you wearing any underwear?" She glared at the naked chest still staring her in the face. It was almost more of an issue than the rest of him put together. Broad. Toned. A tiny sprinkle of hair scattered over the shadowy scars marring his skin in a way that made him seem even more masculine.

More real.

But men like this one weren't real. She'd been fooled before and swore never to let it happen again.

That's why she had to leave.

Dutch pulled down the waist of his pants, revealing a scar that was bigger than the rest peppering his skin. "They rub against this. The nerves still haven't calmed down. Drives me crazy."

She understood the feeling.

Every day Dutch found a new way to soften her resolve.

Hell, it was happening more like every second at this point.

He pulled one of the button-ups he always wore up his arms, eyeing her as he worked the buttons into place. "You ready?"

"I guess." Harlow adjusted the hem of her sweater. Dutch wasn't the only one with a variety-less wardrobe. She wore oversized sweaters and baggy jeans almost every day. They were comfortable to work in and kept her warm in the cool air that never seemed to fully go away here. "Is he waiting for us?"

"Pretty sure Pierce has enough on his plate to keep him entertained until you're ready."

Dutch pulled open the door and held it, waiting for her to go through first.

Harlow squinted at the man standing outside her room. "What in the hell are you doing?"

"He's making sure your ass stays safe." Dutch tipped his head to Micah, wrapping one arm around her back. "Are you okay going through the walkway?"

Harlow's heart sped up. "Fine." She stared ahead toward the connecting hall. "Not that there's another option."

"That you know of." Dutch's hand splayed over her hip, holding on as he tugged her to one side, toward one of the rooms.

He swiped his badge across the sensor beside the door, waiting for the lock to click open before pushing inside.

Harlow stopped short. "What in the hell is this?"

"It's a stairwell." Dutch pulled her along the dimly-lit space.

"Why's it so dark?" She went down the stairs, shivering a little as the air cooled.

Dutch shrugged. "No reason to keep it bright. We never really use it."

"Then why is it here?" She tipped her head to peek further down the cement hall.

"In case something like last night happened." Dutch pulled her to the left, into a smaller hall that branched off the main one.

"I thought this place was safe." It was part of the appeal of coming here, taking this job. A secure location where she could bide her time.

Wait out anyone who might be trying to find her.

"It was." Dutch swiped his badge at a steel door before pulling it open. "And it will be again." He tipped his head, indicating she should go through the door.

Another staircase was on the other side, one too narrow for them to go up side-by-side.

"You go first." Dutch hung back. "I don't want you checking my ass out the whole way and tripping."

Harlow scoffed. "You're awfully full of yourself."

Dutch was suddenly much closer, his body warm and solid as it rested against hers. "Just when it comes to you, Darling." He leaned in close, trailing the tip of his nose along the side of hers. "If you really want me to go first I will. Just be sure to be careful so you don't fall."

"I won't fall, because I won't be looking at your ass." She stood a little taller, trying to be unaffected by his closeness.

By his constant certainty. His consistency.

Tod was never like that. Not even in the beginning. Looking back there were always breadcrumbs she should have been smart enough to follow out of the woods.

But she wasn't. And now she had to confess all her sins.

All her mistakes.

155

Dutch's hands came to cup her face. "Everything will be okay, Mowry. I promise."

Harlow stared up into his eyes, wishing that she could have just a tiny bit of Dutch's confidence in the situation. "That's not a promise you can make."

He would judge her. See her differently after this.

Everyone would.

He smiled softly. "You'd be surprised what I can make happen."

Before she could argue any more his mouth was on hers, warm and strong. Unwavering in the claim it made.

It's what he'd been this whole time.

Unwavering in his pursuit.

Didn't matter what she said. How she tried to act. The barriers she tried to erect.

Dutch didn't give a shit about any of it.

And it made it hard as hell to keep trying.

Especially right this minute. When she needed his certainty so much.

Harlow wrapped her arms around his neck, pulling Dutch closer as she breathed in his scent, soaked in his heat. Tried to pull it all the way to her bones so it could shore up the very structure of her.

Fill in the holes. The weak spots always threatening to snap.

For the first time she kissed him back with purpose and intent.

In a heartbeat she was pressed tight to the wall, the cool concrete chilling her back as quickly as Dutch warmed her front.

Normally something like this would make her panic.

Leave her feeling pinned.

Threatened.

But not today. Not with him. Not anymore

All she felt was safe. Protected.

Nothing could get to her when he was there.

Not Tod. Not the pain he buried under her skin until it invaded her brain.

Her soul.

Dutch's hands still held her face, keeping it in place as he broke the kiss. His eyes were on hers, then moving across her face as if it was the first time he'd seen her.

The mouth that so easily laid her bare lifted at the edges. "You ready now, Mowry?"

"Are you suggesting that sucking your face made me more prepared?"

"One hundred percent that's what I'm suggesting."

She pursed her lips, knowing she should come back at him again, use a verbal jab to try to shove him back a little.

But it wouldn't work. Not even a little bit.

"Fine."

"So we're in agreement?" His lips suddenly descended on hers, catching them in a short, but thorough kiss.

She leaned forward as he pulled away, earning a shit-eating grin from the man still holding her.

Harlow shot him a glare. "I should bite you next time."

Dutch leaned his body into hers a little more. "You definitely should." His lips came close, but this time avoided hers, instead sliding along her jawline to nip at the spot just below her ear. "I'll be looking forward to it all day." He pulled her earlobe between his teeth and gently scraped. "I love the way you taste, Mowry."

Any fight she might have been able to conjure up left her completely as his horrible mouth continued down the column of her neck, teasing her skin with his tongue and teeth as his hands moved from her hips, following the barely-there curve of her waist to ease up the ticklish span of her ribs.

Harlow wiggled under his touch.

Dutch froze. "Talk to me, Mowry." His head lifted, eyes focused on her face. "Too much?"

Yes would be the easiest answer. One that would guarantee Dutch taking his hands off her and a step back.

But both of those things sounded terrible. More terrible than the truth.

"I'm ticklish." She pressed her lips together, knowing this was one more tiny step she never intended to take. "You tickled me."

One brown brow lifted. "Ticklish, huh?" His hands were back on her, this time going straight to her ribs.

158

"I swear to God I will kick you in the dick if you tickle me on purpose, Dutch Mackey." She clenched up, arms locking down, pinning his hands in place.

Dutch's head fell back and his laugh echoed off the concrete walls. "You are fucking fantastic, you know that?"

Before she could catch the breath the threat of being tickled seized in her lungs, he was back against her, his body hard and unyielding. "I promise never to tickle you on purpose, Harlow." His hands moved up without hesitation, passing over her ribs to tuck under the fullness of her breasts. "What else can't I do to you? I need to know the rules."

"Right now?" Her voice was a little pitchy. A little breathless as his thumbs slowly slid higher.

"Right now." His lips were back on her skin, the feel of them on her neck making it harder to focus on what she was supposed to be doing.

Which was telling him she had rules.

She did, but so far he'd broken all of them.

Because she let him.

"I don't—" Her eyes rolled closed as one thumb ran across the nipple secretly straining for his touch.

"You do. And that's fine. I just want to be sure I work with them."

She fought her eyes open. "You mean follow them."

Dutch's gaze lifted to meet hers. "That's definitely not what I mean."

His thumb and finger found the rebellious nipple, working it through the thick knit of her sweater. "If I followed your rules we wouldn't be here, would we?"

Harlow barely whimpered at his touch. The deep need it stoked.

"No." The whispered word was a confession. One she wished she didn't want to make. "Asshole."

He smiled. "I wish I could say I was sorry." His hand moved from her breast. "I'm not."

"Then why are you stopping?"

Dutch kissed her again, his hands moving to catch the sides of her face as his mouth made her legs weak and her stomach tight. His breath was choppy and sharp when he pulled away.

"Because I don't have any desire to fuck you in a hallway, Mowry."

CHAPTER 12

HARLOW'S PUPILS WERE dilated and her lips were pink and swollen as she stared up at him.

A direct result of his bad behavior. Hell, maybe it was good behavior. At this point it could go either way.

Whatever it was, somehow it helped her turn a corner.

One he hadn't seen coming.

"How much does Pierce know about my history with Tod?" Harlow reached up toward her hair, trying to smooth it down.

It wouldn't do her any good. All it would take was a single look at her glassy eyes and pink cheeks and Pierce would know exactly what took place.

"I don't know." Dutch watched as she tried to erase the evidence of the past five minutes. "He won't tell me."

Harlow's dark eyes darted to his. "You tried to find out?"

"Of course I tried to find out." He lifted his brows as she scoffed. "You saying you've never tried to find dirt on me?"

"Tried?" Harlow straightened, tugging at the hem of her giant sweater.

Of course she wouldn't have simply tried.

She would have succeeded.

"Find anything interesting?"

"No." She looked him up and down. "You're boring as hell."

Dutch was still laughing as he knocked on the final door.

Pierce pulled it open, standing back as Harlow passed into his office. She walked around him to peer at the backside of the door. "That's some old-school castle shit you have going on."

"Doesn't mean it doesn't work." Pierce smiled at her. "Did you know there was a hidden door in this office, Ms. Mowry?"

Harlow lifted a brow at him. "No, but I did question your taste in literature." She grabbed one of the aging books on the decoy shelf, testing to see if it moved. "You better hope no one comes in with a hankering for Moby Dick."

Pierce's eyes barely sparkled as he watched Harlow. "No one has yet."

Dutch understood Pierce's appreciation for Harlow's willingness to say what she thought, no matter who she was talking to. Most people walked on eggshells around the owner of

Alaskan Security. He was an intimidating guy. Between the suits and the formal way he spoke, most men watched what they said and most women fell all over him.

Not Harlow. She didn't give a shit and Pierce clearly appreciated that fact.

"Lucky you." Harlow flopped down in the chair across from Pierce's desk.

"Indeed." Pierce's gaze barely flicked to Dutch before going back to Harlow. He took a slow breath. At least the man understood this was going to be a fine line he had to walk.

Pierce rounded the desk, slowly lowering into his chair. "How are you feeling this morning, Ms. Mowry?"

The flush on Harlow's cheeks barely deepened, but her eyes stayed on Pierce. "Fine."

"That is good news." He leaned back in his seat.

"How are you feeling?"

Pierce's jaw barely went slack. He recovered from the surprise of Harlow's concern quickly, nodding his head in appreciation. "I am sore, but otherwise fine."

"That's cool." Harlow's eyes moved around the room, passing from one spot to another. "So are we here to talk about shit or not?"

Pierce's attention shifted to Dutch. "We are definitely here to talk about shit." He motioned to the chair beside Harlow with an almost invisible move of one finger. "Specifically the piece of shit named Tod Talbot."

163

Harlow's gaze leveled on Pierce. "He *is* a piece of shit."

"I agree." Pierce sifted through the files on his desk. "Even before the events of last night."

"I heard he was here." Harlow's eyes narrowed on the files. "Is one of those on him?"

"Yes." Pierce pulled one free and without opening it, slid it across the top of the desk to Harlow. "It appears our piece of shit has been busy since you left him."

Harlow snapped the file from the desk and flipped it open across her lap. She stared down at the top paper. It was the same court document Eva found last night. Harlow was silent.

Dutch watched to make sure she was breathing, waiting for the rise and fall of her chest or shoulders. When it didn't come fast enough, he reached for her, sliding one hand across her back.

Harlow's eyes came to his, wide and searching.

He scooted his chair closer, leaning into her, looking at the file she held. "Did you find out who the victim is?"

"Based on the limited access Eva could obtain, it appears he had a short-term relationship that recently ended badly." Pierce's eyes never left Harlow. "Can I assume your relationship with him ended similarly?"

Harlow's head shook slightly. "No." She took a deep breath. "I left while he was gone one day. Just walked away. Left almost everything."

She flipped to the next page in the file, squinting down at the grainy photos. It was a series of stills from Tod's visit to Alaskan Security's headquarters. When she reached one clearly depicting the brawl the ensued one finger came out to slide across the scene. She peeked Dutch's way under her lashes before continuing to turn pages. "Where is he now?"

"I assume he is in the same place the rest of the men we're hunting are." Pierce steepled his fingers, elbows resting on the arms of his leather chair. "Did he abuse you, Harlow?"

She slowly closed the file. "I don't know how to answer that."

"Did he cause you physical, bodily harm?" Pierce's gaze was intense as he waited for her answer.

Harlow's back slowly straightened, chin lifting. "Yes."

"Did he cause you harm in other ways as well?" Pierce's right eye twitched and the press of his fingers turned the tips white.

The flush on Harlow's cheeks was gone now, drained away by the pain of her past. "Yes."

Pierce nodded. "Thank you for sharing that with me."

Harlow's brows came together. "You're welcome?"

Pierce leaned forward, resting his forearms on the desk surface. "I understand how difficult it can be to come to terms with something like that, Ms. Mowry. I understand the desire to hide it from people out of fear of judgment. I appreciate that you trust me enough to discuss this matter."

"I don't have a choice."

Pierce barely smiled, but it didn't reach his eyes. "You, Ms. Mowry, are a woman who knows she always has a choice."

Harlow glanced Dutch's way before turning back to Pierce. "Tod is a hacker too. It's how we met."

"Is he any good?" Pierce's shoulders barely relaxed at the change in conversation.

Harlow lifted one shoulder and let it drop. "He's alright."

"Not the best."

She shook her head, lips barely lifting into a smile. "No. Not the best."

Pierce smiled back at her. "Lucky me then."

Harlow's lips pressed into a frown. "You got shot because of it."

"I got shot because of my own mistakes. During the time we were focused on the piece of shit's bad behavior, one of their men was able to access the property." Pierce's gaze was unwavering on Harlow. "I am the one who deserved that shot, Ms. Mowry. I was at fault. I was responsible. No one else."

Harlow's eyes dropped to her lap. "Mona could have been killed."

Pierce's nostrils flared and the twitch in his eye was back. "I am very aware of that fact, and you can believe I lost no small amount of sleep over it." He jumped up from his seat and paced to the other side of his office, where bookshelves lined the walls and two armchairs flanked a floor-to ceiling window. "I can promise you the piece of shit will not have the opportunity to attempt to harm another woman."

"You're going to kill him?"

Pierce turned, eyeing Harlow with one hand tucked into the pocket of his pants. "Wouldn't you?"

Harlow sat perfectly straight, unblinking. Her head slowly tipped in a nod. "I would."

"Good." Pierce looked to Dutch. "Is she armed?"

"Armed?" Harlow spun in her seat to face Dutch. "Armed?"

"You want to be able to kill him if the opportunity presents itself, correct?"

Harlow's head turned back and forth as she looked from him to Pierce. "I'm not really a gun person."

Pierce made a quick frown of indifference. "Suit yourself. It's probably better Dutch is the one to take care of him anyway."

Harlow's eyes were wide as they moved down his body. "Do you have a gun?"

"Always." Dutch reached back to pull out the pistol tucked in the waistband of his pants. Harlow leaned back as he held it between them. He reached down to the hem of the pants covering his injured leg, unholstering the smaller gun he carried there.

"Two? You carry *two* guns?"

"It's the perk of missing part of a leg." Pierce came closer. "No one can tell anything is hiding there." He propped against his desk.

Harlow eyed Pierce's suit. "What about you?"

"What about me, Ms. Mowry?"

"Do you have a gun too?"

Pierce's smile was easy. "You can rest assured that if I am the one to find Mr. Talbot first I will be more than capable of resolving the situation."

"How are we going to find him?" Harlow sat up a little straighter, scooting toward the edge of her seat.

"I was hoping that you could help us come up with a plan for that."

The door to Pierce's office opened and Shawn walked right in. "Brace yourself."

A woman strode in right behind him. "Stop being dramatic." She marched straight to Pierce's desk. "You the boss?"

Pierce's gaze flicked to Shawn. "For now." He stood, holding one hand toward the woman. "Pierce Barrick."

"Heidi Rucker." She grabbed his hand in a firm shake. "You're pretty hot too." Her gaze traveled the room until it landed on Dutch. She dropped Pierce's hand and pointed at him. "I know you." Her finger moved to Harlow. "You too." She smacked her gum and gave Harlow a grin. "You're super pretty."

"Thanks." Harlow tipped her head back just a little. "So are you. I like your pants."

"Right?" Heidi twisted from side to side, showing off her knit joggers. "I freaking live in these things. Comfortable and flattering for us thick girls."

Harlow nodded. "They make your butt look great."

"My butt is great." She gave Shawn a once over. "Innit, hot stuff?"

Shawn stared at her, a mixture of horror and embarrassment fighting through his expression.

Heidi snorted out a laugh as she turned back to Pierce. "Where's my office? I got shit to do."

"I can take you there." Harlow jumped up from her chair, taking a few steps before turning back to Pierce. "Unless you need anything else from me."

Pierce blinked.

Dutch smiled. She'd surprised him twice. Shown Pierce she was so much more than even he realized.

And it made him fucking proud as hell.

"No." Pierce stood. "Please get Ms. Rucker set up with anything she needs."

Heidi's brows lifted. "Ms. Rucker?" Her gaze trailed down Pierce's frame. "Fancy."

"Respectful." The sharpness in Pierce's tone surprised nearly everyone in the room.

With one exception.

Harlow's lips curved in a small smile as she watched him.

"We're going to go find the piece of shit." She hooked one arm through Heidi's. "And then you can go make good on your promise."

The women walked out of the office arm in arm, leaving the men left behind staring in their wake.

"She's—"

"A fucking tornado." Shawn finished Pierce's sentence.

"What did she mean when she asked—"

Shawn held a hand up, cutting off Dutch's question. "Shut it."

"I was just wondering—"

"I said shut it." Shawn closed his eyes, taking a short sharp breath before opening them again. "What did Harlow have to say?"

"She confirmed what we expected." Pierce picked up the file on Talbot. "These charges might be his first, but it's definitely not his first offense." He dropped into his chair. "I want to be sure he suffers for what he did to her." His gaze lifted to Dutch.

"He'll get what he gets." Dutch understood Pierce's anger. It came from a wound as deep as his own.

One that no one could see, but was no less painful.

Pierce leaned forward. "What he gets will be what he deserves." The words came through clenched teeth.

"Right now we need to focus on finding him. Until then this conversation is pointless." Shawn stepped to the desk and plucked the file from

Pierce's hand, passing it to Dutch. "Take this to the ladies and keep us in the loop."

Dutch took the file. "What have we collected on the new location?"

"Shadow has a couple guys doing basic monitoring until we can get more men trained on the nuances of covert operations." Shawn dropped into Harlow's vacated seat. "I sent Reed, Tyson, and Jamison over to help Shadow train. We'll send Alpha and Beta out in batches with Shadow and Rogue so they can get a feel for it without being on their own."

"I should have had Alpha and Beta trained before now." Pierce rubbed his face with his hands.

"No one could have seen this coming." Shawn stood. "Rogue is reconvening as we speak. I'll have the whole team here within the week."

"The whole team?" As far as Dutch knew, Wade and Bess planned to stay in Florida until this all passed, keeping their son Parker far from the mess.

Shawn's jaw tensed. He leaned back in his seat, eyes moving from Pierce to Dutch. "Late last night Wade received a call on his personal cell."

"Shit." Dutch rubbed his eyes. He was tired. Fucking exhausted from weeks of being on edge. Worried about everyone here. The team he called family. The men he called brothers.

Harlow.

"Yeah, shit." Shawn's head dropped to his hands as he rocked forward, elbows to knees, fingers raking the longer dark hair at the top of his head. "It was fucking Talbot."

Pierce was still, watching Shawn with the same intensity that he'd had since he and Dutch met almost fifteen years ago. "Get them here. Send all of Shadow to bring them from the airport. Whatever it takes." He stood. "Then we're going to find Talbot and whoever he's working for and end every one of them."

"Um." Mona took a step back from where she stood in the doorway. Her eyes were wide where they fixed on Pierce. "I'm sorry. I will come back later." She continued to back away.

Pierce jutted his chin to the door, eyes on Dutch. "You two, out." He crossed the room, his steps more hurried than normal. "I am always available to you, Ms. Ayers. What can I help you with?"

Mona's still-wide eyes landed on Dutch. "Harlow just sent me down to tell you we found something."

Pierce stopped. "Already?"

Mona's head bobbed in a quick nod.

Pierce's mouth split into a smile he directed only at the small blonde woman still watching him with uncertain eyes. "Amazing news."

Mona's gaze dipped to Piece's chest. "How's your—" She reached out, but pulled her hand back just as quickly. "Do you have a bruise?"

Pierce's smile softened. "Well worth it."

Mona's fair skin flushed as she turned away, walking ahead of them down the hall toward the office for the newly formed Team Intel.

"I think she's scared of you." Shawn stepped in at Pierce's side, watching Mona's hasty retreat.

"I promise you she is not." Pierce started walking, each step quicker than the last, his shoulders pushing back more the closer they got. "She simply isn't sure how to assert herself yet."

"It won't be long considering the company she keeps."

"Let's hope." Pierce pushed the partially-open door wide, stepping into the room.

"About time you showed up." Harlow didn't even look up from her computer as she bit off a chunk of—

"Are you eating Twizzlers?" Dutch stepped in and snatched the candy from her.

Harlow's head snapped his way. "Did you just take my breakfast?"

Dutch bit off a chunk of the cherry-flavored licorice. "Seems like."

She stared at him a second, her face twisting around as she tried to give him a dirty look.

Unsuccessfully.

When her smile finally snuck free she glared along with it. "Asshole."

Heidi watched the interaction, keeping her eyes on Dutch as she leaned into Harlow's side. "I think he's hot for you."

"I am." Dutch wiggled his brows at the newest recruit. "One hundred percent."

"He's always one hundred percent. It's not as impressive as it sounds." Harlow's focus was back on her computer. "Do you want to know what we found or not?"

"That's why we're here, Ms. Mowry." Pierce eased closer to the desk where Harlow and Heidi sat close together.

Harlow glanced up, eyes lingering on Mona as Pierce eased in at her side. "Obviously."

She blew out a breath, plugging her computer into the cable that broadcast it across the main screen on the wall at her back. "We found the piece of shit."

CHAPTER 13

"YOU'RE SURE THIS is where he is?" Pierce stared at the screen.

"I'm sure this is where he has been recently." Harlow tried to shrug in a way that made it seem like she was indifferent. "I can't promise you he's there now."

"How did you find him?" Dutch moved in close, perching his ass on the desk she sat at as he studied the same screen.

Heidi spun her chair a couple rotations. "He's not smarter than one of us, let alone two of us." She leaned to peek around Dutch. "Where's Shawn?"

Dutch turned to look behind him. "He was right with us."

Heidi lifted her brows. "Doesn't seem like it now." She gave Dutch a slow grin. "Seems a whole lot like he's hiding."

"Where exactly is this location?" Pierce's tone was sharp as he snapped Harlow's attention back his way.

"It's about fifty miles out, toward the Canadian border."

"What led you to this address?"

"It's not exactly an address." Harlow switched windows on her laptop, bringing up the map that would more accurately explain where she believed they would find Tod. "It's a town."

"How large?" Peirce stepped toward the screen, hands in his pockets as he studied the map.

"About a thousand." Harlow zoomed in on the map, showing the layout of the small town of Junction, Alaska.

"There's a base ." Pierce pointed to Ft. Greenly. His eyes snagged on Dutch's.

"What?" Harlow looked between the men. "Why does that matter?"

Dutch's stance was tight, almost rigid.

"It means anyone who wanted to recruit trained men would have a supply." Dutch's eyes slowly lowered to hers. "Means we might be dealing with someone just like us."

"Well they're not *just* like us." Heidi leaned back in her seat, kicking her feet up on the desk. "They're the bad guys, right?" Heidi suddenly sat up straight, her eyes going wide. "Wait. Are we the bad guys?"

"We are not the bad guys." Pierce pointed at her. "We are *not* the bad guys."

Heidi held up both hands, palms facing Pierce. "Okay fine. I believe you." She kept her eyes on Pierce as she leaned into Harlow's side. "Are we the bad guys?"

"No." Harlow shook her head. "We're not."

Heidi nodded. "I just need to know. So I can decide how to dress."

Harlow turned the new hacker's way, leaning back to take in her casually cool attire. "How would you dress if we were the bad guys?"

Heidi looked down. "Probably like this, but maybe like in black." She shrugged. "Some grey for variety."

"We're definitely the good guys." Dutch's leg barely brushed her from his spot perched on her desk. "So far our intel has led us to believe this other group is trying to secure routes to smuggle drugs into Canada."

"Like the cartel?" Heidi didn't seem fazed by the possibility that they were dealing with big players in the drug trafficking world.

"Potentially exactly like the cartel." Pierce took one final look at the screen. "Possibly someone working with them in some capacity."

Heidi slow rocked her head in a nod. "Cool. Cool." She scanned the room. "Is this where I'm gonna be working?"

"It is." Pierce frowned at the empty doorway before crossing to Dutch. "Since Shawn is otherwise occupied, can you assist the ladies, make sure they have everything they need?"

Dutch's eyes found hers. "I'm happy to make sure they are properly taken care of."

"He's talking about you." Heidi leaned into her side again, watching Dutch. "He means he's happy to service *all* your needs." Her head tipped Harlow's way. "If you know what I mean."

"Yeah. I caught what you meant." Harlow's face was hot as she turned to the computer in front of her. "We need to find more information. See what else they've been shipping out through the post office."

It was how they'd found Tod. He'd sent a package out and paid for it using a card connected to one of the other addresses they'd identified as being part of the same conglomerate as the warehouse outside town. An easy hack into the post office's security system and they had footage of him from four days ago, standing in line like anyone else. Fooling the people around him into believing he was a normal human.

He was not.

"So this guy's crazy?" Heidi was kicked back in her seat, computer on her lap, scrolling through the footage from the post office in Junction.

"Real fucking crazy." Harlow scanned the street view of the little town, looking for anything else that might have a wireless security system she could find her way into. A newer gas station caught her attention.

"How do you know?" Heidi yawned, her eyes never leaving the footage.

Harlow barely stiffened. She glanced up at Dutch where he still stood in the doorway talking quietly with Pierce.

His gaze almost instantly came to hers, holding it for a few long seconds.

She gave him a little smile. One that didn't feel as forced as she remembered them being.

· "I used to have bad taste in men."

****

"SO HE GOES to the post office every day." Eva paced the floor at the front of their office. Her shoes were off and she held a can of grape soda, occasionally taking a sip as she walked. "What the fuck is he mailing?"

"Something that fits in an envelope." Mona rolled her head from side to side.

"He's paying for the most expensive delivery possible." Heidi flipped through the charges made with the credit card. "It's the only thing he uses the card for besides one fuel transaction."

"Fuel?" Harlow sat up a little straighter. She'd spent the morning trying to find her way into the surveillance system at the gas station, but came up empty. "From where?"

Heidi pulled up a paper from the stack, holding it closer to her face. "Alaska Petroleum Co."

"APC." Harlow pulled back up the map of the area. "If we can figure out what he's fueling we can do a DMV search. See if it leads us anywhere."

"Super pretty *and* super smart." Heidi smiled at her. "Tod is fucked."

"That's the plan." Harlow squinted at the street view as she moved it around.

Heidi took a bite of a carrot from the veggie tray Brock brought in around lunchtime, chewing as she spoke. "What about that?" She pointed at a flat-topped building on the opposite corner of the gas station.

"What about it?" Harlow scanned the nondescript structure. From the top it appeared to be a fast-food restaurant.

"Isn't it a bank?"

Harlow tipped her head to one side. "You think?"

"It's got that overhang for the drive-thru." Heidi popped an olive in her mouth followed directly by a chunk of cheese. She looked pointedly at Eva. "Your new man makes a wicked-good veggie tray, boss."

"I make a good everything." Brock strode in, decked out in his tactical gear, with Dutch following right behind. He went straight to Eva's side. "I gotta go out."

She took a short sharp breath. "Be careful." Her smile was tight as he leaned in for a kiss.

Harlow's eyes immediately went to Dutch, scanning down the full gear he wore. "Why are you wearing that?"

"Because we need all hands on deck for this one, Mowry." Brock moved into Dutch's side, wrapping one arm around his shoulders. "I promise to take good care of him."

180

"No." She stood up. "No. He can't go."

"He has to go." Brock's tone was softer. Gentle.

Which took the agitation crawling over her skin and sent it into overdrive. "You're not the fucking boss, Brock Star." She rushed around her desk and to Dutch. "You're not going."

Brock slowly backed away.

Dutch glanced up, scanning the room over her head as he caught her hand in his. "We need men trained in covert ops, Harlow. Alpha and Beta aren't ready."

"What about Shadow? They're ready." Her heart rate picked up as panic set in.

He couldn't go out there. It wasn't safe.

"Shadow is coming."

"Then you have plenty of men."

"We have to be careful Harlow. The more men we have, the more careful we can be. We will have eyes everywhere." Dutch caught her hand, pulling her out the open door. He tugged her into one of the small conference rooms along the hall, closing the door once they were in. "They're my team." His eyes fixed on hers. "I can't help them from here. I need to be there."

She swallowed at the lump clogging her throat. "What happens if you don't go?"

"Then I send them out one man less. I can't do anything to help them. To keep them safe."

Harlow swallowed again, trying to clear the upset strangling her. "What will happen to you if you stay?"

181

His eyes went far away for a second. Sliding to a moment in time she would never want to see.

But could almost understand.

"Go." Harlow pushed back her hair, straightening. "Go do what you need to do." She lifted her chin up, trying to focus on anything besides the man making her struggle in ways that were more than a little unfamiliar.

Dutch stepped closer.

Harlow took a step back, putting one hand between them. "Nope. I can't do that right now."

She was hanging on by a string. An almost non-existent thread.

Dutch reached out, tipping her with one finger until she finally looked him in the eye. "I left a present in your desk."

"Okay." She sniffed in a breath. "Go do your thing."

Dutch backed to the door, opening it and slipping out in near silence.

"Shit." She dropped her head back to stare at the ceiling, breathing deep. Trying to find some sort of way to go back into the office and act like everything was fine.

Like she didn't just make a big deal out of nothing.

Harlow wiped her face with both hands before shaking them out. She sucked in a breath and marched out of the room, finding the hall empty. No sign of the men who were there seconds ago.

"Hey." Heidi stood in the doorway. "You alright?"

"Fine." Harlow straightened her shoulders. "We should get back to work." She strode past the newest addition to their team and into the office they shared. "We need to check out that bank and see if they have cameras we can access." Harlow lowered into her chair and stared at the top drawer of her desk. She hesitated a second before pulling it open.

"What's that?" Heidi leaned over her shoulder.

Harlow picked up the small item, pressing her lips together. She blinked a few times. "It's an earpiece."

She held it between her fingers, rotating the device, looking for a way to turn it on.

Activate it.

Whatever made it work.

A note in the drawer caught her attention.

All you have to do is put it in.

The writing was neat and even. Perfectly legible.

Harlow slowly and carefully tucked the device into the proper ear. Voices immediately carried through.

Familiar voices.

"She got it yet?" Brock's words were a little muffled, but still audible.

"Hello?"

"There's my girl." Dutch's voice was clear and crisp. "My feelings would have been hurt if you'd taken much longer."

183

"I don't know if this is a good idea."

"Then all you have to do is tap it once and it will turn off. Tap it again and it will reconnect." Dutch paused. "Only stay with me if it helps you."

"Can I stay on the whole time?" She glanced around the room, realizing she was having a conversation no one else could hear. "Won't I distract everyone?"

"I'm the only one you're connected to, Darling." Dutch's voice changed, lowering as he said something about the best route to take.

"Will I distract you?"

"How about I tell you before I have to go do something where I could be distracted, and you can either stay quiet or turn your piece off?"

Harlow nodded. "That would be okay."

"Good." His voice carried a smile she wished she could see.

"Where are you now?"

"We're headed to the warehouse just outside town. The other team that went to Junction left earlier. We should both get to our locations at the same time." Dutch was quiet for a second. "I'm glad you're here with me, Mowry."

"Me too."

The next two hours was spent listening to Dutch as he and the rest of Rogue staked out the warehouse, spreading across the area in a wide net, recording activity and photographing vehicles and plates.

"Have you seen anyone?" Harlow tapped into the few traffic cameras scattered through the area. It was a recent upgrade Fairbanks made as a way to combat the dwindling numbers of their police force. It made it easy to catch speeders and drivers who didn't like to wait for green lights. The city collected cash without burdening the force.

It also worked out well for Alaskan Security.

"There are a few vehicles parked in the lot, but so far no one's gotten eyes on anyone." The sound of snow crunching barely sounded through the connection. "It's all shoveled so I can't tell how many might be inside."

"Are there any prints in the snow?" Harlow found a speed camera set up less than a quarter mile from the warehouse and pulled it up on her screen.

"Just ours." Dutch's voice was softer. "I gotta go silent now, Mowry. You staying?"

She watched the feed as her stomach twisted. "Yes."

Her heart beat in time with the sound of his steps, the only sign Dutch was still there.

Still safe.

Being this concerned for his well-being was a problem she would deal with at a later time.

Right now she just wanted him back in one piece.

Movement on the screen caught her eye. Heidi slapped her on the shoulder then pointed at the screen.

Harlow slowly stood. "Dutch, I think someone's coming."

A black Dodge Charger with tinted windows slowly rolled across the camera's view.

The footsteps stopped.

"I'm going to talk. You don't have to answer." Keeping calm was almost impossible now that the car was out of sight.

Harlow turned to Heidi and mouthed the words 'find it'.

"A black Charger is headed your way on A3. It's not moving fast." She pointed to Eva and motioned to the recording of the footage.

Eva nodded, moving in to scan through the stills until a plate was partially visible.

"Eva's trying to see if we can get a plate and Heidi's trying to find it on another camera." Harlow grabbed her personal laptop and pulled it out, adding it to the desk. Eva was squeezed in close, flipping through screens on Harlow's work laptop.

"I got a partial." Eva's voice was low as she worked through the same system law enforcement used to run plates.

Harlow stood silently, listening for any sign Dutch was okay. A footstep.

An inhale.

Anything.

But the line was silent.

She squeezed her eyes closed.

"I got it." Heidi's whisper sent Harlow spinning her way to watch the Charger as it closed in on the warehouse.

Harlow scanned the surroundings for any sign of Rogue.

Nothing moved.

"This is where they are, right?" Heidi leaned closer, squinting at the screen. "They're fucking hide and seek champions aren't they?"

"God I hope so." Harlow stared at the scene as four men got out of the car.

She sucked in a breath. "That's him." She pointed to Tod.

"The one walking like he's the shit?" Heidi wrinkled her nose.

Harlow nodded. "That one."

Footsteps sounded in her ear again, this time faster than before.

"Dutch?" She straightened. "Dutch don't do any—"

A flash blipped in the upper right of the screen and the men walking toward the entrance to the warehouse toppled toward the ground, scrambling in the direction of anything they could use for cover.

The line in her ear went dead.

"Dutch?" Of all the fucking times for the damn thing to malfunction.

Harlow looked around the room, heart racing, stomach churning. "Dutch!"

She tapped on her earpiece, trying to reconnect the line.

"Weren't they wearing white when they left?" Heidi tilted her head as she watched the screen.

Harlow rushed to her side. "What the—"

A trio of figures in head-to-toe black moved through the trees surrounding the warehouse as pinpoint flashes burst across the screen, sending the men who just arrived back into the car, the wheels turning before all the doors were closed.

"That's a lot of shooting." Heidi glanced up at Harlow. "Can you hear anything?"

Harlow shook her head. "No."

And she wouldn't.

Because fricking Dutch cut her off.

CHAPTER 14

"YOU ASSHOLE." HARLOW came down the hall at him, legs working fast as she almost broke into a run.

Dutch braced himself for the impact.

He knew she'd be pissed, but letting Harlow listen to men die wasn't something he was willing to subject her to.

"I can't believe you did that to me." She was almost on him. A few steps later she launched, her Converse sneakers leaving the floor as she jumped at him, wrapping both arms around his neck as she held him tight. "I hate you right now." She buried her face in his neck.

Dutch pulled her close. "I know." He pressed his lips to her temple, breathing deep. "I'm sorry."

"You should be fucking sorry." Harlow squeezed him tighter. "I didn't know what was happening."

Dutch wrapped one hand around her bicep, trying to get a little more breathing room. "I didn't want you to hear what might have happened."

"I said I was staying with you." She held fast as he worked his fingers around her arm.

"I can't breathe, Mowry." He leaned forward, setting her feet on the ground, hoping it might give him better leverage.

"Choke him out."

Harlow's grip immediately released. She rushed to the woman who made the less than ideal suggestion and wrapped her in a hug. "You're back."

Bess's eyes widened. "I'm back." She returned Harlow's unexpected embrace, patting her back with one hand. "We had to come back."

"What sort of place have you brought me to?" An older woman filed in behind Bess, cradling Parker in her arms as she peeked out the window toward the mountains. "It's pretty." She glanced back over one shoulder as Wade rounded the corner. "It's not Florida, though."

"It's better than Florida because you get to be with your grandson." Wade took Parker from his mother. He pointed around the group of men gathered, introducing each. He thumbed his mother's way. "This is my mom, Gloria." He pointed to Harlow. "And that's Harlow."

Gloria's smile brightened. "I've heard a lot of good things about you, young lady."

"None of them are true or you wouldn't be calling me a lady." Harlow eyed Dutch over one shoulder, scowling his way.

Gloria wagged one finger in Harlow's direction, her eyes on Bess. "You're right. I'm going to like this one."

"Told you." Bess blew out a breath. "I'm exhausted."

"Come on, Sweetheart." Wade wrapped one arm around her shoulders. "Let's get you and Little Man situated in our room." He tipped his head at Gloria. "You too, Mom."

Gloria went to grab her rolling suitcase, but Tyson beat her to it. "I'll bring it up for you, Miss Dennison."

Gloria patted his cheek. "Aren't you a sweet boy?"

"I need a shower, Mowry." Dutch rested one hand on Harlow's back. All he wanted was to be alone with her.

"I'm still mad at you." She crossed her arms, but not in the tight, protective way she did before. This time it was more a statement.

One that left little to interpretation.

"You can take it out on me all night, Darling." He pushed her toward the door leading to the underground hall.

"Where are we going?" Harlow peeked back in the direction Bess and Wade left.

"I didn't think you'd want to take the walkway just yet."

"Shows what you know." Harlow's head tipped back and she looked him right in the eye. "I've gone through the walkway twice today."

Fear settled in his stomach, cold and heavy. "I showed you how to access the tunnels. Why didn't you take them?"

He had to go out with the team today. Leaving Harlow was damn near impossible, but this wasn't a time to be short handed in the field. And Alpha and Beta were all on campus. They might not be trained in covert techniques, but they could sure as hell put a stop to an unwanted visit.

But he was split. Wanting to be there to keep his team safe and needing to be here for her.

Knowing she was in the same spot where Pierce was shot just a short time ago made his ears ring and his eyes unfocused.

Harlow's expression changed, softening as she stared at him. "I just wanted to prove I wasn't scared." She backed toward the heavy door leading to the descending stairs. "We can take the tunnel."

He spent years getting to a functional point. Hours in therapy, learning how to cope and self-soothe.

And right now he felt on the edge of falling back.

Crashing back into the thick of it.

"I can't handle it if you get hurt, Mowry." Dutch shook his head. "I won't come back from not keeping you safe."

Harlow stopped, her eyes roaming his face. "It's not your fault, Dutch." She stepped toward him, stopping just in front to press her palms against his cheeks. "It's not your fault that Jack died and it wouldn't be your fault if I got hurt."

"I promised to keep you safe, Harlow."

She shook her head. "I don't remember that happening."

"Maybe I didn't say it out loud because I knew it would piss you off." Dutch's lungs moved a little easier with the banter. It pulled his thoughts from the dark depths they used to drown in, navigating the way to safer waters. "But I will keep you safe, Mowry. You're mine to protect."

"I never remember discussing that either." She pressed his cheeks a little more. "You can't just say it and expect it to be true."

"I feel like I can." His shoulders eased down, relaxing under the weight of his vest. "I made you a sandwich."

Harlow's hands slid from his face, easing down the front of his chest, over the bulletproof vest. She poked at it. "How much does that thing weigh?"

"A lot. That's why I'm ready to get it off." He caught one of her hands with his, lacing their fingers together. "Come on."

Dutch didn't have to direct her this time. Harlow stayed right at his side as they passed down the stairs and into the main passageway leading to the rooming building. The hall was quiet as they stepped out, with just a few members of Team Rogue making their way to their own rooms.

Dutch went toward Harlow's room.

"Don't you want to go to your room?" She scanned him from head to toe. "So you can change?"

He tipped his head in a nod. "Good call."

Dutch unlocked his door and opened it wide, letting Harlow go in first. She took slow steps, moving across the low-pile of the carpet. "How long have you been staying here?" She lowered to perch on the edge of his bed.

"A few years." Dutch worked his way out of the vest, setting it on the chair in the corner opposite where Harlow sat. "It's better for me to stay on site in case anything happens."

Harlow's lips pursed, twisting to one side. "Don't you get tired of working?"

He lifted his brows at her. "Don't you?"

"I work to forget." Her eyes were focused on him completely as she strategically set the observation out for his perusal.

Dutch turned, needing some space from the moment. He shucked the rest of his gear, lining it along the top of the dresser as Harlow sat silently behind him.

When he finally found the balls to turn and face her again, she was still watching him.

Still waiting.

The woman who never waited for anything, was waiting for him to admit he wasn't as far along as he tried to pretend.

That he wasn't really any better off than she was.

That he didn't have shit to offer her after all.

Harlow stood, slowly walking his way. Her eyes stayed locked on his as she closed the distance between them.

He couldn't look away as she stopped, standing close enough he could breathe in the soft scent of her skin. Her fingers came to his front, brushing across the fabric of his white shirt, skimming over the knit in a touch so soft he could barely feel it. "The ear piece wasn't for me, was it?" Her eyes dropped to follow the path of her fingertips. "It was for you."

He'd tried to fool himself. Pretend it was a way to help Harlow.

But she was right.

"I didn't want to leave you."

Her hands slowly gathered the hem of his shirt, pulling it up and out of the waistband of the tactical pants he still wore. "There were at least twenty men here who would have done whatever it took to keep me safe."

Dutch nodded. "I know that." He studied her face as she worked. "But none of them would be willing to do what I'm willing to do."

Her eyes immediately lifted, catching his as her palms flattened over the skin of his exposed stomach. "Why did you cut me off then?"

"Just because I'm willing to kill for you doesn't mean I want you to hear it happen."

Her touch stilled. "Did you kill anyone tonight?"

It was something he was hoping to avoid discussing with her until later. "No."

"Did the other men who showed up realize you were there?"

Dutch tipped his head. "What do you mean the other men?"

He'd cut her audio off before she should have known the other men showed up.

Her lips pressed to hide the curve of a smile. "Heidi and I found a camera that showed the warehouse." Her hands slipped higher, moving over the puckered spots where shrapnel was picked from his flesh.

"Did you, now?" He fisted the shirt, dragging it up and over his head. "Sounds like you were worried about me, Mowry."

"I had to do something when you shut me down." Her pointer trailed over one of the larger scars on his chest, softly passing over the shiny skin before continuing on. "Who were they?"

"Don't know yet." He reached out to rest his hands on her hips. "But this wasn't their first rodeo."

Harlow nodded. "But they weren't as good as Rogue." The line of her mouth softened into a little smile.

"Is that pride I see on your face, Mowry?" The thought that she might be proud of what he could do never occurred to him.

"Are you always going to make a big deal out of everything?" Her lips twisted into an almost frown.

"I definitely am."

Harlow huffed out a dramatic sigh, but the smile she had was back as her touch slid higher. "We couldn't even see you on the video."

"That's the point." Dutch sucked in a breath as one finger skimmed across his nipple.

Harlow's eyes jumped to his, fixing as she repeated the move.

"I didn't like not knowing where you were." She eased a little closer. "I didn't like that I couldn't help you if you needed me."

"You did help me, Harlow." Dutch pushed the tips of his fingers into the thick sweater covering her hips as she continued to pet him with calculated strokes. "I wouldn't have known anyone else was coming if you hadn't seen them."

"Then maybe next time you'll keep me on the line." She lifted one dark brow as her hands moved down. "Keep me in the loop so I don't have to punish you when you get back."

"Is that what you're planning on doing? Punishing me?" He gave into the need he'd been fighting, pulling her close. "Because so far this doesn't feel anything like that."

Her head barely dipped to one lifting shoulder. "I guess you'll find out."

"Not until I've had a shower I won't." Dutch dug deep, finding the strength to let her go as he backed away. "If you want to torture me you're going to have to wait five minutes."

"I can be patient."

"Can you? Because I haven't seen that side of you yet."

Her eyes narrowed as he shut the door between them, locking it just in case she decided to give him a little more hell before he was ready.

He peeled off the rest of his clothes, tossing them into the hamper before climbing under the water and rushing through the process. He was opening the door less than four minutes later.

"That was quick." Harlow was perched on the chair in the corner where he'd tossed his vest, looking much more hesitant than she had before he'd gone into the bathroom.

"I don't waste time, Mowry." Dutch went to the dresser and pulled out a pair of sleep pants, dropping his towel before pulling them on.

Her eyes never left him. "What does that mean?"

"Means I like to get shit done. I don't like sitting around waiting for something to happen. It makes me—" He couldn't finish the last of it.

He'd been working his way through shit for what felt like forever and thought he was finally in a place where he could give more than he took.

But tonight was making him rethink that.

Harlow was quiet for a minute. "I don't expect you to be perfect, you know that, right?"

"I'm not trying to be perfect." It was a knee-jerk response, one that sounded like a lie, even to his own ears.

He *was* trying to be perfect.
Completely recovered.
For her.

For himself.

"I don't know that I'll ever fully get over what happened to me, Dutch." Harlow stood from the chair. "I was abused. Verbally. Physically." Her chin tipped just a little. "He held me down and spit in my face when I disagreed with him. Squeezed my neck so long everything blurred to black and white." She stepped toward him, lifting one hand. "Broke my fingers, broke my glasses." She swallowed. "Tried to break me." She took a long, deep breath. "I will never forget the look in his eyes when he hurt me, Dutch. It will haunt me for the rest of my life."

Harlow stood in front of him. "I think it's unrealistic to believe that all that will go away if we just work at it hard enough." She shrugged a little. "I guess that's why I never tried."

Dutch reached out, smoothing back the mass of dark hair he'd thought of night and day for way too long. She was everything he'd imagined a woman would have to be to put up with him. Smart. Funny. Deadly with a comeback.

But her being right for him didn't make him right for her.

And that was where he stood now, stuck with the possibility that he might not be the best thing for Harlow.

But the worst.

"I don't want to hold you back, Mowry."

Her eyes widened. "What?"

"If I'm not over my shit, how can I be there to help you with yours?" The realization made him sick to his stomach, twisting the lingering self-doubt he tried to control until it spread and grew.

"I'm a grown woman, Dutch Mackey. I don't need you to fucking coddle me." She shoved him hard in the center of his chest. "Is that what you think I want? Some man to come in and fix the mess the last one made?" She pushed him again. "Cause if you do, then you can kiss my ass."

Dutch stood still. "I just—"

"You just what?" She pushed him again, sending him taking a few more steps back. "Thought I couldn't handle it myself?" Another shove. "That I need a savior?"

Her next shove sent him toppling backwards and onto the bed.

But Harlow didn't stop coming at him.

"I don't expect a man to save me. Especially not from myself." She climbed over him, crawling up his body before grabbing his face with one hand braced across his chin and jaw. "I just want someone who understands why I am the way I am and doesn't try to make me something I'm not." Her eyes dropped to his mouth. "That's all I want from you."

A second later her lips were on his. But the kiss Harlow started wasn't sweet or careful or hesitant.

It was strong and confident and in control.

Her teeth scraped along his lower lip as her hands shoved into his hair, fisting it tight.

She broke the kiss, her mouth still hovering just above his.

"Is that something you can give me?"

.

CHAPTER 15

THE WHOLE WORLD went sideways, flipping on its head as Harlow's back hit the mattress.

Then Dutch's lips were back on hers, his weight resting heavy against her chest and legs. His mouth moved to her ear. "How are you doing, Mowry?" He eased more weight onto his arms. "You feeling okay?"

"I'm fine." She wrapped both arms around his neck, pulling his mouth back to hers, breathing deep as the scent of him surrounded her.

It's why she wanted to be in his room. She'd only been there once, but remembered it vividly. The smell. The way his sheets seemed warmer. His mattress seemed softer.

The whole thing just felt better.

It was a big part of the reason she ran the hell away the last time she was here.

"Never cut me off like that again." She tried to say it against his lips, but the words ended up muddled.

"I can't promise that."

Harlow smiled at Dutch's immediate understanding.

"Didn't expect you to smile about that."

"You told me the truth even though you knew it would piss me off." Harlow slid both hands over his chest. "I respect that." Her touch moved over his face, fingers skimming the short hairs he'd neglected shaving off the past few days. "And just so we're clear, I fully plan on figuring out how to override that earpiece."

He leaned up to frown down at her.

"You don't want me to lie to *you*, do you?"

Dutch growled low in his chest as his body eased back over hers.

"Oh my God." The words rushed out on an exhale.

Dutch froze. "What's wrong?"

Holy hell. Was he going to be like this the whole time?

Probably.

"Nothing is wrong. You growled. I thought it was sexy and said 'oh my God'."

His lips quirked in a smile. "You think I'm sexy?"

Did that question even warrant an answer?

The man looked like fucking Chris Evans in tactical gear. Anyone with a heartbeat would think he was sexy.

But the odd shift in his features made her wonder if Dutch knew how she really felt. Which made sense, considering she'd done her best to hide it from everyone, including herself.

"I think you are sexy as hell." Harlow brushed her fingers across his lips. "Even that first day I wanted to sleep with you."

"Use me for my body?"

She nodded. "Women have needs."

"I'm sort of banking on that right now, Mowry." One of his hands found the hem of her sweater, slowly shoving it up.

"We'll see."

Dutch barked out a laugh. "You're fucking amazing, you know that?"

She'd lost herself before. Smothered who she was in an attempt to make a man like her.

"You're the first one to think that." A tinge of sadness crept into her voice.

"Liar." He caught her lips in another kiss as his hand pushed her sweater higher. "That's not true and you know it." His fingers barely grazed the underside of one breast. "There's been many men who wanted the real Harlow Mowry. You just didn't want them to have her."

"I didn't trust them with her."

Dutch's eyes came to hers, lingering. The hand teasing her breast came to her face, curving along her cheek as he kissed her again. It was almost overwhelming. The feel of his lips. The brush of his barely-there beard. The careful way he handled her.

Because Dutch knew she was breakable in spite of what she showed him.

It was the first time she'd ever felt completely safe with a man.

With anyone.

He knew her secrets and never once judged her. Never questioned how she got where she did.

Why she didn't leave earlier.

Why she didn't press charges.

Dutch just let it be what it was.

"I like you." Harlow didn't open her eyes when she said it, but the weight of his gaze on her was heavy.

"I know that, Mowry." Dutch's voice was soft.

"Okay." She rubbed her lips together. "That's good then."

The tip of his nose ran alongside hers. "It is good." The hand on her cheek moved to her hair, sliding down the strands. "You should know I'm in this for the long haul."

She dared a peek at him. "What does that mean?"

"Means I want to be with you. I want you to be with me."

"That's all?" He made it sound so simple. Like all they had to do was decide to be together and that would be it.

They would be.

"That's all." His smile made her heart skip a beat. "For now."

"I knew there would be a catch."

His grin turned devilish. "I am a catch, Mowry." Dutch was back to pushing up the heavy knit of her sweater. "I know how to make coffee." He worked her shirt a little higher. "I know where to find cookies."

Harlow lifted her arms over her head. "You can carry a tiny pistol no one knows about."

He chuckled. "Another good point."

Her sweater hit the chair in the corner.

Dutch stared down at the long-sleeved shirt she wore under it. "You always have this many clothes on?"

"Usually." Harlow ran one hand down the shirt. "It's cold here."

"I'll talk to Pierce about raising the thermostat in our office." His fingers worked up the cotton shirt, dragging over her exposed belly as they went.

She'd had sex since…

But it was always her running it. She was the initiator. The dominating partner.

It kept things on her terms.

She got what she wanted and nothing more.

But this was not that. Not by a long shot.

Dutch was not the kind of man who would be fine with that sort of scenario.

He wanted more from this.

And so did she.

But…

"Talk to me, Mowry." His hand stilled. "Tell me what's going on in that head of yours."

"Nothing." She held her breath, expecting his hand to start moving again.

Dutch shook his head, the hand on her belly backing down. "This isn't going to work if you aren't honest with me."

Harlow caught his hand. "Don't stop. Just keep going no matter what."

"This isn't a band-aid, Harlow." His body eased off hers, stretching out at her side. "You can't just rip it off and think everything will be fine."

"Maybe it will be."

"Maybe for you." He shook his head. "Not for me. If you think I would ever do this if you weren't one hundred percent comfortable, then you don't know me as well as I thought you did."

She did know that.

Damn it.

"I want to do this." Harlow rolled onto her side, curling closer to him, missing the feel of Dutch's body on hers. "I want to do this with you, but it's different. It's more..." She fished around for the right word. "Difficult than normal."

"I'm going to not be offended that you think sex with me is difficult."

She couldn't help but laugh at the serious look on his face. "I have been careful to only have sex with men I don't care about." She rolled her eyes up to look at the ceiling. "Unfortunately, I care about you."

Dutch smoothed down her hair, his hand continuing down to rub her back. "We don't have to rush anything, Mowry."

Her eyes leveled on his. "That's not what this is about." It had been so long since she'd tried to explain how she felt, and it was not turning out to be like riding a bike.

"Then what is it about?" His hand stroked over her spine in slow circles. "Talk to me."

"I want to have sex with you." She pursed her lips, considering holding the next bit in. "A lot. I want to do that a very much lot." Harlow took a slow breath, trying to calm the nervous energy making her words come fast and choppy. "But I don't seem to have the same…" She motioned between them. "Distance with you as I have with other people."

"Other people?"

"Other men."

Harlow smashed her lips together, trying to stop the constant stream of overexplaining running through them.

Dutch probably *loved* hearing about her past sexual partners when they were lying in bed.

And still hadn't managed to have sex with each other.

But he didn't look unhappy at all by her oversharing. His grin was back. "Sorry."

"You don't look sorry."

"I'm not." Dutch reached up to run one finger down the side of her face, tracing the line of her jaw. "What's your plan, Mowry?"

"You didn't like my plan."

"The power through thing? Yeah. That's not happening." Dutch's touch moved down her arm, making her wish he'd managed to get her shirt off.

Harlow sat up.

She wanted him to touch her, skin to skin, and clearly she'd made him hesitant about this whole thing.

Dutch was trying to be careful with her, and while she appreciated it, right now it wasn't coming close to giving her what she needed.

The fitted long-sleeved t-shirt was not as simple to get off as the oversized sweaters she always paired it with, which left her wrestling the damn thing off in the most unsexy of ways, the snug neckline sucking the skin of her face back as she yanked it off her head.

Laying back and waiting for him to touch her was not going to go well. The anticipation was too close to stress, and stress was too close to panic.

Harlow chucked the shirt, tossing it in whatever direction her hands aimed as she climbed on top of the man she'd been lusting after since her first day in Alaska.

At least until lust turned into something very different.

Dutch's eyes widened as she pressed her hands to his chest, rolling him to his back as she straddled his hips. Her attention immediately dropped to the jeans blocking the feel of his body under hers. "Damn it." She tucked and

210

rolled, unbuttoning her jeans as she went before standing and wiggling out of them too.

Definitely not a memorable disrobing, but that's not what this was about.

She wanted to be close to him. Feel his body with hers and clothes were getting in the way of that desire.

"I think you need to slow down, Mowry." Dutch held his hand up as she came back at him.

"Shut up, Dutch." Harlow climbed back onto him, the thin fabric of her panties doing nothing to buffer the feel of what she'd seen with her own eyes.

Twice.

"I just think—"

Harlow dropped forward, pressing her lips to his as she spoke. "Stop talking."

He was being a good man, she got that.

But all the reminders of what might happen only made it more likely it would, planting a seed she didn't want to grow. Not tonight.

Not with him.

Because Dutch was different.

"I like you, Dutch." Harlow forked her fingers into his hair. "I like the way you take care of the people you care about." She ran her hands down the sides of his face and over the stubbly hairs she'd imagined tickling the inside of her thighs. "I like that you worked hard to be a better man than you were." She ran her tongue over his lower lip, nipping it. "I like that you want to protect me from everything." Her hands slid over his shoulders and down his chest as she sat up, watching him. "I like that you switched my coffee for decaf.

His brows popped up.

"You thought I wouldn't notice I suddenly wasn't climbing the walls all day long?" She'd figured it out eventually. Not as quickly as she would have expected, but there was a lot going on.

Harlow trailed her fingers across his perfectly scarred skin. "I knew you were taking care of me." Her gaze lingered over the marks that proved his suffering.

His pain.

The pain Dutch used to understand hers.

"I tried to pretend you weren't." She could barely whisper it as her throat tightened. "I wished you would stop."

Dutch was quiet, his eyes never leaving her face.

"I knew you wouldn't, though." His skin was warm under her palms, his body solid where she explored. "I knew you would ruin it."

"What did I ruin, Harlow?" His tone was soft.

She met his gaze. "Me."

Dutch sat up abruptly, knocking her off balance. Before Harlow could tip over he had her, one arm wrapped tight around her back, holding her close as his hand caught the back of her head, cradling it as his lips covered hers. This time the press of his mouth was different than all the times he'd kissed her before.

It was a little rougher. A little less controlled.

A little less careful.

And it was everything she wanted in this moment. For Dutch to just be there with her. Not thinking of her past or his.

Dutch's hands were in her hair, on her back, sliding over her thighs, tickling over the skin of her ribs.

Harlow caught his hand just as it reached the spot that might make her accidentally retaliate. "Watch it."

His mouth smiled where it pressed against her neck. "You're really that ticklish?"

"I will assault you and not feel bad about it."

Dutch's chuckle was low and easy.

"Just avoid the ribs." She gripped his other wrist and lifted both hands higher, resting his palms over her breasts, ready to feel the heat of his touch there.

But they were still covered in a sports bra.

"Damn it." One more freaking thing to wrestle her way out of.

Harlow grabbed the banded bottom and worked it up and over, doing her best to not just flop her tits out.

But it was what it was at this point. Her boobs were big and flopping was just what they did.

"Oh." Dutch leaned back a little.

"What's wrong?" She'd been careful not to elbow him in the face. "Did I hit you?"

"No." His eyes dipped to her chest. "I did not realize..."

She followed his line of sight to the double-D's she'd wrestled with since her freshman year of high-school. "Yeah. I usually strap them down as much as I can so no one can tell they're like this."

She'd been proud of them when she was younger, but hearing it was all men would ever want you for sort of took that away.

Created one more thing she tried to force into nonexistence.

Harlow pushed her hair back, tucking it behind one ear. The mood had shifted, and this time it was her fault.

She was the one bringing in the past.

"I'm sorry. I just—"

"Don't." Dutch caught her face, tipping it up until her eyes met his. "This isn't going to always be easy, Mowry."

She frowned at him. "What have the easy parts been?"

He smiled. "I'm sure we'll have some eventually." His thumbs stroked her cheeks, eyes moving over her face. "You are so fucking beautiful." Dutch's smile was a little softer. "I'm so damn proud of you."

"I haven't done anything." If nothing else, the past five minutes made it clear she still let her past affect almost everything in her life.

Including this night with Dutch.

"That's not even close to the truth." He leaned back, taking her with him as he went. "You are here with me."

"So you're proud I'm having sex with a stupidly sexy man?"

"Stupidly sexy?"

214

Harlow rolled her eyes a little. "You don't have abs without recognizing women will find you sexy."

"Maybe there's only one woman I'm worried about." He rolled, taking the top position again. "I don't give a shit about what the rest of them think."

"Heidi thinks you're sexy." The jealous edge to the words was clear enough to make her eyes widen.

"I'll pretend you're not considering stealing all her gas points in retaliation."

Harlow rubbed her lips together. "I put all yours back."

"I know you did." He leaned down to brush his lips over hers. "That's when I knew you liked me."

"Then you knew before I did." She hadn't wanted to like him. Part of her still sort of didn't. It was the scared bit that wanted to shut the world out. Build a wall so high no one could get past.

She thought she had.

But even that small part of her knew it was no use when it came to this man.

He made her want to climb her own damn walls. Scale them and chase him down waving the white flag.

Dutch nosed his way down her neck. "At least we're finally both on the same page."

"Were you getting tired of chasing me?"

He lifted up, his eyes darkening to the color of stormy seas.

"I chased you through three feet of snow, Harlow. If you think I was even close to being tired of trying to catch you, then you are very mistaken."

CHAPTER 16

"I SHUT DOWN." Harlow's eyes dropped, her mood shifting immediately. "I should have done more to try to stop what was happening."

Dutch pushed back the dark hair caught against the side of her face. "You couldn't have stopped it, Mowry. Fighting might have made it worse."

She stared up at him, silent for a second. "I know that."

He thought the desire to find and slaughter Tod Talbot couldn't get any stronger, but knowing the son of a bitch tried to smother the fight out of Harlow made his skin burn with the need to return the favor.

"Why are you so quiet?" Harlow's question was hesitant.

"I'm just processing." Dutch took a slow breath, working through the reaction. She'd just started opening up to him and one wrong move could steal all that away.

"I didn't mean to—"

Dutch caught her lips before Harlow could issue another apology he didn't need or want. He inhaled the soft scent of her hair and skin. The layers of clothes she usually wore almost smothered it out, but now that she was nearly bare, the sweet smell of vanilla and lavender was stronger. "I like the way you smell, Mowry." Dutch kissed a line toward her neck, breathing deep against the drape of her dark hair.

"That's good." Her body relaxed just a little under his. "I read that lavender is supposed to be calming."

He chuckled against her skin. "How's that working out for you?"

"Meh." She relaxed a little more.

Dutch leaned up. "I'm gonna need you to keep talking to me, Mowry. I need to know you're okay."

"You want me to talk the whole time we fuck?"

"First of all." He held her gaze. "I'm going to need you to not refer to this as fucking."

Her eyes slowly trailed down to look at where his body pressed tight to hers. "It seems like you enjoyed the reference."

"Liking how it sounds coming out of your mouth and wanting to make it clear this is more than that are two different things, Mowry." Dutch caught one of her hands, lacing her fingers with his as he held it against the mattress

218

just beside her head. "I'm not just here for a fuck." He traced the swell of one breast with his free hand. "I want more than that from you."

"I know." Her eyes fell closed as his touch moved, palm curving to slide up the fullness.

"I want it all from you." His fingers found the darkened peak, rolling it until she whimpered. "I want you at my side in everything, Mowry. Not just the bed." Dutch tipped his head to catch the puckered peak between his lips, her sharp inhale shooting straight to his dick.

He reached down to grab her thigh, ready to pull it wide.

Harlow's leg locked up, her body going rigid under his. Dutch froze, waiting her out for as many heartbeats as he could stand before slowly relaxing his grip.

Her eyes were wide on his when Dutch lifted his head. "Talk to me, Darling."

She shook her head, blinking hard.

"No talking means we stop." Dutch started to move away.

Harlow grabbed his shoulders latching on. "I don't want to stop."

"I appreciate that, but I can't do it like that, Mowry. I told you I'm not that guy."

She eyed him for a few seconds. "I'm ashamed."

The soft admission was the most perfect and awful thing he'd ever heard. "There's no shame here. Not with me."

Her gaze moved down, focusing on his chest as one hand came to brush over the scars marring his skin. "I don't want to bring the past in here."

"Your past goes everywhere you go, Harlow. It's part of you."

She chewed her lower lip as one finger gently moved back and forth over one of the angrier-looking scars. "I don't like spreading my legs."

Harlow's eyes avoided his, which was probably for the best.

"He," she cleared her throat, "he said that was how I got where I did. Spreading my legs."

Dutch closed his eyes, counting to ten faster than he had in his life. No one deserved his attention besides the woman in front of him. When he opened them, Harlow was watching him.

Waiting for his reaction.

"Do I need to tell you that's not true?"

She shook her head.

He leaned closer. "Good." Dutch brushed his lips over hers. "Anything else I need to know?"

She shook her head, eyes still locked onto his.

Dutch dared running one hand down the line of her body, being careful to keep his touch firm enough to keep any potential tickling to a minimum. "What about earlier? When you climbed over me?"

"That's different." She lifted one shoulder. "Maybe because I'm the one doing it."

"I can work with that." Dutch rolled to his back, pulling her with him. "Get comfortable, Mowry."

She rested her hands on the mattress at either side of his head, her long hair falling into his face.

Dutch leaned up to wrap his lips around one of the nipples tempting him, pulling it into his mouth to tease the tip with a few strokes of his tongue before moving to the next.

Harlow's hips rolled into his, rubbing the line of her pussy against his aching dick, dragging a groan from his chest. She gasped, her eyes dropping to where he still held her nipple captive, caught gently between the line of his teeth. Her pupils were dilated, lids hooded as she watched his every move. The pace of her breathing picked up as he lifted one breast, sliding his fingers over the soft skin until they held the puckered tip, presenting it perfectly for his tongue.

Her body rocked against his, the soft tickle of her hair dragging over his skin with every move she made.

He reached between their bodies, rubbing over the heated mound of flesh still hidden behind the last scrap of fabric she wore. Harlow sucked in a breath as his fingers tucked into the side, immediately sliding between her swollen labia to find the hardened nub of her clit.

"Dutch." The soft roll of his name off her tongue sent him scooting down the bed, determined to hear her say it as many times as he could earn.

Harlow went stiff over him. "What are you doing?"

"Working within the parameters I currently have." He tugged the crotch of her panties to one side, holding them in place with one hand as the other braced against her backside, pressing down until her pussy brushed his lips. "That's my girl. Just like that. Bring it to me."

Harlow whimpered as his mouth met the warm slick of her body, tongue sliding to rub over the single spot he knew would give her what she needed.

A release. A way to set it all free.

"Dutch, I—" Harlow's voice broke as he gently sucked her clit, her hand coming down to tangle in his hair as she rocked into him. "That's—"

He pulled her closer, licking at her clit as he worked a finger inside her, stroking slow and steady until he found the spot that made her thighs clench around him, and then he stayed on it, the sound of her soft cries making his dick ache with need.

But it could fucking wait.

Harlow's grip on him tightened as her legs locked against his ears, her pussy pulsing around his fingers as she came, head pressed to the mattress, body grinding helplessly against his face.

He gripped her hips, holding her in place as he eased from under her, rolling to kiss his way up the back of her thigh and over the swell of her ass cheek. "How you doing, Darling?"

Harlow's face rested against the mattress, her mass of dark hair hiding most of her features. "I wasn't expecting that."

"Glad I could surprise you." He worked his way up the small of her back and between her shoulder blades. "You ready to go to sleep?"

Her head popped up, one eye peeking out through the blanket of hair. "What?"

Dutch eased to one side, stretching out on the bed beside her. "You've had a long day. I think maybe you need some sleep."

Both her hands whipped up to slap at the hair in her way, shoving it back until finally her whole face was in view. Harlow's blue eyes narrowed at him. "Are you messing with me right now?"

Dutch shook his head. "Not messing with you, Mowry." He reached for her, intending to pull her close.

She slapped at his hand. "Why don't you want to fuck me?"

"Don't call it that."

Her jaw shifted to one side. "I can call it whatever I want." She crawled toward him, glare sitting strong on his face.

"You can call it whatever you want, but calling it a fuck won't get you what you're gunning for."

Her gaze skimmed his face. "Calling it a fuck doesn't mean it's not more than that."

"Does in my book."

Her nostrils barely flared. "What if I think the word fuck is hot?"

She wouldn't be the only one in the room. The sound of it coming from her mouth so many times was killing him, but she'd made it clear more than once that was her MO. No emotions. NO attachments.

Just fucking.

"I'm willing to negotiate." He eyed her as she came closer.

"What are your terms?"

"You make it clear this is more, and I'll let you call it whatever you want."

Harlow's movements stilled. "Of course this is more than that."

"You're sure?"

Her expression softened. Harlow came close, one palm resting on the center of his chest as her lips hovered over his. "I'm sure."

Dutch pulled her against him, the soft press of her body to his reigniting the ache he'd intended to ignore. Harlow reached down, running her hand over the length of his dick through the fabric of his pajama pants before tucking her fingers under the waistband. "I want you, Dutch." She tugged at the pants, managing to get them to his thighs. Her hands immediately went to his straining cock, stroking it with a perfect touch.

"Fuck, Harlow."

"We're not allowed to say fuck." She tipped her head just enough to make her plans clear.

Dutch reached up, fisting one hand in her thick hair. "Nope." He scooted away, rolling up onto one side.

Harlow started to scoff at him, but the sound turned to a yelp as he wrapped one arm around her, tugging her down beside him. "If you think I can handle watching that mouth wrap around my dick right now, then you would have been in for a disappointing surprise." He pulled her close, her back to his front then reached for the condoms he stashed in his bedside table. "I can't even think about it if you want this to be remotely satisfying."

"It's already been satisfying." Harlow curved her spine, pressing her ass back against him as he tried to work on the condom.

"You're distracting as hell, Mowry." He struggled with the rubber, finally managing to get it in place.

"You're slow as hell." She wiggled her backside. "I'm starting to think you're stalling."

"Maybe I'm trying to buy some damn time." He gripped the ass she kept shaking at him. "And you aren't fucking helping with that." Dutch leaned into her, sliding the tip of his dick along her slit. "You're going to regret it when this only lasts two minutes."

"Two minutes?" She peeked over her shoulder at him. "It takes longer to microwave popcorn."

"I thought you hated popcorn." Dutch notched his cock in place, pressing his hips into the curve of her body. He gritted his teeth as her body stretched around him.

Her hand came to rest on the back of his neck. "Shut up. I'm busy." A soft moan slipped through her lips as he eased out and pressed back in. "You're still being slow as hell, Pretty Boy."

"You're still being distracting." He leaned into her, pushing Harlow's front toward the bed. He braced one knee on the other side of her body, finally getting a little more leverage. Enough to give her a proper thrust.

"Oh God." She fisted one hand in the blankets.

He leaned into her ear. "Better?"

Harlow nodded, eyes squeezed shut.

"Good then." He ran his lips over the soft skin of her back. "I don't want to hear any complaints later." Dutch skimmed one palm down her spine and over the fullness of her bottom, following the jut of her hip around to her belly before sliding down to cup her mound. "How you doing? You okay?"

"Shut up and do what you're supposed to be doing." She gasped when he pushed a little deeper. Thrust a little harder.

"Are you always this demanding in bed, Mowry?" His fingers pressed deeper, finding her still-engorged clit.

"Yes."

"Fan-fucking-tastic." Dutch worked the tiny nub in time with his hips, moving faster as she bowed under him, her spine curving as her muscles went tight. Harlow's whole body went still for a heartbeat.

Suddenly she bucked back against him, her pussy clenching tight as she cried out. It was pure and unrestrained. Complete surrender to what happened between them.

Dutch buried his face in her hair, breathing the soft scent of lavender and vanilla as he fought through a few more seconds, trying to give her as much as he could manage before his balls pulled tight and his dick swelled, the heat of his cum filling the condom between them.

Harlow went limp. "Holy shit."

Dutch sucked in long breaths. "Yeah."

Harlow leaned her head up a little. "I think we should do this again sometime."

****

"SO NOW YOU want us to hunt down yet another unknown group of dudes with guns." Harlow scowled at Pierce. "Do you at least have a starting point? Some sort of fricking idea of where in the hell those other men came from?" She sat close at Dutch's side, eyes on the front of the large room they used for all-team meetings. "Or do you just want us to look everywhere?"

Dutch grinned at Pierce, shifting to wrap one arm around the back of Harlow's chair.

Pierce scowled at him before turning to Harlow, his expression softening. "There must be some connection, Ms. Mowry, or they would not have been there."

"So now we're just looking for someone with some random connection to the other unknown group who has some random connection to Alaskan Security." She smirked Pierce's way. "Makes complete sense."

"What if the connection isn't *to* Alaskan Security?" Mona sat on Harlow's other side, a notepad perched on her lap, pen hovering over the top sheet.

Pierce's attention eased to Mona. "I'm not sure I follow your thinking, Ms. Ayers. Please enlighten me."

Mona's shoulders barely straightened. "Maybe this is about someone who *works* for Alaskan Security." Her eyes darted around the room before snapping back to where Pierce sat at the front of the room, the team leads at his side. "Maybe this is personal."

"You mean me." Harlow didn't ask.

Mona shook her head. "I think we haven't been giving whoever this is enough credit." She rocked the pen in her hand like a teeter-totter. "What if they're recruiting people close to the ones you hire because they will know us well enough to be able to guess our next move?"

Pierce's lips barely lifted at the edges. "What about Chandler Larson and Howard Richards? Unfortunately it appears they were part of the problem before we were lucky enough to cross paths with you and Ms Tatum."

Mona barely deflated. "I'm sorry. I thought—"

"Don't ever be sorry for having an idea, Ms. Ayers." Pierce's eyes fixed on her. "And you may still be onto something. I think we should put that on our list of possibilities."

Mona's head dropped as she gave a small nod.

Harlow rocked back in her seat, tucking one leg under her butt as she tapped her own pen against her lips. "Well..."

Pierce's gaze dragged from Mona. "Yes, Ms. Mowry?"

"Technically Chandler and Howard were already involved with the other team before Eva came here, but didn't they basically bring her here? Drop her in your lap?"

Eva leaned around Mona to nod at Harlow. "Chandler is the one who chose Alaskan Security. He pressured me to come here." She pointed to Mona, a wide grin on her face. "I think you're onto something."

Mona's head lifted and she smiled a second before pressing it down.

Harlow's head tilted as she continued the slow tap of her pen. "It just seems odd that they would come for us so blatantly and we had no clue they even existed."

Everyone looked to Pierce.

He sat perfectly still.

Mona's head barely turned. "You knew."

Pierce was silent as the men at his sides shifted in their seats.

"Holy shit, you all knew." Harlow's head slowly turned toward Dutch. "Did you know about the other team before they shot at Bess?"

Dutch held her gaze. He hadn't lied to her yet, and now wasn't the time to start. "Yes."

She blinked. "What the fuck?"

"Our knowledge was very limited, Ms. Mowry, and therefore I chose to keep it well-contained." Pierce's tone was sharp. "If you wish to be upset with someone, then you should direct your anger at me."

Harlow's head spun his way. "Oh, I plan to." She stood up from her seat. "Well-fucking-contained, Pierce?" She walked to lean both hands against the edge of the table between them. "So well-fucking-contained that you chose not to tell the team you assembled specifically to find these bastards?"

"That's not the only function of your team and you know it." Pierce held her glare without flinching. "The information we had was limited to the knowledge this group simply existed. That's all we had. Would that have been helpful to you, Ms. Mowry? To know that they existed?"

"Yes." She straightened, head high. "Ladies, I believe we should be done with this meeting."

"Agreed." Mona stood first, chin tipped up, cool blue eyes trained on the man at the head of the room.

Both women looked to Eva, who was scrambling to collect her cup and the folio perched on her lap. "I'm coming, hang on." She leaned in to press a kiss to Brock's lips, glancing

230

Harlow's way when she scoffed. "What? He didn't know." Eva turned back to Brock. "You didn't, right?"

"He did not." Pierce's tone was short and flat.

Eva gave Brock a wink. "Give him hell." She stood up, reaching out to tap Heidi on the arm. "Come on. We're leaving."

Heidi's head popped up from where she'd been glued to the screen of the computer perched on her lap. She reached under the drape of her blonde hair to pop one wireless headphone from her ear. "What?"

Pierce's dark brows lifted. "Were you wearing headphones during this meeting, Ms. Rucker?"

Heidi snorted. "Uh, yeah." She stood. "I've got shit to do."

Pierce stared at her.

"Regretting your life choices, Pierce?" Harlow smirked at him as she followed the rest of her team out of the room.

"Fuck." Pierce wiped his hands down his face.

"I told you we needed to tell her." Dutch stood. "I said it her first day here."

"We didn't have any concrete information." Pierce's jaw set.

"She could have found us some." Dutch made his way to the door.

"Where in the hell are you going?" Pierce's tone was tight. The closest to being on edge Dutch had heard it in years.

Dutch turned to his friend. "I'm with them."

Slowly, the men in the room stood one by one. Men who also should have known of the intel they had.

Pierce leaned back in his seat. "This is how it is?"

Brock's mouth was in a thin line as he stood, Wade joining him. "Seems like."

Wade almost lost the mother of his child during the first shots fired in what appeared to be a turf war.

Alaskan Security versus the unknown.

Unless Mona really was onto something.

Then this could be infinitely more dangerous than a simple war over drugs and the territory required to transport them.

Dutch walked out of the room as Pierce's eyes narrowed on the mass of men filing through the room toward the door, leaving him with only his team leads at his side.

Harlow was leaned against the wall when he walked out, propped into place, arms crossed. "I'm still mad at you."

"I know." He wrapped one arm around her shoulders and pulled her in close to his side. "You can kick my ass later." He pressed a kiss to her temple. "Right now I need you to do what you do best." They walked into the room where Eva, Mona, and Heidi sat at their desks.

He and Harlow went straight to their adjoining workspaces, sitting down in unison.

Harlow tipped her head his way. "We need access to the public transit camera system. I want all the footage we have starring this fucking circus of rejects we're dealing with."

Mona snorted a little. "I like that."

"Me too." Eva rocked her head from side to side. "I think we should start with the known members." She held up one hand counting off on her fingers. "Chandler. Howard. Tod."

"Don't forget Chris." Wade and Brock walked into the room. "Bessie's ex was connected to them somehow."

"He was *trying* to be connected to them." Harlow was already on her computer. "Anyone else?"

"We need to figure out who showed up yesterday." Heidi eyed Wade where he stood just inside the door. She tipped her head at him, giving him a dimpled smirk. "Hey."

Brock thumbed over his shoulder. "Taken."

"Damn it." Heidi dropped her head back. "I thought the ratio of women to men here was better than this."

"Any ideas about who that might have been?" Harlow continued on with the line of questions. She rolled her eyes to Dutch. "Or am I not supposed to know that either?"

"We have zero intel on the men who showed up yesterday. Rogue attempted to follow them after they fled, but lost them." He leaned in close to her. "And for the record, that is the only information that has ever been contained."

"And it wasn't just from you, Mowry." Wade's nostrils flared as his gaze landed on Dutch. "You are in the majority on this one."

Obviously the fallout from this wouldn't just be with Harlow. "What the fuck did you want me to do?"

"I want you to do what's best for the team."

"Rogue wasn't the only team that I had to keep safe. Sharing that intel would have potentially exposed another team in a way we were hoping to avoid." This was why he'd been pushing Pierce to hire additional staff. He couldn't handle all the team's needs and lines started to blur as Alaskan Security grew and diversified.

"Holy shit." Heidi's head popped up. "I think I found something."

CHAPTER 17

"ALREADY?" DUTCH STARED at the newest recruit.

Heidi scrunched her nose up at him. "What's that supposed to mean?"

"Means he's not used to the way we work." Harlow leaned into her desk. "What did you find?"

"I tapped into Howard's phone records and there's a number he was calling a bunch." Heidi rattled off the number.

"Wait." Dutch held up his hand. "How did you get into his phone records already?"

"Well I just found the cell number associated with him and looked them up."

"Yeah. That's what I'm asking. How did you already get into the provider's system?"

Heidi's eyes moved from side to side. "I don't think I understand the question."

"I'm just a little concerned that it's so easy to get into a cell company's records."

"No one said it was easy." Heidi's lip curled as she glared at him. "And I've been in this particular system before." Her mouth curved into a sly smile. "Cheating on a hacker's friend isn't a good idea."

Mona leaned forward to peek around Eva at Heidi. "That's a little crazy."

Heidi threw her hands out. "I know, right?" Her eyes dipped back to her computer screen. "He should have known better."

Mona lifted a finger. "That's not what I—"

"Whose number is it?" Harlow once again pulled the conversation back. Keeping these girls on task was starting to be like herding fucking cats.

"Oh." Heidi squinted. "Chris Snyder." She glanced at Wade where he stood in the doorway next to Brock. "That's the one you were talking about, right?"

"How do you already know everyone's last names?"

Heidi blinked up at Dutch. "Do you really want me to answer that?"

"She has clearance. She didn't have to completely hack into our system to find it." Harlow continued on, pointing at Heidi. "Keep looking into Richards' records. See what else you can find." She moved her finger to Eva. "You look into Chandler. Find anything you can about what he was up to for the past six months." Next was Mona. "Chris Snyder Jr. Find anything." Harlow took a long deep breath. "I've got Tod."

"I don't think this is a good idea." Dutch moved in close at her side, keeping his voice low.

"I don't care." She turned his way, huffing out a sigh. "That's not entirely true." She took another breath, settling the nerves eating into her skin. "I'm the only one who will be able to find anything on him. I know how he hides, and now that I have some information to work with, I might be able to find something."

Dutch's eyes sharpened. "You've tried to find information on him before?"

Harlow rubbed her lips together, not really wanting to have to answer the question. "Maybe."

"And did you find anything?"

She looked away. "Only the basics. Where he lived. Where he worked. Social media bullshit."

Dutch's head dipped lower as he dropped his elbows to his knees, facing the floor for a second. After a few heartbeats his eyes lifted to hers. "How did he find you?"

Harlow barely shook her head. It was a question she'd asked herself a thousand times over the past couple days. "I don't know."

"Shit." Dutch sat up straight in his seat, his eyes meeting Brock's over Harlow's head.

"Got it." Brock and Wade turned, walking from the room, pulling the door closed behind them.

Harlow watched them go before spinning back to the man at her side. "What's wrong?"

"Maybe nothing." Dutch's voice was so low she could barely hear it, forcing her to lean in closer.

He caught her lips with his in a kiss that was longer than it should have been, considering they weren't alone in the room. When his mouth left hers it slowly moved over the cheek facing away from the women sitting across from them, until it rested against her ear. "We might have a mole."

Harlow stared straight ahead, fighting not to react to the obvious implication.

That it might be one of the women only a handful of feet away.

"Gross." Heidi didn't look up from her computer. "Get a room." She sighed loud and long. "I'm sorry. I'm just jealous." She waved one hand in their direction. "Carry on. I'll put on some Taylor Swift and pretend like it's not happening." Her waving hand grabbed an ear bud off her desk and poked it in place.

"Taylor Swift?" Eva stared at Heidi as she kicked her feet up on her desk in the same relaxed post Harlow used to assume.

But on Heidi it appeared to be simply a comfortable stance instead of a show.

"Better than New Kids on the Block." Heidi tapped her phone and started humming along with whatever was playing in her ears.

"Better than New Kids on the Block my ass." Eva was on her own computer. She rolled her

238

shoulders. "Time to see what all Chandler's been up to."

The rest of the day passed in a blur. Dutch focused on scouring the footage they had of any identified members of the rejects, looking for anything that might help them figure out who they were or where in the hell they came from.

By the end of the night they each had a handful of leads to track down.

Everyone but her.

"He's gotten better at this shit." Harlow's eyes burned as she kept working long after Eva, Mona, and Heidi left. She let her lids drop, hoping to ease the sting. "He didn't used to be this good at hiding."

"Is that why you didn't know he was here?" Dutch was still with her. Still working on running down any bit of information Shadow could collect, trying to find any possible players.

"I check on him once a week." The admission came out, sliding past her exhausted brain and out into the world.

"Don't blame you on that one." Dutch reached over, closing the screen of her laptop. "I'd keep an eye on him too."

"It made me feel safer." She watched as he packed up her things. "Knowing he was far away from me."

Too bad she was wrong.

"You have to do what it takes to stay sane, Mowry." Dutch stood, slinging her bag over one shoulder. "It's one day at a time."

"What about tomorrow?"

"We deal with that tomorrow." He held his hand out to her. "Come on. You need sleep or you won't be worth shit when tomorrow gets here."

"I might not be worth shit now." She was supposed to be the best at what she did.

Better than anyone.

Especially fucking Tod.

But she'd spent hours hunting him like the animal he was, and came up empty.

No cell numbers.

No addresses besides the one in Texas.

No new friends.

Nothing more than a post office visit and a fill up at a gas station using a card attached to the address of the warehouse they found to be abandoned.

Dutch leaned down, his eyes leveling with hers. "You will find him, Mowry." He caught her chin, holding it while his mouth passed across her lips. His face stayed close to hers. "And when you find him, I will kill him for you."

She smiled. "Thanks."

Dutch grinned back at her. "The pleasure is all mine, I promise." He wrapped his arm around her shoulders and led Harlow out of the room and through the underground tunnels leading to the rooming building. When they finally reached her room, Harlow stared down at the new lock on her door. "What in the hell is that?"

"An extra precaution." Dutch pulled a key from his pocket and unlocked the deadbolt before punching a set of numbers into the keypad.

Harlow glanced down the empty hall before stepping inside.

She came all the way to Alaska because it seemed like it would be an escape. The ultimate disappearing act.

Why would anyone look for her in Alaska?

They wouldn't. Shouldn't.

"Have you talked to Pierce?"

"Not me." Dutch set the key on the dresser. "Wade and Brock met with him."

"I'm sure that was a fun discussion." Harlow pointed to the key. "Don't I get one of those?"

"There's only one key to the lock." He kicked off his shoes. "I'm not fucking around with your safety, Harlow."

"I'm not sure it will help." She flopped down on her bed. "If someone at Alaskan Security is working for the rejects then I'm not sure there's anything that will keep me safe." Harlow fell back to the mattress and stared up at the ceiling.

She should be more panicked about this than she was. For years the thought of Tod finding where she was kept her up at night.

Stole countless hours of her days.

It's why she kept tabs on him. It made it possible for her to function, knowing he wasn't close enough to find her.

But right now the panic she used to struggle to control wasn't fighting into her stomach.

"That hurts my feelings, Mowry." Dutch peeled off his shirt. "I thought you had more faith in me than that."

She rolled her head his way, scanning the width of his chest. "Sorry."

"It's understandable." He crawled onto the bed, leaning down to press a kiss to her lips. "How about a bath?"

"You're going to run me a bath?"

"No." Dutch stood from the bed. "I'm going to run *us* a bath." He moved to the bathroom, his limp a little more pronounced than normal. "I need it and I'd like to have your ass in there to help distract me from how much it fucking hurts."

Harlow sat up. "If it hurts why do you want to do it?" She watched the steam lifting off the water as he twisted the faucet on.

"It's sort of a hurts-so-good kind of thing." He worked open the button of his pants. "It helps my muscles relax, but makes the nerves that never quite got their shit together go crazy."

His pants hit the floor and one brow lifted. "You coming?"

Her eyes lingered on his naked body. Being wet and slippery against that was definitely tempting. "Is it going to burn my skin off?"

"Maybe." Dutch backed toward the tub. "I'm not going to lie. Seeing your ass bright pink might be part of the appeal for me."

She widened her eyes at him.

Dutch held his arms out wide. "Come on, Mowry. It'll be fun."

242

She tried to work the smile off her face. "I think you're trying to distract me."

"Does that sound like something I'd do?" His easy grin tempted her more than even his body could. "Come on. You need to relax."

She sighed, pushing off the bed. "I'm not convinced this will be a relaxing experience."

"I'll bet everything I have that you get out of that tub relaxed as hell." Dutch circled her as she stepped into the small bathroom, his hazel eyes moving over her. "You're not wearing the same kind of bra you usually do."

"How in the hell can you tell—"

He was so close his naked body brushed against her. "I don't miss anything when it comes to you, Darling." Dutch caught the mass of her hair with his hand and pushed it to one side, leaning into her exposed ear. "Why are you wearing a different bra, Harlow?"

She shivered at the heat of his breath on her skin. "Because I wanted to."

Dutch hooked his fingers under the hem of her sweater, working it up as his lips trailed over her neck. "Why?"

The cool air of the bathroom hit the bare skin of her belly. Dutch wasn't just taking off her sweater, he was peeling off both layers she wore, taking them up her body and over her head at once.

He swore under his breath, moving to stand in front of her, his eyes on the swell of her breasts where they spilled from the low, lacy fabric of the single sexy bra she owned.

That was why she wore it.

Because she wanted Dutch to have the same reaction to seeing her that she had to seeing him.

Dutch shook his head. "You might have to go back to the other ones, Mowry. I don't know that I can sit next to you all day knowing this is what's hiding under those fucking sweaters you wear." His hands moved up her middle, spanning the skin of her stomach, his touch moving faster, but still solid as it passed her ribs, stopping just under her breasts, palms cupping their weight through the stabilized fabric. "I'll fucking stroke out."

"You should have told me what you knew about the rejects."

His eyes lifted to hers. "Well-played." Dutch's touch didn't move as he eased closer. "I should have. I'm sorry."

She studied his face. The strong line of his jaw. The straight slant of his nose. The indescribable color of his eyes. "Is that all there is?"

He nodded.

She inhaled, the soft scent of lavender filling the humid air of the bathroom. "Okay."

Dutch's mouth lifted on one side. "I planned to go to some pretty great lengths to make it up to you, Harlow. You probably shouldn't let me off that easily."

"You'll make it up to me anyway."

Dutch's hands moved to her back as he hefted her body to his. "Every fucking day."

She sighed into his mouth as it came to hers. All the fear, the frustration, the anger she'd fought for so long eased back.

Subsided.

Because how could she keep being upset about what brought her to a man like this?

One she understood like no one else could.

On who understood her back.

Dutch worked her pants past her hips and thighs, far enough that the baggy cut allowed them to drop to the tile floor, leaving her in the matching bra and panty set she slid on this morning after her shower, feeling a little more comfortable with the body she tried to hide.

Dutch pulled his lips from hers and leaned back, eyes raking down her front, his chest rising and falling as he took her in.

"Fucking incredible."

His hands ran over the barely-there slope of her hips, fingers squeezing the not-so-womanly part of her frame. Her narrow hips always made her top look even bigger than it was. Something she tried to even out with pants that added bulk.

She should be self-conscious of it. Especially considering how hard she'd worked over the years to hide what Dutch was so brazenly staring at.

"Why are you looking at me like that?" Harlow couldn't look away from his eyes. The way they drank her in. Passed over every inch of her skin.

Those same eyes slowly lifted to hers. "It's how you look at me."

Her stomach tightened. "Is it?"

The mouth that tortured her in the most excruciatingly amazing way last night curved into a wicked smile.

One that said it might be about to do it again.

"It is." Dutch hooked his thumbs under the waistband of her panties, skimming them down her legs as he dropped to the floor along with them, leaving his head right in line with—

Dutch leaned in, wide hands spreading over her hips and gripping tight as his mouth met the bit of her pussy peeking from the junction of her thighs. His tongue probed deeper, immediately finding her clit.

Harlow tried to push her feet apart, but Dutch's hands moved down, pressing her legs tight together as the tip of his tongue continued to ease back and forth over the sensitive bit of flesh. Her knees buckled and she grabbed around, looking for something to hang onto.

Dutch held firm, lifting up just a little as he walked her back until she was pressed to the wall.

Then his mouth was back on her, hands still holding her in place as he continued to torture her that single spot.

She rocked against him, trying to get just a little more.

His hold on her tightened, stopping the tiny bit of movement she'd managed.

"Asshole." Harlow's head fell against the wall at her back as he chuckled, the low vibration rumbling through her most sensitive area.

Dutch's probing tongue pressed a little harder, rubbed a little faster. His hands stayed steady when her legs lost their ability to hold her, that damn tongue never missing a freaking beat, even as she fisted his hair and threatened to shut down every credit card he had.

Her thighs fought his hold, jerking as the constant slide of his tongue became too much, tossing her over the edge hard and fast.

Dutch's mouth finally relented, sucking and biting its way up her body, over her belly and the swell of her breasts where they peeked out of the bra he still hadn't removed.

"What the fuck was that about?" She grunted as his arm wrapped around her waist, taking her from being pressed against the wall to being pressed against him.

His wicked lips twisted into a smirk. "Just trying to keep you comfortable, Mowry."

CHAPTER 18

HER SCOWL WAS sexy as hell.

Dutch pulled Harlow toward the tub, working the clasp on her bra with his free hand. "You keep frowning at me like that you're not going to want to get out of bed in the morning."

Her eyes widened. "What's that mean?"

"Means I'll go to great lengths to be sure you relax." He stepped into the tub, good leg first, before hauling her over the side.

Harlow sucked in a breath. "That's hot."

Dutch reached for the faucet.

"Is it better for you if it's hot?"

Her question made him pause long enough she figured out the answer on her own.

"I'm fine." Harlow pushed him a little. "Get in."

He lowered into the heat of the water, keeping his legs at the sidewalls of the tub, before reaching up to her. "If it's too hot we can cool it down. I'll be fine."

"I don't want you to be fine." She dropped into the water between his legs in a quick move, sucking in a sharp breath. "Holy shit. How the fuck do you have skin left?"

Dutch closed his eyes as the heat sank into the knotted muscles of his injured leg, easing the constant ache there while also making his scarred skin sting like fire.

Harlow went quiet. The water sloshed a little. The wet heat of her fingers slid over his face, stroking his forehead and temples. Sliding over the line of his brow.

"I'm okay."

"You don't look okay."

He barely lifted his lids to find her frowning at him. "It just takes a minute for everything to get used to the heat."

Her touch left his face to move down his chest and stomach. One hand slid down the thigh of his mangled leg, fingers pressing gently into the muscles there. "Holy shit, Dutch." Her thumb circled a particularly painful knot. "What in the hell is all this from?"

He slowly opened his eyes.

Harlow sucked in a breath. "It's from carrying me, isn't it?"

Answering her was out of the question. She wouldn't understand how little the pain mattered compared to the fear he felt over what might have happened to her. "It'll be fine." Dutch pulled her close. "Stop worrying about it."

"No." Harlow's gentle but firm touch continued moving down his leg, fingers finding spots of painful cramps and carefully working them loose.

He started to relax, his body sinking into the water filling the cramped space of the tub. "You don't have to do that, Darling."

"I want to." Her voice was soft. "You take care of me all the time. I want to take care of you too." The brush of her fingers moved over his thigh, easing higher.

Dutch caught her wrist. "What are you doing, Mowry?"

Her eyes held his. "I want to touch you."

"You were touching me." He laced his fingers with hers, lifting their joined hands from the water to press a kiss to her knuckles.

"I want to touch more of you." Her eyes dipped to the water.

"Not right now."

"Then when?" One dark brow lifted. "You stopped me last night. You're stopping me now. When do I get to touch you back?"

"You don't have to touch me back." It felt wrong to take from her. She'd been through horrible things. Had so much stolen from her by a man who didn't deserve to share the air she breathed.

He wouldn't do the same.

"That's not what this is about." Harlow pulled her hand free of his grip. "You're the one who wanted this to be more than just fucking." Her hand dipped under the surface of the water. "More than fucking means I get to touch you back." She turned, facing him on her knees. "I get to touch you the way you touch me."

He stared her down. "That's not what it means."

"Oh really?" Harlow's hand moved through the water, the tips of her fingers dragging over the skin of his stomach. "Because I'm positive more than fucking means a mutually emotionally satisfying situation." Her touch dropped lower. "And I'm not feeling very emotionally satisfied right now."

"How's that?"

She leaned in, her hand wrapping around his dick in the heat of the tub. "You're making me a taker."

Harlow's eyes held his as she fisted his stiffening length. "I'm not selfish, Dutch, and I don't want or expect a man to fill my needs without getting anything in return."

"Obviously you forget last night." He definitely got more than enough in return. "I didn't go to bed unsatisfied, Darling."

"I did." She eased closer. "I went to bed not knowing how it felt to have your cock slide over my tongue." Harlow's grip on him tightened. "Not knowing if I could please you the same way you please me." Her eyes narrowed. "And now you want to take that from me again." On the next glide of her hand Harlow's thumb slicked across the head of his dick, sending his head dropping back against the wall.

"You don't have to do this, Harlow."

"I want to do this." Her voice was low in his ear. "I want to watch you come because of what I did. Because of how I made you feel."

His dick twitched against her palm. "You don't have any clue how you make me feel."

"Then let me find out." Her strokes moved faster. "Let me see how I make you feel."

Dutch's hips jerked, shoving his dick into her palm as his balls pulled up tight, the need to come burning across his skin.

"Open your eyes."

He lifted his lids, his eyes meeting hers just as heat speared down his cock, sending spurts of cum into the water between them.

Harlow's lips were parted, eyes glazed as she watched him. "Thank you."

Dutch reached out to pull her close. "I'm not sure you're the one who should be saying that right now, Darling."

****

PIERCE STARED AT the window, the fingers of one hand slowly falling against the surface of his desk.

"There's the possibility someone decided to defect." Roman, the newly-appointed technical coordinator of Alpha Team, was leaned back in his seat, one leg crossed over the other. He'd been a member of Alpha since its inception, which made him an easy choice to fill the spot

253

as far as Dutch was concerned, and in light of recent events, Pierce finally came to the same conclusion. "Money can make a man do stupid things."

"It's definitely stupid." Seth, the team lead for Alpha sat at Roman's side, his expression grim. "I swear to God if one of these men—"

"Then you will let me handle it." Pierce stood, crossing his office to stand at the window that ran from the floor to the ceiling. A single, huge plant sat on a lone table in the center of the two armchairs at each side.

"Where in the hell did that plant come from?" Dutch had never seen anything green and growing in any of the buildings, let alone front and center in Pierce's office.

The owner of Alaskan Security glanced down as if he wasn't sure what Dutch was talking about. His eyes stayed on the leafy vines for a second as his shoulders slowly relaxed. "It's a gift." Pierce turned. "I will have Intel begin looking into the potential of a defector."

Dutch shifted in his seat, eyes moving to meet Shawn's. "I'm not sure that's our best idea."

Pierce's brows lifted. "Why is that?"

"What if our mole is part of that team?" Shawn voiced the concern he and Dutch shared.

Pierce barely tipped his head in a nod. "I see." He focused on Dutch. "Then let's start with her. Have Harlow look into Heidi's background. See what she can find."

"I don't mean Heidi." Shawn paused for a heartbeat, probably trying to work up the nerve to say what needed to be said. "I mean Mona."

Pierce's whole body went still, the only movement coming from the throbbing of a vein in the side of his head. "Ms. Ayers has no part in this."

"I hope you're right, but the timeline fits. She has motive. She has the potential connections—"

"Shut up." Pierce's words snapped through the air. "She has no motive and no possible connect—"

"Money. She could still be in touch with Chandler. We still haven't found that bastard yet." Shawn held his ground.

Pierce's jaw clenched tight. "It is not Ms. Ayers and anyone I hear suggesting she is involved will be shown out of the front gates." His attention snapped to Dutch. "Have Harlow look into Ms. Rucker." He strode to the door, opening it. "Let me know what she finds."

"So we're done?" Shawn scoffed out a laugh as he stood. "Whatever." He stared Pierce down as he passed, the first one out of the office, with the other team leads following in his wake.

Dutch stayed put, waiting for the room to clear.

Pierce glared at him. "What?"

"I wanted to tell Harlow everything we knew, and do you remember what you told me?"

Pierce's nostrils flared.

255

Because he sure as hell remembered what he said.

"You've gotta let her look into Mona." Dutch glanced to the doorway, ensuring it was still empty. "But not just because we have to do what's best for the safety of the company, but because it's what's best for Mona."

"How is invading her private life what's best for Ms. Ayers?"

"Shawn and I aren't the only ones who considered her as a possibility, Pierce. That means you've got a whole line of men who think it's plausible she's the one trying to get them killed. You think she's safe here?"

The color drained from Pierce's face.

"You've gotta let us look. It's the only way she will be protected."

Pierce's shoulders slumped as he walked to his desk and opened the bottom drawer, pulling out a bottle of top-shelf scotch and a tumbler. He poured a couple fingers then immediately tipped it back, clearly unbothered that it wasn't even six in the morning. "I can't do that to her. She'll never forgive me."

"If she gets hurt because you didn't, you'll never forgive yourself."

Pierce leaned back in his seat, his normally perfect posture, sloped and rounded. "Let me think about it."

"You don't have long." Dutch shook his head when Pierce offered a drink. "And considering the rumor going around Shadow about who showed up the other day, you may not just be protecting her from the men here."

Pierce rubbed his eyes. "The government is still claiming it wasn't them."

"Bullshit. You and I both know that was a covert op." Dutch leaned forward. "If the CIA has their hands in this mess and she's a part of it then there's a good possibility she will end up dead."

Pierce's eyes snapped to his. "She's not involved."

"Then you've got nothing to worry about." Dutch stood. "And if she ever finds out about it, I'll take the heat for you."

Pierce stared at him. "I'm not authorizing this."

"Understood."

Dutch turned and walked from the office. One hurdle down, one to go.

****

"I'M NOT DOING that." Harlow shook her head. "Not happening."

"You have to." Dutch leaned back against the headboard, resting one arm behind his head. "It's the only way to keep everyone safe."

Harlow squeezed her eyes shut and pulled the covers higher. "It's just wrong."

"I know it feels like that."

Her eyes popped open and immediately landed on him. "Not just *feels* wrong. *Is* wrong. It's her life. I shouldn't just go digging around in it."

"What if she's the one who led Tod to you?"

Harlow's gaze didn't flinch. "What if she's not? Then I've dug through her whole life for nothing."

"You've got to decide what you can live with, Mowry." Dutch knew this would be a hard sell. Even harder than Pierce. "But you need to understand there's more than a few men who think she might be the one."

Harlow let out a long, loud, groan of a sigh as she rolled to face the ceiling. "Fuck."

"You've got to do it."

"Shit." Harlow flipped the covers off her body and stood up.

"Whatcha got on there, Mowry?"

"Shut up. I hate you right now." She marched to the bathroom, slamming the door as she went in.

"Those look like my pants." Dutch said it loud enough she'd be able to hear it through the door she put between them. "And my shirt." He closed his eyes, relaxing for a minute. He woke her up before he went to meet with Pierce, making sure she was okay before slipping out to the early-morning meeting. Knowing Harlow was behind a locked door only he could get in made it easier to do what needed to be done, but his stomach twisted in knots until she was back at his side.

Especially now that he didn't know who he could trust.

Harlow yanked open the bathroom door, a toothbrush sticking out the side of her mouth. "What about Heidi?"

"She just came on. We're looking for someone who's been involved from the beginning."

Harlow huffed out another groan as she went to spit in the sink, running the water a few seconds before coming back out. "What if she's clean?"

"Then we move on, including the rest of the team in the search." It would be the best, worst thing if Mona wasn't their mole. Pierce and Harlow would both be happy, but it would also mean the hunt continued.

Harlow stomped back into the room, rounding the bed with one more groan. She flopped onto the mattress beside him, dragging her bag up the side as she went.

"Fine."

CHAPTER 19

"I'M NOT HAPPY about this." Harlow worked her way through Mona's bank records.

"You said that already." Dutch scooted closer to her, switching on the television.

"Don't you have something to do?"

"Not without you." He settled back, kicking off his shoes. "Not until we get this figured out."

"Just because I don't find anything doesn't mean she's not messy." Harlow blinked, trying to clear the blurring of the lines of information.

"If you can't find something then there isn't anything." Dutch sounded completely confident in her abilities.

"Maybe Tod fixed her." A transfer caught her attention, sending Harlow to open another window where she could track down the account the money was sent to. "But so far it looks like Miss Mona is sensible as hell with her money.

The woman must have spreadsheets on spreadsheets. All her bills came out automatically. She had a savings account that appeared to be her emergency fund, an IRA, and donations that all distributed on a specific day each month. "I should have her teach me how to budget." Harlow scanned through the system at Investigative Resources, the business Eva and Mona owned with Chandler. When he turned out to be on the wrong side of the equation, the women filed a temporary restraining order, locking down the assets. Everything appeared to be in line with what it should be, given the circumstances.

"She's got ten grand in her checking. Thirty in a savings account. Fifty in an IRA and another hundred in her 401K through Investigative Resources."

"Damn." Dutch rested his head against her arm as he scanned the computer screen. "Any strange deposits or transfers?"

"Not a single one. Her paychecks are all direct deposit. All her bills are paid online. There's nothing suspicious financially." Harlow opened her mouth. Dutch fed in a chunk of the French toast Brock brought down. "Eva's going to be pissed when she finds out he was in on this."

"She'll understand." Dutch held a fork with a strawberry stuck to the tines in front of her mouth while she chewed. "She might be mad at first, but she's a smart woman. She'll get it."

"Are you saying I'm smart?" Harlow opened her mouth as he moved the berry her way. "I'm still mad at you, by the way."

"I know." Dutch held up her coffee, waiting for her to take it and swallow some down before setting it back on the table at his side. "Once you're done I'll make it up to you some more."

Her cheeks heated. "Once I'm done here, we have to go find the girls and tell them we have to investigate every fucking member of Alaskan Security."

"Not every member." Dutch popped a slice of banana in his mouth from the plate they were sharing. "We know it's not Pierce. Not Wade or Brock or me."

"Maybe I should check anyway." She peeked his way. "Just to be sure."

"I'm an open book, Mowry." Dutch stabbed at a hunk of sausage and held it up. "You can look into anything you want."

"Hmph." She chewed, scrolling through addresses and phone numbers, intending to see which numbers she needed to dig deeper into.

The finger on her mouse stopped.

Harlow struggled to swallow down the wad of meat that was suddenly much larger than it was a second ago. "I think we might have a problem."

Dutch went still beside her. "How big of a problem?"

"Not very big. Just the size of a PO box." Harlow pulled up the USPS system and within a few minutes she was in and staring at the information for PO box 87469 in Fairbanks, Alaska.

"Shit." Dutch sat up, straightening as he peered at the information. "Why would she have a PO box?"

"Maybe she doesn't want everyone knowing where she is." Harlow's stomach churned. "Maybe she likes to have her mail in a single, localized spot."

"Or maybe she's getting mail she doesn't want anyone here to know about." Dutch's eyes moved to her face. "Can you find out what she's receiving?"

Harlow shook her head. "There's no way to backtrack. They don't keep records of every piece of mail's destination."

He let out a long breath. "Pierce is going to lose his shit."

"Only if we tell him." Harlow turned back to the screen. "It's just a PO box. There's a million reasons she could have it. This isn't proof of anything."

"It's proof we can't clear her." Dutch set the plate down on the bed beside him and rubbed both hands over his face. "Damn it."

"I need to keep looking into it." Harlow closed out of all the windows. "We have to find more before we say anything." She scooted off the bed, closing her laptop and pushing it into her bag.

"What are you doing?" Dutch's eyes narrowed.

"I'm going to work." She opened her closet and pulled out a turquoise sweater and a pair of jeans. "We've got more than one problem to deal with, in case you didn't remember."

"You're just going to let Mona keep working like nothing's wrong?"

"There's a chance nothing *is* wrong." Harlow worked the sweater over the long-sleeved shirt she put on after her shower, continuing to talk as she went. "There's a chance poor Mona just wanted to order a fucking vibrator without having to explain it to one of you assholes." She popped her head through the neckline.

Dutch's brows were up. "We don't scan your mail, Mowry."

Harlow shot him a grin. "Sure."

She wiggled out of Dutch's pajama pants and into her jeans before dropping her butt to the bed so she could lace on her Chuck's.

"So maybe we go get into her PO box." Dutch stood and started to pace. "Say we want to get one of our own and when they leave us we can get into hers."

"Or." Harlow held her hands out. "And just hear me out on this one. We can *not* do that." She grabbed her bag and hooked it over one shoulder.

"We've got to do something."

"We are doing something." She switched the deadbolt and yanked open the door, sucking in a breath and jumping back at the sight of someone on the other side.

Not just any someone.

Mona.

Her hand still hung in the air, fist ready to knock. "Oh. Hey." She gave Harlow a tight smile as she slowly lowered her arm. "I was just coming to make sure you were okay." Her eyes drifted to where Dutch moved in at Harlow's back. "We hadn't seen you yet and I was worried."

"I'm good." Harlow stepped out, dropping her free arm around Mona's shoulders. "How are you?"

"Good, I guess." She glanced over her shoulder as Dutch followed them down the hall. "Tired. I stayed up last night working."

"Find anything interesting?" Harlow kept going, moving toward the front of the building.

"Mowry." Dutch was stopped at the door leading to the underground tunnel. "This way."

"What's that?" Mona leaned to peek through the door as they backtracked.

"He doesn't like me taking the front pass-through since Pierce got shot." Harlow watched Mona's reaction from the corner of her eye.

Mona reached up to tuck the short swing of her blonde bob behind one ear. "I can understand that." She hesitated just a second before stepping through the door, tipping her head back to peer up the stairs leading to the second floor. "I didn't even know this was here."

"It takes longer and you've got to go up and down stairs, so it's sort of a pain in the ass." Harlow led Mona down the stairs.

"You won't get shot, though." Mona twisted her lips to one side. "So I guess that's a perk."

Harlow nodded, pointing one finger at Mona. "Solid point."

"You never said if you found anything about Chris last night." Dutch's deep voice bounced around the concrete-lined corridor.

"Oh." Mona twisted his way as she continued to walk at Harlow's side. "He's a mess. Had all sorts of money coming and going. I made a spreadsheet of all the accounts he dealt with so I could dig into those today." She shook her head. "It didn't stop after he was killed either. Someone else has access to all the accounts he was using."

"That's interesting." Harlow hurried to keep up with Mona as they took the stairs up to the door leading to their office. "Look as far into that as you can. Check for anything that's happened since he kicked it." She pushed through the door and turned toward their office, stopping after a few steps when she realized Mona wasn't still beside her.

Mona stood just outside the stairwell door, staring down the hall. Pierce was walking away from them, back straight, looking just as fucking proper as always.

With Heidi at his side.

Mona's head dropped, one hand coming to tuck her hair into place. "Um. Yeah." She turned to Harlow, a smile frozen on her face. "I will do that." She strode straight to the office, back stiff.

Harlow shook her head at Dutch as Mona disappeared. "It's not her."

"You sound awfully sure of that." Dutch stood just behind her, resting his hands on her hips.

"Did you see the look on her face just now?"

"When she saw Pierce with Heidi?" Dutch shrugged. "He meets with everyone when they first start. Tries to get a read on them." He leaned in close, his nose trailing along the line of her neck. "Don't you remember? You told him you were too busy for his bullshit?"

Harlow laughed, jabbing an elbow gently into Dutch's stomach. "I'm too busy for yours too." She wiggled free of his hold. "I've got an asshat to find and destroy."

"We've got a whole pile of asshats to find and destroy." Eva came down the hall, wearing a giant kitten printed sweatshirt over a pair of ripped-up black jeans. She followed Harlow's eyes, tipping her head down to look at the glitter-accented feline taking up most of her upper body. "What?" She glanced back up at Harlow. "This is my ass-kicking sweatshirt."

Dutch squinted at the innocently meowing face. "Why is that your ass-kicking shirt?"

Eva gave him a grin. "Cause no one expects the chick in the cat sweater to kick their ass." She bumped him as she walked past. "Watch your back, Dutchie boy."

"If you kick his ass then I have to kick Brock's ass." Harlow followed Eva into the room. "And I'll have to change because I didn't wear my ass-kicking shirt today."

"You guys have ass-kicking shirts?" Mona rested one hand on the front of her tailored three-quarter-sleeve sweater.

"We'll get you one." Eva dropped into her seat. "We'll probably have to order one, though. Shopping is shit up here."

"And no one's leaving campus until we have this shit sorted out." Dutch sat at his desk, rolling the chair into place.

"You're allowed to leave." Harlow eyed him.

"I'm allowed to leave because if I get killed it's my own fault." Dutch didn't glance her way as he logged into the system.

"Whose fault is it if we get killed?"

"Mine." Pierce strode into the office with Heidi following right behind him.

Mona didn't look his way, instead staying focused completely on the screen of her computer.

"Have you found anything?" Pierce's gaze rested on the woman completely ignoring him.

Harlow leaned back in her seat, kicking her feet onto the surface of her desk. "Mona found out someone's still using Chris Snyder's bank accounts.

Pierce moved closer to Mona's desk. "Anything else?"

"Chandler has definitely had help locking down his information." Eva opened her laptop. "I was able to find everything I already knew, but there's nothing that gives me any clues about his life here."

"Maybe he left." Dutch watched Mona for any sort of reaction. "Decided it was too dangerous and skipped town."

"He's not that smart." Eva wrapped her hair into a wad at the top of her head and banded it with a glittery scrunchie. "And he's way too greedy to walk away from something like this."

"Something like this might involve more than we realized. There's a rumor the other team who showed up two days ago could have ties to the government." Dutch continued to watch Mona. "And the government doesn't like to leave loose ends. He's just as likely to end up dead as he is to end up alive. These aren't people you fuck with. They'll kill you without thinking twice."

Mona shot up from her seat. "I have to go to the bathroom."

She marched from the room without looking at anyone around her.

Harlow stood up. "Dick." She hurried after Mona.

"What?" Dutch held his arms out.

Harlow paused to glance back into the office. "I wasn't talking to you." She shot Pierce a glare before turning and heading to the bathroom at the end of the hall. She rapped on the door. "Mona? It's me. You okay?"

"I'm fine."

"You didn't seem fine." Harlow propped against the door. "You want me to change the lock pad code to his office?"

It was quiet for a second.

"No."

"Can I come in?" Harlow waited.

The door lock clicked open.

Harlow opened it and stepped in, locking it behind her. She lifted a brow at Mona. "You're sitting on a bathroom floor."

Mona's head tilted to one side as she peered at the tile floor. "It looks clean enough."

"I'm not sure that's ever true." Harlow backed up against the wall and slowly lowered to a crouch beside Mona. "He's not into her, you know."

"I have no idea what you're talking about." Mona stared straight ahead.

"Listen." Harlow eased a little lower as her thighs started to burn. "Heidi's cool as hell and cute and funny and—"

"Are you saying this to be helpful?"

"I thought you didn't know what I was talking about?"

Mona's nostrils flared. "Continue."

"But she's not his type."

"She's every man's type." Mona stretched her legs out. "She's pretty. She's smart. She's got a ton of personality." Mona sighed. "And she's all—" she made an hourglass shape with her hands in the air, "womanly."

"She does have a nice ass." Harlow cringed as her butt hit the tile floor. "I swear if I get piss on me I'm never forgiving you.

Mona turned to look at the floor between them. "Who would pee all the way over here?"

"I don't understand the ways of the wiener, Mona. Stop giving me shit." She gagged a little as more of her ass cheek met the floor. "Ugh."

"You didn't have to come in here." Mona tipped her head back against the wall. "I just needed a minute."

"He's going to think you have the shits or something."

Mona's eyes opened wide at the ceiling. "Lovely."

"I'll tell him it was me." Harlow curled her arms up against her chest as she glanced down, scanning the tile for any signs of urine. "That I'm the one with the shits."

Mona lowered her brows. "I ran out of the room because you have the shits?"

"What's he gonna do?" Harlow sniffed the air, the clean, bleachy scent making her feel slightly better about her ass being on a bathroom floor. "Call me a liar?"

Mona sighed. "It doesn't matter anyway." She dropped her head back to the wall. "I don't know what I'm even upset about."

"You're upset because the boy you like was hanging out with another girl." Harlow leaned her head back beside Mona's.

"He's not a boy. That one's a full-grown man." Mona rubbed one thumb over the nude-painted tip of her pointer. "I thought when he jumped in front of me the other night that maybe…" She shook her head. "But I think he would have done that for anyone."

Harlow tipped her face toward Mona, studying the other woman.

The one who was most definitely not their mole.

"You wanna go work in your room for the rest of the day?"

Mona's lips pressed to a thin line as she shook her head. "Nope." She pressed both hands on the floor and pushed up. "I want to go back in that room like I don't give a shit."

Harlow grinned at her. "That's my girl." She pointed to the sink. "Now wash your hands so you can help me up."

The office was quiet when they walked back inside after making a stop to grab some snacks and drinks to get them through the morning.

Heidi glanced up as they came in. "You're back."

Harlow scanned the room for Dutch. Both he and Pierce were missing, leaving Eva and Heidi the only other ones in the room. "Where's Dutch?"

"He and Pierce left right after you did. Marched right out." She scissored her fingers to mimic walking. "Like they had someplace to be."

Mona went straight to her seat and sat, back perfectly straight as she went back to work."

"Well…" Harlow sat in her own chair, looking around the room. "Okay then."

"Oh." Heidi lifted one hand. "Also, I found the connection between Howard and Chris."

CHAPTER 20

"SHE HASN'T FOUND anything yet." Dutch held Pierce's gaze.

"Nothing?" Pierce didn't look away. "You're sure of that?"

"Positive." Dutch relaxed back into his seat. Chances were good Pierce knew damn well he was lying.

But he promised Harlow he would wait until she dug deeper, and that's what he was going to do.

Pierce stared him down for a minute longer before inhaling long and slow as he turned to Shawn. "Have you come up with any other options for me from Rogue?"

"Are you asking me if I think any of my men have turned?" The scowl on his lips was unmistakable. "No. I don't."

"It's a fair question, Shawn. Don't get so pissy about it." Seth, the team lead for Alpha was about as relaxed as it got. "It's just as likely to be your team as it is anyone else's."

Shawn shook his head. "It's not."

"You saying my team is more likely to be filled with a bunch of pussies who would do something like this?"

"Not a bunch." Shawn held up one finger. "Only one."

"Fuck you, Shawn. You think you're something because your team handles the covert shit." Seth's eyes narrowed. "I'd like to see how they handle fucking crowd control when there's a thousand people trying to get hands on the celebrity they think they should be able to touch."

Shawn snorted. "Sure, Seth. It's the same fuckin' thing."

"God you guys are bitches."

The whole room turned.

Heidi stood in the doorway, with the rest of the women at her back. She leaned toward Harlow. "Are they all on the same cycle or something?"

"Probably." Harlow thumbed Heidi's way. "Hot stuff here found the connection between Howard and Chris."

Pierce waved one hand toward the chairs occupied by the team leads. "Then by all means, join us."

Dutch stood, giving Harlow a wink as she came his way. He positioned himself behind his vacated chair as she sat in the seat, and rested both hands on her shoulders.

Heidi came through, a stack of papers in one hand. Seth jumped from his seat. "You can sit here."

Heidi gave him a dazzling smile, showing off the deep dimples in her softly rounded cheeks. "What a gentleman." She plopped into the chair as Mona sat in Shawn's now-empty chair and Eva leaned against the back.

"Ms. Rucker, the floor is yours." Pierce's gaze shifted to Mona, lingering for a second before moving back to rest on Heidi.

"So Mona and I found a shit-ton of bank accounts that Chris was moving money into and some he was getting money from. I tracked down all the other accounts and one of them belongs to Howard." She flipped the papers around, showing where she'd highlighted the rows of account information. One finger poked at a line toward the bottom of the sheet. "This one."

"Snyder sent Richards money." Pierce's gaze sharpened. "Interesting."

"What?" One of Heidi's brows lifted at him. "No. Howard sent money to Chris."

The room went quiet.

"Howard was the one financing Chris?" Dutch leaned into Harlow's ear. "Is that what she's saying?"

Heidi shot Dutch a glare. "I'm right here. You can just ask me to explain."

"He just wanted an excuse to sniff my hair." Harlow lifted a wad of her dark strands and smacked them over her shoulder in the direction of his face.

Heidi rolled her eyes. "Rub it in some more." She turned her attention to Pierce. "I'm not saying Howard was funding whatever this Chris guy was doing, but he definitely sent him money."

"How much are we talking?" Shawn made his way toward Heidi, taking the paper from her hands as she shot him a wink and a smile.

"Hey."

Shawn glanced at her before taking a small step back as he scanned the information. "Twenty grand?"

"On-the-dot." Heidi punctuated each word with a tap of her pen to the paper in Shawn's hands, beaming her dimpled smile on him the whole time.

When he finally lifted his eyes her way she gave him an exaggerated wink.

Shawn held the papers out, barely waiting for Heidi to take them before he put half a room's worth of distance between them.

"Did anyone else on our list send Chris money?" Pierce turned his attention to Mona and Eva.

"I still haven't found anything on Chandler. He's definitely got his shit on lock down." Eva straightened, stretching her arms over her head. "Mona did find a few more accounts for Howard that we're in the process of analyzing."

"We also pulled all the phone records for the known numbers for each man." Harlow lifted her shoulders and let them drop. "Unfortunately they're probably using burners at this point, so I'm not sure it will be any help."

"It's worth a shot." Pierce stood. "Let me know what you find."

The room began to clear out.

"Ms. Mowry. I'd like to have a word with you."

Harlow barely paused. "Sorry, Pierce. I've got shit to do." She walked out of the room, leaving the head of Alaskan Security staring after her.

"She's not going to tell you shit, man." Dutch hung back. "It's not worth pissing her off over it."

Pierce rocked back on his heels, shoving both hands in his pockets. "She needs to get this done so we can have Intel focus on finding our problem."

"You're the one who wanted a team of women who wouldn't take your shit." Dutch backed to the door. "Still seem like a good idea?"

"We would be fucked without them." Pierce rounded the desk. "Make sure Ms. Ayers has everything she needs."

"Why don't you make sure Ms. Ayers has everything she needs?" Dutch kept walking toward the door. "I've already got my hands full."

"I'm confident Ms. Ayers is not a fan of mine right now." Pierce went to stand by his window, but instead of staring out, his eyes went straight to the giant plant on the tiny stand. "And I'm not sure I blame her."

"You have to do what's best for everyone, Pierce. You have fifty people to protect. Not just one."

Pierce's eyes lifted to his. "Would you put Harlow in danger to protect fifty men?"

"That's different." He and Harlow had something. Something that wasn't like what most people had or wanted, but it was perfect for them.

"Is it?" Pierce turned away, falling silent.

Dutch backed out of the room, leaving Pierce to his own misery. Shawn fell into step with him as he headed to the office. "We've got a problem."

Dutch scanned the empty hall. "What now?"

"It's Richards."

Dutch stopped short. "What the fuck's wrong with Howard?"

Shawn's gaze settled on his. "He's gone."

Dutch blinked hard a few times.

No way he heard what he thought he just heard. "Gone where?"

Shawn walked to his office, leaving Dutch to follow.

"How the fuck is he gone?"

Shawn closed the door to his office. "Stop fucking yelling." He locked the door. "After the shooting we decided to move him to a secure location."

"What?" The vault at Alaskan Security was as secure as it got. "There was no way for him to get out of here."

"Him getting out wasn't our primary concern." Shawn went to his computer, pulling up the recording of Richards in his make-shift cell. "Does he look like a man who is being held indefinitely in a nine by twelve box?"

Richards was stretched out on his cot, hands behind his head, looking relaxed as shit.

"You think he believed someone was coming for him?" Dutch watched as Shawn set the feed to fast-forward and Howard zipped through different areas, reading the pile of books stacked in one corner, jogging in place, doing jumping jacks. "That's the most physical activity that prick's gotten in years."

"Every time he was brought food he asked what time it was." Shawn slowed down the footage as Howard took a tray of food to the small table, waiting until the deliverer was gone before pulling out a paper stuck to the underside of the table and scribbling across it with the tines of his plastic fork. "He was keeping track of the days and times, scratching it into a page he tore from a book."

"So you decided to move him." Dutch wiped his hands down his face. "Without telling anyone."

"It was a need-to-know basis." Shawn paused the feed. "Shadow took him out at night."

"What fucking good did that do?" Dutch almost laughed. It was almost funny. "If they still think he's here, they're still going to try to come get him."

"I didn't say it wasn't clear we moved him." Shawn's jaw clenched. "It was the night Pierce was shot."

Dutch dropped his head back toward the ceiling. "Christ."

He thought that bullet was meant for Harlow. Fucking agonized over it thinking she was the target in all this.

"We made a show of taking him out. Anyone who was watching would know what was happening."

"And didn't that just piss them off?" Dutch scrubbed his face again. "That move almost got Mona killed."

"Maybe Mona's part of our problem." Shawn's eyes were unflinching. "Any news on that?"

"Nope." Dutch unlocked the door. "Brock's going to shit when he finds out Howard's gone."

"He'll get over it. It's better than losing lives trying to keep him here." Shawn lifted one hand. "There's a reason I shared this information with you.

"Yeah? Why's that?"

Shawn stood from his desk. "I want you to find him."

****

"WHAT'S WRONG?" HE hadn't even made it to his desk before Harlow was questioning him. "What happened?"

"Nothing." Dutch grabbed the front of her sweater and pulled her close, pressing a chaste kiss to her lips. "I just missed you."

The sound of retching came from Heidi's desk. "I'm going to ask for my own office if you two don't stop. You're making us single girls miserable." Heidi's eyes narrowed on her screen. "Uhhhh."

"What?" Harlow pushed off the center of his chest as she turned to Heidi.

"Someone's in Howard's accounts now too." She frowned at the screen. "Spending money like crazy from his checking account."

Harlow slowly turned to Dutch. "That's interesting." She leaned back in her seat, eyes never leaving him. "Who would have access to Howard's bank account besides Howard?" She lifted her brows. "Because there's no way Howard could be the one spending, is there?"

"I'll look into that."

Eva's attention left her own computer to go to Dutch. "Why would you have to look into that? He's locked up here until this is all over."

"Isn't it illegal to lock people up in your basement?" Heidi's brows came together. "Because if not then I've been dating all wrong."

"Dutch." Eva stood up. "Where is Howard Richards?"

"Oh shit." Heidi's eyes widened in surprise at her computer. "I'm guessing all the cameras in that section of the property didn't just accidentally shut down a few nights ago." She sucked on the straw to her cup, eyes glued to her computer. "Has he gotten uglier?"

Eva jumped up from her chair, nearly tripping in her haste to watch whatever was on Heidi's screen. Her face went pale as she stared. "Why are all the camera's turning off?"

Harlow's scowl stayed on Dutch. "Probably because they moved Richards and didn't want us to know."

"Not just you." Pierce walked in looking less polished than normal. His hair was dropping out of the perfectly combed slick-back it usually fell into. His eyes were tired. His mouth was downturned. "Mr. Richards was a security risk. Keeping him here was inviting problems."

"Problems like what?" Eva's glare turned to Pierce. "Like having him locked down so he couldn't do anymore damage?"

"I believe Mr. Richards is more valuable than we first believed. There was concern an attempt would be made to free him of this location." Pierce stood in the center of the room. "I was unwilling to risk the safety of everyone here in order to continue to house him on the premises."

"Where did you take him?" Eva gripped the edge of Heidi's table, her knuckles turning white.

"We initially took him to a safe house we've successfully used in similar circumstances." Pierce glanced Mona's way before continuing on. "Unfortunately, there was a failure of the power grid supplying that location, and we were forced to move him again.

"Where is he now?" The edge to Eva's voice might be fear.

Or it might be rage.

It was a fine line for the women in the room.

"That is the million dollar question." Pierce started to step toward Mona but instead moved Dutch's way. "I would like for you to put all your effort into finding him."

"*All* our effort?" Harlow lifted a brow at him. "Don't we have more important things to deal with?"

Pierce stood straight, all his attention on her. "No. We don't."

"So freaking dramatic." Harlow rolled her eyes as she reached into the bag of chips on her desk to pull out a handful.

"That's what I said." Heidi snorted. "Men."

Mona kept her eyes on her computer the whole time, never once acknowledging Pierce's presence.

"Are you done?" Harlow lifted her brows at him. "Because apparently now we have even more to do."

Pierce's gaze lingered on Mona. "If anyone needs anything from me, please don't hesitate—"

"Yeah." Harlow waved one hand around. "We know."

Pierce pressed his lips together before turning and striding from the room.

"You too." Harlow turned to Dutch. "Get out. We need to talk."

"Are you serious?" He almost laughed.

But the look on her face stopped him short.

"I'm real fucking serious." Harlow grabbed his face with both hands. "I need to handle some shit."

Dutch shook his head. "This is a bad idea, Mowry."

She smiled. "I have no idea what you're talking about."

"You do." Dutch lowered his voice. "You can't do what you're thinking of doing."

"Why not? Because it's not what's best for Alaskan Security?"

"Yes."

Her eyes were serious as they locked onto his. "You're wrong."

"What if you're wrong?"

"I'm not." She held his gaze. "I promise."

He kept his eyes on hers a second longer before standing up. "Damn it, Mowry." Dutch walked to the door, leaving her smiling at his back.

"You can make this up to me later, Darling."

"Sick." Heidi's nose crunched up. "Hey, Dutch."

He turned, lifting a brow in question.

She gave him a grin. "Tell Shawn I said hi."

286

CHAPTER 21

HARLOW STOOD UP as soon as the door closed behind Dutch. "So apparently lots of people think we have a mole."

"I can see why." Eva was still a little pale, but at least she was pissed. Pissed was always easier to deal with than scared. "I can't fucking believe they let Howard get loose."

"How could that even happen?" Mona's skin wasn't much pinker than Eva's. "Isn't Shadow supposed to be some sort of super team?"

"They're the team that deals with covert ops when the government wants one more degree of separation between them and the garbage they're taking out." Harlow stood up from her desk. "Unfortunately, the mole issue isn't the biggest problem we currently have to deal with."

"How in the hell is that not our biggest problem?" Eva's hands went out at her sides. "Because that's a pretty big fucking problem."

"Some people think they know who the mole is." Harlow rocked on her feet. This was not going to be pretty, but it had to be done.

Mona wasn't their mole. No way was that woman behind any of what was happening.

She'd bet her life on it.

Basically was.

"Awesome." Eva leaned forward. "Let's get them and lock their asses in the hole Richards was supposed to be in."

"They think it's Mona."

The room went quiet.

Eva blinked a few times. "What?"

"There are a few people who think Mona is the mole."

Eva's mouth hung open.

"Mona?" Heidi started laughing, trying to smother the cackle with one hand as she leaned to peek around Eva. "No offense."

"It's fine." Mona pursed her lips. "Well, that's fantastic."

"So what we have to do is prove you're not." Harlow hated the way Mona slumped down in her seat. She'd just started to find a little bit of the spine Harlow knew she had.

"You can't prove a negative." Mona's head dipped lower. She turned to Eva. "I should go."

"Yeah, that's not happening." Harlow went to stand in front of Mona's desk. "Because I like you, and I'm not letting you walk away from this." She tipped her head from side to side. "Also because you'll probably get killed if you leave."

Mona's eyes went wide. "What?"

"Yeah." Harlow looked down the line of women. "I'm pretty sure we are on the kill list at this point." She shrugged at Heidi. "Sorry."

Heidi leaned toward Eva. "You didn't tell me that part."

"The only way to get off the kill list is to take down whoever this is." Harlow straightened. "And as pretty as the boys are, I'm not confident they are capable of doing that on their own."

"They are awfully pretty, though." Heidi chewed on the end of her pen. "I think I'm going to go after Shawn, what do you think?"

Eva's brows came together. "I think we should probably focus on the whole people want us dead thing first."

"Says the woman getting boned regularly." Heidi sighed. "Fine." She scratched at one of the two buns her hair was wrapped into. "You want me to look into Mona? Find all the reasons she's not a mole?" Heidi glanced Mona's way. "Besides the obvious?"

Harlow backed toward her desk. "Full-disclosure." She winced. "I already started."

Mona's head snapped up. "What?"

"Pierce was worried you wouldn't be safe until—"

"Pierce thinks it's me?"

"Fuck him." Heidi straightened, leaning on her desk so she could look straight at Mona. "Fuck him and his nice ass."

All three women looked Heidi's way.

"That came out wrong." She shrugged a little. "I mean, if that's what you're into, though."

"It's fine." Mona sucked in a breath, shoulders straightening as her eyes came to Harlow's. "What do you need from me to get this over with?"

"Maybe start with the PO box you have."

Mona's pale brows came together. "What PO Box?"

"The one in downtown Fairbanks." Harlow pulled up the information she found earlier. "It looks like you got it right after you came here."

Mona turned to Eva. "I don't have a PO box." She looked back to Harlow. "I haven't been off campus at all."

"You're shitting me." Harlow pointed at Heidi. "Get us into the system at the post office."

Heidi didn't say anything as her head barely bobbed to some sort of unheard rhythm.

Harlow picked up a pencil and threw it at her. "Hey."

"What?" Heidi pulled out one of the earbuds the loose bits of her blonde hair concealed.

"We need in the USPS system."

"I know." Heidi shoved the bud back into place. "I can read lips, you know."

Harlow shot Eva a look. "Is she always like this?"

"*She's* only like this when *she* isn't getting any dick." Heidi frowned as she continued to stare at her screen. "Makes me bitchy."

"Most of the time her music isn't even on." Eva tossed a pen Heidi's way.

Heidi caught it as it bounced off her boob and fell toward her lap. "I'm keeping these."

"I still like her." Harlow leaned on her desk, eyes wide as she stared at Heidi, raising her voice. "As long as she gets into the freaking system so we can see who rented that PO box."

"We probably won't be able to see." Heidi chewed one nail for a second before holding it out in front of her. "Where can I get a manicure around here?"

"That's what you're worried about right now?" Harlow pointed Mona's direction. "Our friend is being accused of fucking espionage—"

"I'm your friend?" Mona's voice was quiet. Hesitant.

Harlow turned her way. "Of course you're my friend." She hesitated as the truth sunk in.

She trusted Mona. Enough to put everything on the line to make sure she was protected and safe.

"You're all my friends."

"Even me?" Heidi tossed the pencil Harlow threw back her way.

"Maybe." Harlow gave her a smile. "It's early in the game though."

Heidi shrugged. "Fair enough."

Harlow focused on Mona. "You are kind and caring and smart as shit. Don't let anyone ever make you think anything different."

Mona's spine straightened. "You too."

Harlow rocked back in her seat. "Thanks."

"You're gonna be pissed." Heidi's nose and lip lifted in a curl. "I can only go back two weeks." She tapped on her keyboard a few seconds. "Yup. No video from the day it was rented."

"Shit." Harlow tapped the tips of her fingers against her chin. "How was it paid for?"

Heidi's brows lifted as she scanned the screen. "Looks like it was cash."

"Fuck a duck." Harlow shoved her fingers into her hair, digging the tips into her scalp.

"Anyone know a dude who looks like a ken doll?" Heidi's head tipped to one side. "But not in a hot way?"

"Chandler." Eva jumped up from her seat to rush to Heidi's side, watching the screen. "Motherfucker."

Harlow rounded her own desk to join them. Sure enough, Chandler moved across the screen, walking through the lobby to the wall of PO boxes in the small post office, using a key to unlock one before pulling out a stack of envelopes and tucking them into the pocket of his suit coat.

"Does this dick always wear a suit?" Heidi sucked on the straw of the cup always at her side.

"He thinks he's something." Mona stood at Eva's side, arms crossed over her chest. "That son of a bitch."

"But if it's in your name then you should be able to go get into it, right?" Heidi bobbed her head as she grinned Mona's way. "Go steal whatever he's got being delivered there."

"Nope." Harlow shook her head. "I think we need to pretend we don't know anything."

"What if it's a shit ton of cash?" Heidi lifted her shoulders and held them there. "We could have hella fun with a shit ton of cash."

"First of all, I can guarantee you no one is going to let us leave the property." Harlow counted off a finger. "Second, I can promise you they are able to get into this system almost as easily as you just did."

"What's the third reason?" Heidi's eyes bounced from Harlow's fingers to her face.

"Do you need a third reason?"

"I just expected more than two reasons when you started counting." Heidi shrugged. "That's all."

"But clearly the PO box isn't mine." Mona held her hand out to the screen. "That proves I'm not the mole."

"If there even is one." Heidi leaned to dig around the pile of crap stacked across her desk. "Maybe no one is being a dick." She unearthed a bag of jerky, pulling it free of the chaos and ripping the top open.

"No." Harlow shook her head. "There's definitely someone feeding them information."

"How do you know?" Mona sounded almost hopeful. Probably thinking Harlow didn't have a good explanation.

"There's no way Tod could have found me." Harlow leaned against the desk, unease making her stomach turn.

It was easy to judge someone from the outside looking in. Simple to say you would have handled things differently.

Left sooner.

Pressed charges.

Murdered him and buried his body in the woods.

She swallowed down the fear that kept her from letting people close. "Tod is a piece of shit." Harlow shifted on her feet, trying to find words to explain the things she'd endured.

Accepted.

Tolerated.

Until she didn't.

"He was abusive." Harlow looked to the ceiling, unable to face the women she thought of as her friends.

She was about to find out if she was theirs.

"He always said he would find me if I left, and for a while I believed him."

Heidi snorted. "I've seen what you can do. No way could that prick find you if you didn't want him to."

"Couldn't he find your tax records? Be able to find you here that way?" Mona picked up a stack of files on Heidi's desk and tapped them against the surface, evening up the edges before setting them at the top corner.

"Pierce hired me on as a private contractor through an LLC I formed." Harlow shook her head. "None of it traces back to me."

"You're super smart." Heidi pointed her way. "If I hunt this Tod guy down and castrate him can you help me disappear?"

"Definitely." Harlow watched as Mona continued straightening Heidi's mess of a desk. "I checked in on Tod regularly. Watched to see if he started spending money out of state or making calls from a new location."

"About a week ago he went radio silent. No calls at all. No money going out. No money coming in."

"So he's a new recruit." Eva pursed her lips. "They needed someone who could help them get in since we had Howard." She rocked her head from side to side. "Then they realized he knew you and decided to capitalize."

"You've got it backwards." Mona's pointed finger bobbed in Harlow's direction. "They're trying to fill their staff with people connected to us." She grabbed a trash can and started tossing empty wrappers and crumpled sticky notes into the bin. "Chandler was the reason Eva and I came onto Alaskan Security. Howard knows how we work. Knows how we work through cases because it's how we trained him to do it."

"They wanted someone who understood how you work." Eva met Harlow's gaze. "They found Tod."

"Why?" Harlow rubbed her eyes. "Are they just trying to—"

She tipped her head to one side.

Chris Snyder was the son of a senator. Chandler was part owner of a digital investigation firm. Howard worked at the firm.

Tod was a hacker.

"I just don't see how the dots connect."

"Maybe they're trying to take us down to steal all Alaskan Security's business." Heidi chewed a chunk of jerky. "I mean, Pierce is rich as fuck. Who wouldn't want to be rich as fuck?" Heidi turned Mona's way when the other woman looked her up and down. "What? Are you trying to say you didn't look into him before agreeing to take this job?"

Mona blinked. "It didn't even—"

"You're way more trusting than I am." Heidi grabbed a bag of almost empty chips as Mona tried to throw it away, tipping it back to catch the last couple bits with her mouth before passing it back. "I wanted to be sure this dude was for real."

Harlow had done the same. Probably knew more about Pierce than most people at Alaskan Security. It's part of the reason she treated him the way she did. "Pierce isn't a bad guy. He's just trying to build a successful business."

"Maybe someone else is too." Eva glanced at Heidi. "I don't remember you being this messy."

"She was." Mona grabbed the last of the trash from the desk and tossed it.

"Cleaning is boring." Heidi was back on her laptop, eyes focused. "This Chris guy knew that Bess chick, right?"

"Chris and Bess dated until right before she got pregnant with her son, Parker." Harlow paced to her desk, sitting down in front of her own computer. "He's the reason her parents hired Alaskan Security. He was not thrilled that she didn't want to be with him."

"Is he her kid's dad?" Heidi grabbed a marker off her desk and walked to the only wall not covered in monitors or windows.

"No. His father is Brock's friend Wade." Eva turned in her seat to watch as Heidi laid her sharpie to the paint.

Heidi turned. "Wait. So her baby daddy is a guy who works here?"

"It's a long story." Harlow pointed to the wall. "Whatcha doin' there?"

"This shit is confusing as hell." Heidi pushed up on her tiptoes and wrote ALASKAN SECURITY in big blocky letters across the wall. Then she drew four lines coming down, adding Harlow, Mona, Eva, and Bess at the ends. Then she added a line from Bess, writing Chris at the end. Harlow's line got Tod. Mona and Eva's lines connected to both Chandler and Howard. When she was done Heidi took a few steps back and studied the web they had so far. "What else?"

"Howard and Chris are connected by money transfers." Mona walked to the wall with a red marker, adding in a line to connect the men. "And Chandler and Howard are connected because they worked together."

Harlow studied the names and lines. "And here I thought Howard was just a lackey." She turned to Eva. "Is it possible Pierce is right and he's more involved than we thought?"

Eva crossed her arms as her eyes moved across the wall. "He's manipulative as hell, I know that much."

There was a sharp knock at the door. A second later Pierce strode in.

"Missed us already?" Heidi turned to him, capping her marker and staring him down.

Harlow moved in to Heidi's side, taking the same stance. If Pierce thought he was coming in to get information from them then he was about to be real surprised. "Can we help you with something?"

Pierce stared at the wall a second before turning their way. "I will have a white board installed first thing tomorrow morning." He eyed the line of women in front of him. "I spoke with the individuals you recommended hiring from Investigative Resources and informed them we would be postponing their arrival in Alaska. I think given the current circumstances it's best we delay their addition to the team."

"Agreed." Harlow lifted a brow. "Is that all?"

Pierce looked pointedly at the web of names on the wall.

Harlow tipped her head to one side. "We're kinda busy here, so unless you have something else..."

He held her gaze for a minute. "I would appreciate a briefing first thing in the morning."

"We'll see."

His eyes flicked to Mona before snapping back to rest on Harlow. "I understand your unhappiness with me right now, Ms. Mowry, but any decision I make must be for the good of the company. I have to do what keeps the people I employ safe."

"That's cool." Harlow lifted one hand and waved. "See ya later."

For a second she thought he would argue. Press her for the information he clearly knew they had.

Instead Pierce frowned, turning away and striding from the room stiff as a board.

"I think you pissed him off." Heidi smirked as she said it.

"Good." Harlow turned from the door. "Cause he sure as hell pissed me off."

CHAPTER 22

"SHE CAN'T JUST—"

"Are you going to be the one to tell her that?" Dutch held one hand toward the door of Shawn's office. "Because I'm sure as hell not going to do it."

"You're sure she's telling them?" Brock glanced at Dutch.

"Positive." He could see it in her eyes before Harlow kicked him out of the room. "She's convinced Mona isn't our mole."

"Eva's going to shit." Brock shifted in his seat. "Not looking forward to that conversation."

"They haven't seen the shit we've seen. They don't know what people are fucking capable of doing for money." Shawn rubbed his eyes. "If Harlow's wrong then—"

"Then we're fucked." Wade stood up from his seat and paced to the window overlooking the main courtyard running along the backside of the building.

"If she's the mole then we were already fucked. The woman has access to everything." The more Dutch thought about it, the more he was coming around to sharing Harlow's opinion. "And if Mona was the one feeding Chandler or whoever the fuck is in charge of these bastards information, then they should be acting a whole lot different."

"Would they?" Shawn's eyes were lined with exhaustion. He'd been burning the candle at both ends for weeks now and it was starting to show. "Us not realizing they had someone inside would be essential and I'm guessing they'd do just about anything to make sure we didn't find out."

"Mona knew we were going to that warehouse. If she knew we would be there then why in the hell would Tod show up? Don't you think she'd give him a head's up considering I've made it clear I'll kill the bastard the second I get a chance?" The feds showing up had screwed up more than their chance to gain important intel from the op. He'd also missed the perfect opportunity to end at least a little of Harlow's suffering.

Shawn's eye twitched a little as he stared Dutch's way. "No more field work for you."

Dutch relaxed back into his seat. "You know damn well we don't have enough men trained for covert ops." He'd avoided going out for years, worried that between his leg and his mind he'd be more of a liability than an asset. "I'll go out if my team needs me to go out."

Shawn pointed directly at Dutch's face. "I swear to God if we're left with a fucking mess because—"

"Because what, Shawn?" Dutch leaned forward, returning his friend's warning glare. "Because that fucking piece of shit raped Harlow? Squeezed her neck until she lost consciousness because he wanted to prove she was weaker than he was?" Dutch straightened, leaning back in his seat. "I'll kill the motherfucker the first chance I get."

"We can only kill him if we can find him, so I wouldn't be too fucking worried about it. After being shot at by the feds I'm sure Tod is still cleaning the shit out of his pants." Brock shoved Wade's empty chair toward where his friend still stood in the corner. "Sit down. You're making me fucking nervous."

Wade eyed the chair, but stayed put. "What about the men you eliminated? Any word on their identities?"

Shawn barely shook his head. "Shadow's contact has clamped down tight on this one."

Shadow's purpose as a way for the government to avoid getting their hands too dirty offered Alaskan Security access to certain perks. One of them was the ability to clean up certain messes with no questions asked. Another was being tapped into a world of intelligence most people couldn't handle knowing existed.

"Probably because they've got their hand in the same fucking mess." Shawn opened the drawer of his desk and fished out a bottle of Excedrin, popped open the cap and tossed a couple back, swallowing them down without the help of the bottle of water on his desk.

"This shit giving you a headache too?" Brock held out his hand, taking the medication when Shawn passed it his way.

"Something like that." Shawn rolled his head from side to side. "Unfortunately, we can't wait for the feds to shut whatever this shit is down. Whoever this is had made it clear we are in their fucking way and that they'll do whatever it takes to get us out of the picture."

"But how?" Wade reached for the bottle before Brock could get the cap back in place. "We barely knew they fucking existed and they were hitting our safe houses and trying to take down our men."

"The first shots were fired at Bess." Dutch lifted his gaze to Wade. "Not at us."

Wade raked one hand through his dark hair. "This is bullshit." He tipped back the pill bottle, catching three in his mouth before stealing the water from Shawn's desk.

"There's got to be more of a connection than we've found." Dutch looked around the men in the room. "And if anyone can find it it's—"

"Harlow." Brock tossed Wade the cap to the pills.

"No." Dutch stood up. "She's too close. Harlow's good as hell, but she's a hacker. Hunting down ties isn't her specialty."

"Who are you talking about then?" Wade's brows came low as he looked to Shawn who was still sitting at his desk, head tipped toward the ceiling. He let out a long breath.

"Heidi."

Dutch grinned. "I forgot. I was supposed to tell you she said hi."

"That woman's going to make me lose my mind." Shawn scrubbed his hands down his face. "I thought Harlow was a fucking handful."

"She's a handful all right." Dutch opened the door. "But she knows her shit." He tipped his head toward Shawn. "Come on, big boy."

Shawn shook his head. "You're on their team. You go talk to them."

"Don't be a pussy." Dutch opened the door wider. "You go up against men with assault weapons. You can handle a sweet little hacker."

"That woman isn't sweet." Shawn stood, grabbing his pill bottle from Wade and chucking it into the drawer it came from. "She's vicious."

"You guys talking about me?" Heidi poked her head into the open doorway before stepping into full view. She slowly wrapped her lips around the straw on her giant steel mug, making a show of pursing them as her long-lashed eyes rested right on Shawn's paling face.

His strangled swallow was almost comical.

"We were, actually." Dutch moved to block Heidi's view of Shawn. "We need you to find out how Chris ties into all this. We're missing something big."

"Cool." Heidi tried to lean to peek around him, smirking when Dutch moved along with her. "Hey, Shawn."

"Go back to work, Heidi."

Heidi's smile widened. "I'll do whatever you tell me to do."

Shawn let out a strangled-sounding cough.

Heidi started to walk away but stopped, pointing at Wade. "Oh. I'm supposed to tell you your mom has Parker and Bess is working."

"Working?" Wade's tone was tight. Understandably. He had a family to worry about. One he'd already worked hard to protect.

"Yeah." Heidi squinted Wade's way, looking him up and down. "Did you think she was just going to sit around and wait for you guys to figure this shit out?" She turned her attention back toward Rogue's team lead. "Bye, Shawn."

As Heidi walked down the hall, back to the office she shared with the rest of Team Intel, Dutch turned to Shawn. "You might be screwed, my friend."

"I don't have time for this bullshit." Shawn stood from his desk. "We've got dozens of men to clear. The whole damn property's got to be swept. We've got to send Rogue and Shadow out to freaking Junction to see if we can narrow down the location on Tod and Chandler."

"Are you sure they're both there?" The feds showing up at the warehouse fucked up their whole op. They had to hunker down to avoid being discovered which meant they had no clue who went where. "Maybe the feds caught Tod."

"I need a fucking vacation." Shawn pushed past Dutch. "Look at the footage we can get a hold of. See if you can tell who went where." He turned toward Pierce's office. "I'm headed to get the short list from the other leads for Intel to start on."

"You think they're going to give you one?" Dutch glanced at Wade and Brock before turning back to Shawn. "Would you give them one?"

"Christ." Shawn pressed the thumb and fingers of one hand into his eyes. "This is a fucking mess."

"We've got to look into everyone." It was a painful truth. One no one wanted to face.

One of their own might be selling them out. Putting anyone associated with Alaskan Security at risk.

Dutch fell into step with Shawn. "We have to come up with some sort of system to hold us until the girls can find something." He glanced up as a few members of Alpha passed, nodding their way as the men went into the break room. "How's the training coming?"

Bobby grinned. "Fun as shit."

"Hopefully that also means you're taking it serious as shit." Pierce stepped out of his office, looking perfectly pressed.

Bobby tipped his head. "Definitely. Very serious."

"He just thinks he's a badass now that he knows how to cover his tracks in the snow." Micah elbowed his friend. "Come on. We don't have long before we have to be back."

Seth followed the last of Alpha as they came down the hall on their way to lunch. He stopped at Pierce's side, watching his men as they filed out of sight.

Pierce turned to Seth. "Are you satisfied with how your team is performing?"

Seth gave a half-nod. "Some yes, some no."

"Any standouts?" Pierce motioned toward his door with a jerk of his head.

Seth followed him in. "Micah is definitely taking to it well. He's got the focus it requires. Might be worth considering taking him out next time you go. See how he does in the field."

"Excellent." Pierce sat behind his desk. "What about Beta? Have you heard anything about their performance?"

"Beta is on the backburner. We had to narrow down the herd." Zeke stepped into the office, fully outfitted in his gear. "We couldn't handle training both teams at once."

Pierce's gaze sharpened. "What about the private training session I arranged?"

"That's going surprisingly well." The lead for Shadow flipped the top sheet on the clipboard clutched in his hand to scan the paper below it. "As far as Alpha, we've got maybe two guys who could be ready to test soon."

"How are the rest doing?" Pierce pointed to the clipboard in Zeke's hand. "May I?"

Zeke slid the board Pierce's way. "I would expect we might end up with four out of ten who will be worth a shit."

Seth scoffed. "I'm getting real fuckin' sick of you assholes acting like Alpha isn't just as damn valuable as you are."

"Alpha is valuable in its own way." Pierce's eyes didn't leave the paper he was reviewing. "Unfortunately, that way is not useful in our current situation."

"Then let us go back out and do what we do." Seth shot Zeke a glare as the lead for Shadow stepped in to retrieve his clipboard. "My men are itching to get back to work."

"Of course they are." Zeke tucked the clipboard under one arm. "Can't wait to be back on the fuckin' red carpet, standing between some actress and the paparazzi." He clicked his tongue. "Sounds like tough fucking work."

Seth's nostrils flared as his gaze slowly dragged Zeke's way.

Dutch stepped between the men. "Fighting isn't going to help our cause right now." He pressed one palm to the center of Seth's chest as the lead for Alpha pressed forward. "Don't do it, man."

Seth stared Zeke's way, eyes narrowed. "When this is all over I'm fucking coming for you, dick."

"I'll be waiting." Zeke's tone was dry as he turned his attention back toward the clipboard in his hand. "Send your men back in when they're done eating. We've got shit to do."

Seth stood a few seconds more, still clearly considering starting a brawl in Pierce's office. Finally he tipped his chin up, scanning the room before walking out.

"That was uncalled for." Pierce waited for Zeke to look his way. "I'd appreciate it if you kept your opinions on Alpha and their assignments to yourself."

"Or what?" Zeke faced Pierce down.

"Or I will dissolve your team." Pierce stood, one brow lifted. "Considering your team is the most likely reason we are where we are, it might be for the best anyway."

Zeke snorted. "You think this place could continue to be what it is without Shadow?" He shrugged. "Fine. Do it and see what happens."

"If you believe Alaskan Security wouldn't be just as financially successful without the added liabilities of what your specific specialties involve, then you would be very wrong." Pierce moved in close to Zeke. The head of Shadow stood a full three inches taller than Pierce and at least that much wider. "I have risked more for less, and I'm not interested in retaining men who disrespect me. Do you understand?"

Zeke held Pierce's eyes for a few long seconds. Finally he took a step back. "You know where to find me if you need me."

Pierce watched Zeke leave, waiting a few heartbeats before turning to Shawn. "Prepare Rogue to take the members Zeke recommends out for a trial run. We need to see if they're as ready as he believes."

Shawn nodded. "We can go out tonight."

"Until then I want the property swept. All of it. Check the perimeter, the cameras, I want this place secure." Pierce turned to Dutch. "Go find me something. Anything."

Dutch gave him a single nod. "We will handle this."

Pierce's expression shifted, showing the fatigue he expertly hid. "We have to."

Dutch left Pierce with Shawn, heading straight to the office and straight to Harlow. When he walked in she was standing on a desk, scribbling on the increasingly chaotic web the women scrawled across the wall.

"How's it going?" Dutch walked to the edge of the desk and squinted up at the jumble of names and information Harlow was adding to.

"This is a freaking nightmare." She turned, capping the purple marker in her hand as she sat down, dangling her legs over the edge as she leaned into him, resting her forehead in the center of his chest. "Whose idea was it for me to work here?"

"Yours." Dutch wrapped his arms around her. "If I remember correctly, you were pretty excited about it."

"I was excited about the money." She tipped her head back, resting her chin against his sternum. "I'm not sure it's worth it anymore."

He smiled down at her. "Good thing you're not just getting money out of the deal then."

"Are you arguing that you are enough added value that I should be excited to be risking my life?"

"When you say it like that—"

Harlow's lips twisted into a smile as she reached up to wrap her arms around his neck. "How's Pierce?"

"Not having a great day." Dutch leaned in to press a kiss to her forehead. "He's got it coming at him from all sides."

"Well he can stop worrying about one side." Eva sat at her desk. "We found enough to make it pretty clear no one in this room is doing anything they shouldn't be."

Mona didn't look up from where she worked on her computer.

"That is excellent news." Dutch pulled Harlow off the desk as he turned toward the women in the room. Bess now had a spot set up on the other side of Mona. She sat in her chair, staring at the wall of insanity. "How's Wade's mom doing?"

"Fine." Bess didn't look his way, her eyes moving slowly across the mess of a diagram. "She thinks everyone is overreacting."

"That's because she hasn't been kidnapped." Harlow leaned into his side, the hand gripping his shirt tightening just a little. "It's not as fun as it sounds."

Dutch pulled her a little closer, turning his attention to Heidi. "She found anything interesting yet?"

"Not that I know of." Harlow slowly pulled from his arms, turning to face the same board Bess still studied.

"She's still looking." Heidi's head popped up. "Do you realize how big of a fucking mess you people are in?"

CHAPTER 23

"KEEP LOOKING." DUTCH turned to Harlow. "I need to help Rogue sweep the property. Pierce wants to be sure it's secure."

"Secure?" Mona glanced up from her computer for the first time in an hour. "Did something happen?"

"We want to be sure nothing else happens." Dutch pressed a quick kiss to Harlow's lips before backing away and out the door. "Why don't you guys just solve this whole shit show while I'm gone?"

"That's the plan, Stan." Heidi snorted, her smile wilting when she realized no one was laughing along with her. "Bunch of freaking downers."

"I'm sorry we don't find this as amusing as you do." Eva's skin was still a little pale. Had been since she learned Howard slipped Shadow.

However in the hell that happened.

Harlow turned to be sure Dutch was out of earshot before moving in closer to the women she worked with.

Her friends.

The people she trusted most outside Dutch.

"Hey." She kept her voice low just in case someone might be in the hall. "How did Howard get away from Shadow?"

Eva shook her head. "I haven't heard anything."

"No one hears anything about Shadow." Mona scooted her chair closer.

"Isn't that the point?" Heidi's voice carried through the room as she continued to work.

Harlow stepped to the newest addition, reaching up to yank out one of Heidi's ever-present earbuds. "If you're going to be a part of this then get over here."

Heidi peeked toward the door. "Why don't we just close that?"

"Because then they will want to come in here to see what we're doing." Harlow moved back to the spot where Bess, Mona, and Eva were sitting close together, motioning for Heidi to follow.

"Ugh. Fine." Heidi slid her computer from her lap to her desk before dropping to sit on the floor beside Eva's chair. "Obviously Howard's fat ass didn't give them the slip all by himself."

Bess lifted one hand, eyes on Harlow.

"You're allowed to talk." Harlow glanced to the door. "Just be quiet."

"Do we know which safe house they had Howard at?"

Harlow shook her head. "Shadow is a pretty self-contained unit. The original plan was for me to start helping them at some point, but so far they've resisted."

Mona raised her hand.

Harlow shot Mona a wide-eyed look. "I said no one has to raise their hands."

Mona's hand slowly dropped. "I think I know where he was."

Harlow's stomach clenched. "How would you know that?"

She'd been positive Mona was not involved in this shit. So sure she put everything on the line because of it. Suddenly that was seeming like it might have been a bad idea.

"I, um—" Mona's eyes moved to the faces of the women around her, "I was having a conversation with one of the members of Shadow when another one came up and said something about Santa's house."

Harlow blinked. "You've got to be kidding."

Mona shook her head.

Harlow turned to Heidi. "Find it."

Heidi's brows came together. "Now you want me to find Santa Claus?" She scoffed as she shoved up from the floor. "You people are going to make me lose my damn mind. *Find the connection between Chris and Howard, Heidi. Find the connection between Chris and Chandler, Heidi. Find out who's telling people shit about Alaskan Security, Heidi. Find fucking*

Santa Claus, Heidi." She flopped back into her chair, shoving in the ear bud Harlow pulled free before dropping her computer back on her lap.

"You know we're looking for a safe house, right?"

Heidi's head rolled her way, eyes resting on Harlow a second before rolling it back.

"Have I mentioned how much I like her?" Harlow backed toward her own desk. "Once she has the location, find any camera we might be able to get into. See if we can get eyes on how shit went down." She turned to Mona, Eva, and Bess. "You three keep trying to figure out how in the hell Chris, Howard, and Chandler found each other."

Harlow sat in front of her personal computer, rolling her shoulders. "I'm going to find Tod and figure out how to fuck his world up."

****

"IT'S AWFULLY QUIET in here." Dutch took a few steps into the room, Brock and Wade following behind him.

"We're fucking busy." Heidi glanced up from her computer, eyes trailing over the men filling the door to their office. "Where's Shawn?"

"Hiding from your ass." Brock gave her a wink. "You scare the shit out of him."

Heidi lifted one shoulder and let it drop. "His loss."

Wade walked in, going straight to Bessie's desk. "How are you doing, Sweetheart?"

Bess was definitely frustrated. She'd stepped into a mess none of them could figure out and it was clearly frustrating the hell out of her. "This is insane, you know that, right?"

It was a phrase she'd repeated countless times in the past hour.

Wade leaned down, catching her lips in a kiss. "I wish I could change this." He rested his forehead against hers for a second, eyes closed.

Harlow watched, surprised at how intimate the moment seemed. The way Bessie's hands cradled Wade's face. The way he leaned into her.

They way they leaned on each other.

"What's wrong, Mowry?" Dutch's voice startled her.

Harlow snapped her eyes back to the computer she was supposed to be focused on. "You're in your gear again."

"I told you we have to go out tonight." He crouched down at her side. "There's a couple men from Alpha who might be ready to join us and we need to see how they handle it."

"Does that mean you won't have to go out anymore?" Harlow glanced his way, trying not to let the sight of the heavy vest strapped to his chest make her panic.

"The more men we have who are capable, the less chance I will have to go out."

"Okay." She avoided looking his way. "Then I guess you should go."

"I won't be gone long." Dutch eased closer. "When I get back I will make it up to you."

"I'll let you try." She dared a glance Dutch's way. The quick glance turned into a longer perusal of the gear strapped to his broad frame. "You do look kinda sexy in all that."

"Kinda?" Dutch leaned into her ear. "You hurt my feelings with that one, Mowry." One hand ran down the center of her back. "I hoped you found me more than kinda sexy."

"I guess that depends on how long you take to get back here." She smiled as he started to laugh, low and deep in her ear.

"I will do my best to keep this trip short." Dutch opened her top drawer and pulled out the earpiece he gave her. "And you can be with me the whole time."

"That's what you said last time." Harlow took the small device. "Right before you cut me off."

Dutch's face was suddenly very serious. "I didn't want to make things worse for you, Harlow. Hearing what can happen out there—"

"I thought something horrible might have happened to you." She turned to face him. "That's all that I care about, Pretty Boy."

"We're going to have to work on that nickname, Darling."

"We'll see." Harlow leaned into him, wrapping both arms around his neck. "Please be careful."

Dutch rested his head against hers, the same way Wade had done to Bess seconds ago. His hazel eyes closed and he took a long, slow breath. When his eyes opened, she was waiting.

"Everything will be okay. I'll be in your ear the whole time."

"I don't like leaving you." Dutch's gaze was steady on hers. "Especially not knowing what the fuck's going on."

"There's dozens of men here. You swept the property. I can see the whole place from here. If anything weird happens I will lock every door in this place." The smile Harlow gave him was genuine and easy to come by.

For the first time in a long time she felt in control of her life.

And nothing was different. Not really. Tod was still trying to find her. Figure out a way to make her suffer for daring to leave him.

She was still a little broken. Still a little damaged. Might always be.

But it was finally getting better. There was someone at her side who understood and accepted what she really was. Even if sometimes it was ugly and painful.

"If anything weird happens you better lock that damn door and stay the fuck in this room until we come get you." Wade's tone was edgy.

"We will be fine." Bess sat up straight in her seat. "Promise."

Wade's gaze was dark as he scanned the room before turning to Dutch and Brock. "Let's get this over with."

Dutch leaned into Harlow's ear. "Figure out what in the hell is going on so these guys can calm the fuck down."

"Come on, Mackey. I know she's pretty, but the faster we get going, the faster you can sweet talk her into your bed."

Dutch straightened. "Sweet talk gets me nowhere with this one." He gave her a wink. "Be careful, Mowry. I don't want to stay up late killing anyone."

She smiled at him. "I will do my best."

The men filtered out, and the room stayed quiet for a minute. Finally Eva stood up and walked to peek out the door. "They're gone." She grabbed her computer and walked to the front of the room, plugging it into one of the monitors on the wall. "Here's the road just outside our house."

Heidi braced the sucker in her hand between her teeth before coming to the front with her own computer, and connecting it to a separate monitor. "The property technically doesn't have an address. It's listed as vacant land on the auditor's site." She stepped back to look up at the screen. "But clearly there's a building there."

A smallish structure sat in the middle of a thick grove of trees, making it difficult to see from the satellite picture, and probably impossible to see from the narrow road leading past.

Harlow stood to get a better look at it. "Are you sure this is it?"

"It's owned by an LLC that I believe might be associated with our very own Alaskan Security." Heidi turned to face Harlow. "Plus it's the only place in the North Pole that fits the bill."

"So Pierce is buying properties under another name?" Mona's gaze sat on the wooded lot.

"They're safe houses. If any dumbass could trace them back to Alaskan Security then they wouldn't be very safe, would they?" Heidi cracked down on the sucker she still held. "This is the one I had the hardest time finding." She smiled around the candy. "Probably since it's Santa's house."

Harlow turned to Eva. "Do we have footage from the day Howard escaped?"

Eva's gaze held hers. "I didn't check yet."

Harlow took a deep breath. "You staying for this?"

Eva nodded.

Harlow moved to her computer and pulled up the public transit camera Eva found. "Let's see what we can find." She worked through the past few days, scanning all the footage.

There was nothing.

"Shit." Eva shoved her fingers into her hair, shaking it out. "As much as I didn't want to see his face, I was really hoping we could figure out what in the hell happened."

"Uh." Heidi on the floor at the front of the room, her computer perched on her lap. "I think I found it."

Eva moved in at Harlow's side with Mona and Bess following suit, all four women watching as Heidi replayed the footage.

The feed was grainy and dim, making it difficult to make out what exactly was going on.

But not impossible.

"That can't be it." Eva started to lean into Harlow.

"That's him though." Mona squinted at the squatty form being shoved from one group of towering men to another. "They're just handing him over."

"Why would they do that?" Eva's wide eyes moved to Harlow. "He is fucking dangerous."

Harlow shook her head. "I don't know." She faced the screen again, hoping for some sort of an answer, some reason Shadow would simply pass Richards off to whoever those men were. "It doesn't make any sense."

"None of this does." Bess rubbed her eyes. "I can't think about it anymore. It's making my head hurt."

Heidi scooted her butt around until she faced the rest of the women. "What the fuck is going on?"

Everyone's eyes rested on Harlow.

"Does Dutch know?" Mona's question was understandable.

"I don't think so." Harlow glanced at the earpiece on her desk.

"I wouldn't do that." Heidi stood up. "I think we should wait and confront them all at once."

"Pierce too." Eva's eyes narrowed on the still-shot of Howard and the two groups of men still displayed on the screen. "Someone knows something and it's bullshit."

"So Shadow is the mole." Harlow pressed one hand to her head. The potential that it could be more than one person never occurred to her. She'd assumed there was a single culprit, with their own agenda, ready to take down Alaskan Security to get what they wanted.

"Why?" Bessie moved to stand in front of Harlow on the other side of her desk. "What would Shadow gain from passing information to these people?"

Harlow dropped her head back to stare at the ceiling. "Fuck if I know."

"There has to be something that makes it worth it." Bessie's eyes moved to rest on a nondescript spot in the corner of the room. "Otherwise there's no reason to risk it." She tapped her fingers on the surface of the desk. "Chris wanted to be a part of whatever this is but didn't have the cash to play. He thought my family's money would fund what he was trying to accomplish."

"Chris had money, though." Heidi was back at her desk, shifting around the ridiculous amount of trash she'd managed to accumulate since Mona cleaned it. "Remember? Howard was sending it to him."

"What?" Bess turned to look at the screen. "That Howard?"

"Yup." Heidi grabbed a stack of papers. "Here." She held them out to Bess, but pulled them back to swipe off a dusting of crumbs covering the top page. "Sorry. I had powdered doughnuts for breakfast."

Bess took the paper. "What is this?"

"It's his bank records." Heidi leaned in to point out a line. "See that? Those are transfers from an account I connected to Howard."

Bessie's blonde brows came together. "Why would Howard send him money?"

"That's the million-dollar question." Heidi leaned in again. "Well, the twenty-thousand-dollar question."

"So Howard sent Chris money for something." Bess uncapped her marker and strode to the wall of chaos they'd been working on, adding in notes under the line where Howard's name was connected to Chris. She stepped back, staring at the web for a second.

Eva slowly walked to Bessie's side, her eyes narrowing more with each step. She suddenly spun to face Mona. "What's Chris's last name?"

"Snyder." Mona's head barely tipped to one side. "Why?"

"I feel like it sounds familiar." Eva's eyes squinted a little. "Does it sound familiar to you?"

Mona shrugged. "I've been looking at it for days so, yeah."

Eva shook her head. "No. I mean like did we maybe hear Howard talk about him at the office?"

"I didn't deal with Howard at the office. He was on your team." Mona turned to Heidi. "Did you hear Howard talk about him at the office?"

"I stayed the hell away from that weirdo." Heidi's brows lifted. "He creeped me out."

Eva slowly turned to Bess. "Is there anyone who might have wanted Chris investigated, privately?"

Bess snorted. "My dad." Her eyes jumped to Eva's. "Do you think you guys were hired to investigate him?"

Eva rushed to her laptop. "Maybe. I don't remember specifically seeing it happen, but we were so busy that I couldn't keep up with everything." She leaned in, eyes moving across the screen as she accessed Investigative Resources' system. Her face fell. "Shit."

"It was a really good thought." Bessie walked to her desk, dropping her marker into the small container holding all her pencils and pens. "I need to go check in on Parker and Gloria. See how they're doing." Bess grabbed her phone and headed to the door, jumping back a little right as she reached the open frame. "Oh."

Bobby stepped into view, nodding his head at the women still in the room. "Dutch sent us to make sure you all were taken care of." He thumbed toward the other side of the door where another member of Alpha stood. "You guys leaving for the day?"

"Just me." Bessie turned to wave. "I'll see you girls in the morning."

"Kiss your baby for me." Heidi snapped the gum she unearthed from the sucker she had earlier. When Bess was gone she turned to Harlow. "Have you seen her kid? He is so fucking cute."

"He is pretty cute." Harlow wasn't much of a baby fan, but Parker was about as adorable as it got. "I bet she'd let you babysit."

Heidi's eyes went wide. "You think?"

Eva scanned Heidi. "You want to babysit?"

"I love kids." Heidi beamed. "I want at least five."

Harlow wrinkled her nose. "Ew." She lifted one hand. "No offense."

"I've got to catch a dick first." Heidi twisted in her chair, spinning from side to side on the pivoting base. "A nice-looking one. I don't want ugly kids."

"I bet you can find one here. Just stay the hell away from Shadow. Apparently they're—"

"Hey." Harlow turned toward Eva, her eyes wide. "Which tampons did you say you liked best again?"

Eva blinked a few times. "Which tampons do I like best?"

"Yup." Harlow rolled her eyes toward the door where Bobby still stood outside. "We were talking about how sometimes the blood just gushes when we're on our periods and goes everywhere, and you said there was a tampon that could handle all the clotting."

"Oh." Eva's eyes stayed glued to Harlow's face. "Yup. Lots of blood everywhere without them." She rocked back on her heels. "If you want to have a couple to try we can go to my room and I'll give you some."

"That's an amazing idea." Harlow grabbed her computer off her desk. "Because I am

328

having issues with that right now. I might even end up with blood on my shoes." She shoved her computers in her bag. "Mona, do you want to try some of Eva's tampons?"

Mona's blue eyes moved from Eva to Harlow. "I don't—"

"Pack your shit up, Mona." Heidi worked to cram half the stuff on the surface of her desk into a bag. "We need tampons for," her voice got louder as she leaned toward the door, "our heavy, painful, bloody periods." She snapped her gum again as she grinned Harlow's way. "You're amazing."

CHAPTER 24

"WHAT DO YOU think?" Shawn sat at the back of the van carrying half of Rogue from the location they just spent two hours casing. "You think either of them are ready?"

"I think Micah did pretty well. I couldn't find him most of the time." Wade, Brock, and Dutch were assigned to find the rest of the team as they moved around the two-acre property where Howard was kept. "Hunter might eventually get it together, but he's nowhere near ready right now."

Brock leaned into Dutch's side. "You hear anything from Mowry?"

Dutch shook his head. "She's probably still pissed about me shutting her off last time."

Hopefully.

"There's more than enough men there to handle anything that might happen." Brock sounded as confident as Dutch was.

Which was not very. "I don't like leaving them with all this shit happening."

"Pierce is there. So's Shadow. They're fine." Brock leaned back, adjusting the front of his vest. "They're fine."

"We thought that before." Dutch wiped one hand down his face.

"You can't fucking watch them every second of every hour of every day. It's just not possible." Shawn's tone was sharp. "We've got to deal with this shit. It's just how it is."

"You saying you won't feel like a piece of shit if something happens to one of them while we're gone?" Brock faced Shawn down.

"We have to deal with this. We can't just sit at headquarters waiting for these dicks to strike again. We've got to go out and find the bastards so we can end this and everything can go back to normal before I lose my goddamn mind." Shawn leaned back in his seat. "Now, if you don't mind, can we talk about the shit we need to discuss to make that happen?"

Dutch sat up, pressing his earpiece and leaning away from the sound of Shawn's voice as the team lead continued trying to discuss everyone's opinions of how the evening went.

The softly muffled sound of a feminine voice he thought he heard was a little clearer. "Harlow?"

"When will you be back?"

The tension bunching his shoulders and eating the lining of his stomach eased. "We're on our way now. Maybe thirty minutes out."

"We're going to be in Eva's room. Come there when you get back."

"Is everything okay?"

"Yup. Fine." The clipped edges of her words surprised him.

"You sure?" Dutch turned back toward Shawn who had fallen silent.

"Positive. Just come to Eva's room."

"Okay." Dutch glanced at the other men in the back of the van. "I'll see you in a little bit."

"Good." Harlow's voice softened just a little. "Be careful."

"I will do that."

The line went silent in his ear.

"What was that about?" Shawn's focus was all on him.

His best guess was Harlow and the rest of Team Intel found something. Something she didn't want everyone to know about just yet.

"I think the girls are maxed out for the night. Harlow said they're all headed to Eva and Brock's room."

"Shit." Brock dropped his head back against the side of the van. "If they get the margarita mix out my night is fucked."

"At least they're entertaining." Dutch helped move the conversation into safer waters. "Especially now that they've got Heidi in the mix."

"I thought Harlow was hell on wheels." Brock shook his head. "That Heidi makes Harlow look like an amateur."

Shawn was suddenly silent, all his attention focused on the clipboard in his hands. He'd stayed in the van during the op, watching the whole exercise through the body cameras on each member of Rogue.

"I'm going to send Hunter back to Shadow for a few more weeks of training, see if we can get him a little more up to the level we need him at." Shawn scribbled across the top paper. "I'm going to go ahead and say Micah is ready for level one ops, that way we can get Dutch back where we need him." His eyes lifted to the rest of the group. "Everyone in agreement?"

"Fine with me." Dutch stretched his leg out, wincing a little as the ache there intensified with the movement. "It's been nice to get back out, but I'm ready to be back in the comfort of my office, drinking coffee while you assholes do the hard work."

Brock studied him for a minute. "You did good, man. I know it's not always easy for you."

"It's weird. It used to be rough." He worked his foot from side to side. "Now it's just the leg that wants to hold me back."

Brock clapped him on the back. "Even that doesn't slow you down much. It was like old times out there."

"It felt like old times." Being out in the field showed Dutch just how far he'd come. "I didn't think I'd ever be able to do it again."

"I knew you'd come around." Brock gave him a small smile. "I'm proud of you. You worked hard to get here."

334

"It took a long damn time." Dutch settled back into his spot on the long bench-style seating.

"But you did it. That's what matters." Brock's smile widened to a shit-eating grin. "Now you get to reap the rewards."

"I'll tell Harlow you called her that."

"You do and I'll kick your ass. She'll never shut up about it."

Dutch grinned back Brock's way. "I know."

****

"FUCK." HARLOW DUG through her giant bag. "I swear I grabbed it." She started pulling everything out, looking for the external hard drive containing all the video recordings she needed. "It's not here."

She glanced at the door to Eva's room. "I've gotta go get it."

"They're probably still out there." Eva tipped back the glass of wine she'd poured the minute they walked in.

"Do you think they told Pierce we're up to something?" Mona's eyes followed Harlow's to the door.

"Who the hell knows?" Harlow went to the door and pressed her ear to the cool steel. "But if Shadow is the problem, then we're all screwed, because those guys could probably make every one of us disappear." She turned to the women. "I'm going to go grab it and then I'll come right back."

"You can't go alone." Mona stood up, tugging at the hem of her tailored sweater. "I'll come with you."

Mona's offering warmed Harlow. "Thanks."

"Don't get caught. They'll know something is up before we have a chance to figure out what it is." Eva tipped her glass Harlow's way. "Be quick.

"We'll hurry." Harlow turned to Mona. "Ready?"

Mona nodded silently.

She was going to be the perfect co-conspirator.

Harlow pulled the door open, waiting just a second to see if anyone popped out on either side. They'd told Hunter and Bobby their services were no longer needed, but the men seemed hesitant to abandon their post.

Probably because Dutch threatened them within an inch of their lives if anything happened to her.

Harlow smiled.

She peeked her head out into the empty hall before stepping out, Mona sticking to her side as they hustled to the unmarked door leading to the underground tunnel system. They ducked inside and hurried down the never-used staircase. A few minutes later they were at the door leading to the hall of their office.

"It's got to be on my desk. I'll run in and grab it while you keep lookout."

Mona's brows came together. "What do I do if someone comes?"

336

"Hell if I know." Harlow grabbed the handle. "Improvise." She opened the door, slowly stepping out, scanning the space as she walked toward her office.

Luckily, the hall was as empty and quiet as the second floor in the rooming building was. Harlow picked up the pace, fast-walking to the office with Mona right behind her.

The hard drive was right where she thought it would be. Harlow grabbed it, immediately turning to hurry back out into the hall and to the heavy steel door. She grabbed the handle and pulled it open, stepping through just as a familiar voice carried down the silent hall.

"Ms. Ayers. Is everything okay?"

Mona had one hand on the door, holding it open. She didn't even look Harlow's way as her hand dropped, letting the door swing closed, completely hiding Harlow from view.

Harlow shifted on her feet.

Did she stay here and wait for Mona?

What if Pierce came with her? He would immediately know something was up, and right now they didn't know enough to risk Pierce sniffing around.

Possibly alerting Shadow to their suspicions.

And anyone who had any sort of understanding of the male species could see that Pierce would definitely never let Mona go wandering through the building alone late at night. He didn't think she was capable of handling herself. That girl was definitely getting an escort back to her room.

Harlow turned and hurried down the stairs, ready to put as much space between her and them as possible. She was moving so fast she didn't see the shadowy figure until it grabbed her around the middle, one arm clamping across her waist as the other pressed into her mouth.

Last time someone grabbed her like this she didn't fight back the way she should have.

Didn't really put up a fight at all.

Harlow's arms went rigid as bile ran up her esophagus and her body went numb. Sharp memories crowded her brain and seized her lungs, threatening to shut her down once again.

She squeezed her eyes shut, digging deep for that picture Dutch tried to paint for her. Something about a beach and water and...

Dutch.

He was the reason she calmed down. Not a fucking mentally created beach.

He was strong. He overcame.

So could she.

Harlow lifted one foot, raking the side of it down the shin of her captor, shoving as hard and fast as she could. His hold on her loosened a tiny bit. She immediately went limp, letting her arms go up as she dropped to the floor, tucking to roll away.

"Goddamn it." Rough hands grabbed her again, fingers digging deep into her flesh. "Don't make this harder than it has to be."

Harlow tried to place the voice. It was familiar.

338

One she'd heard recently.

She grabbed at his face as the masked man tried to fight her up from the cold cement floor, digging her fingers into the eye holes cut into the knit hiding his identity.

He slammed her hard, knocking Harlow's head back against the concrete, making her see stars in the dim space.

"You are making everything real fucking difficult, Mowry." He grunted as her body lurched upward. "This is your own damn fault."

She blinked hard, trying to clear the throbbing pain muddying her thoughts. "None of this is my fault."

Not this moment. Not any of the similar ones in the past she used to be so ashamed of.

"This is *your* fault." Harlow dug her nails into the skin of his neck, doing her best to get the sharp edges through the weave of the mask covering it. "You are the dick here."

"I might be a dick, but I'm about to be a rich dick." He managed to get her up. "The price on your head is pretty fantastic."

"You can't spend money if you're dead." Harlow kicked at him again, this time missing as he dodged her foot.

"I don't plan on getting caught." He ripped open the Velcro pocket on his Alaskan-Security-issued vest, reaching in to pull out a capped syringe. "I didn't want to have to do this, but you just had to be a pain in the ass."

"No." Harlow tried to back away, pulling against the hold he had on her arm. "Don't you fucking dare."

She had no clue what was in that syringe, but it was definitely not good. Harlow yanked her arm harder as he struggled to uncap the needle with one hand. "Damn it, Mowry. Hold fucking still."

Did this piece of shit really think she wouldn't fight back?

Probably. Tod most likely told everyone how weak she was.

How terrified.

Harlow braced all her weight on one foot and swung the other with everything she had, aiming right for his dick.

The asshole willing to trade her for his soul grunted, but instead of going down his hand moved from her arm to her neck, gripping tight as she shoved her back against the wall.

"Stupid cunt." He squeezed, cold eyes leveling on hers. "I forgot to mention there's no requirement you be alive when I deliver you."

Harlow dug her fingers into his hand, trying to pry it off her throat as her body lifted higher, toes barely staying on the floor. She watched the needle in his hand, fighting for consciousness as he caught the cap between his teeth and pulled it loose.

The sharp point came toward her and she still refused to look away.

Because one quick move might catch him by surprise. Might make him lose his grip. Could give her the opportunity to...

A sudden and deafening sound stopped the next thought from coming and sent Harlow falling, dropping to the hard ground as she gasped for air.

Her ears rang, the bells screaming so loud there was nothing else.

Nothing but the need to get away.

Harlow pushed to her feet, one hand pressing to the throb in her head as she staggered a few feet down the hall, daring a glance to see how close he was.

How long she had before she had to fight again.

But the man wasn't on his feet. The betrayer of all the people she cared about most lay motionless; his body sprawled across the ground.

Harlow turned, finally catching sight of the reason she was conscious.

The person who saved her life.

Mona stared at her across the unmoving form, eyes wide, skin pale. A small pistol hung loosely from one hand. "I think I killed him."

Harlow dared a few steps toward the man, crouching down as she got closer.

Mona moved in from the opposite direction, the pistol she held lifting to point steadily at the dead man.

Harlow reached out, pinching the bottom of the mask and lifting it up, revealing the identity of the person who brought Tod to her doorstep.

"Holy shit."

CHAPTER 25

"WHAT IN THE hell is going on?" Dutch's stomach dropped as a handful of men ran down the hall past him and the rest of Rogue as they filtered into the building from the back lot.

"Got a sensor in the building registering a gunshot." Zeke barely slowed as he passed. "Somewhere in the main hall."

Dutch took off with them, turning to yell back at Brock and Wade. "Go find the girls. Make sure everyone's okay." He turned and ran, Shawn at his side, staying with Zeke as the head of Shadow led his men through the methodical clearing of the main building. The halls were empty, no sign of what might have set the sensor off.

Pierce stepped from his office. "What is the issue?"

"The sensor in this hall registered a potential shot." Zeke stepped into Pierce's office. "Did you do anything in here that might have set it off?"

"I didn't hear anything." Pierce turned to stare down the hall filled with men. "Maybe it's a malfunction."

"Or maybe someone's trying to distract us." Shawn tapped the earpiece still in his ear. "I need everyone available to sweep the buildings. High alert." His eyes lifted to Dutch, narrowing as he listened to whoever was in his ear. "Where did she go?"

Dutch's stomach dropped. "Where's Harlow?"

Shawn shook his head.

"What about Mona? Do we have eyes on her?" Pierce's tone was tight.

Shawn's gaze moved away.

Dutch had his phone out, pulling up the locator app connected to the chip on Harlow's glasses. His lungs stopped working as he waited for it to load. "It says she's right here." He spun, scanning the floor for any sign of her glasses.

But Pierce was already running, racing down the hall to the door leading to the tunnels running under the building. "I know where they are." He was a full flight of stairs ahead of Dutch, taking them two at a time as he raced deeper into the ground.

"Harlow!" Dutch's leg ached, but he pushed faster, catching up to Pierce just as they made the first turn toward the rooming building.

His heart nearly stopped beating at the sight of Harlow on the ground, a fully-geared man right beside her.

Mona swung around, pointing both hands their way, a pistol clutched tight.

Dutch nearly tripped, trying to get stopped as he reached for his own weapon, ready to do whatever it took to keep Harlow safe.

"No." Pierce swung one arm across his chest, immediately stepping in front of the woman holding them at gunpoint. "Everything is okay, Mona. Put the gun down."

"He tried to kill Harlow." Mona's voice barely shook. "He was going to do it."

"I know." Pierce stepped closer, moving slowly. "But he didn't." His tone was soft as he continued moving. "Because of you."

She sniffed, her arms slowly dropping. "I think I killed him."

"Good." Pierce gently took the gun, switching on the safety before tucking it into the back of his waistband. "That's what Zeke trained you to do."

Harlow slowly stood from where she'd been crouched, her small body swaying. Dutch ran to her, grabbing her just as she started to go down.

"I'm not passing out because I'm scared." Harlow's hands gripped the edges of his vest. "He slammed my head into the concrete." She leaned into him, her eyes closing. "Everything hurts."

"I got you." Dutch scooped her up. "I'm taking her to Eli." He tipped his head at Shawn as the team lead ran in behind Pierce. "Tell him to meet me there."

He carried her past the growing crowd of Shadow and Rogue members, and up the stairs to the medical building where Eli's clinic was located. Dutch eased onto the examining table, cradling Harlow against him as he waited for Eli.

"I fought him." Harlow's eyes barely opened to meet his. "I didn't just let him try to take me."

Dutch pushed back the dark hair falling against the side of her face. "What in the hell happened?"

"It was Bobby." She reached up to rest one palm against her forehead. "I guess I shouldn't feel bad that I didn't see it coming since you sent him to make sure we were okay while you were gone."

"I didn't send anyone to make sure you were okay." Dutch forced his hand to smooth down her hair. "All of Shadow was here. You should have been fine."

"Howard didn't get free on his own." Harlow's lips pressed to a thin line. "Shadow handed him over."

"What?" Dutch leaned down to get a better look at her pupils. "Why do you think that?"

"I don't think it." Harlow's eyes closed. "I know it. We saw it happen. Ask Eva."

Dutch looked up as Eli came in. "I think she's got a concussion."

Eli's hair was mussed and he was still in his pajamas as he came into the room. "I heard." He eyed where Harlow was tucked into Dutch's arms. "You gonna put her down so I can examine her?"

"Nope." Dutch held her a little tighter. "You can figure something out."

"Stop being a baby." Harlow leaned up, wincing as she moved. "My head hurts."

Eli carefully felt around the back of her head. "Makes sense considering the size of the lump back here." He moved to shine a light in her eyes. "You hurt anywhere else?"

Harlow pointed to her throat. "My neck." Her blue eyes lifted to Dutch, hanging for just long enough to make the knife in his chest twist.

"That son of a bitch better be dead."

Harlow held her head back as Eli gently moved his fingers along her skin. "Did you lose consciousness?"

She shook her head.

"Good." Eli straightened, grabbing a light from the counter. "Open your mouth."

Harlow did as he asked, one of her hands sliding into Dutch's as the staff physician checked the inside of her throat.

"There's some irritation, but nothing that looks like it will cause problems." Eli went back to her head, moving Harlow's hair to check the bump growing with each passing second. "The fact that this is coming out is a good thing. Better than going the other way." He let the drape of her hair fall back into place and reached into the small fridge in the corner to grab an ice pack from the freezer. "You won't be sleeping on your back for a few days, and you'll probably have a headache for a while, but that should be it." He passed the pack to Harlow. "Come back in the morning so I can see how you're doing."

She pressed the pack into place, wincing as it touched her skull. "Okay."

Eli gave her a grin. "You're way more agreeable this time."

"Sorry." She slid off Dutch's lap. "I'll try harder tomorrow."

"I look forward to it."

Harlow took two steps before suddenly lurching forward; grabbing the trash can and immediately puking into the plastic liner.

Dutch grabbed her hair, doing his best to pull all the strands away from her face and out of the way. Eli held out a stack of paper towels, waiting while Harlow wiped her mouth and tossed them into the can.

"Sorry." She sniffed. "I thought I was okay."

"You've been through a lot in the past week, Mowry. I know men here who wouldn't handle it as well as you have." Eli pulled a bottle of water from the small fridge and passed it her way. "Sometimes you've just gotta let yourself be upset about the bullshit."

"I'll keep that in mind." She tipped back a sip of water. "I'm going to go lay down before I hurl all over the floor."

"Call me if you need me." Eli pointed Dutch's way. "I'm serious."

"Thanks." Dutch tucked Harlow close into his side, holding as much of her weight as he could as they walked toward the rooming building.

Harlow leaned into him, her walk slow. "Why would Shadow just hand Howard over?"

"Is that why you wanted me to come to Eva's room?" He opened the door to the walkway where Pierce was shot. Large barricades were now set up outside to block the view of the space, making him feel slightly better about the fact that Harlow would be using this route for the foreseeable future.

Her head barely nodded where it rested against his side. "We didn't know who else we could trust."

Any other time her admission of trust would have made him smile.

"Don't let it go to your head. That was before Bobby turned out to be a traitor." She peeked up at him. "Didn't you have him camped outside my door at one point?"

"Not specifically him." Dutch opened the door at the other end of the hall, easing Harlow into the building. "Alpha was in charge of the interior." Dutch started to direct Harlow down the first-floor hall.

"I need to go see the girls." She moved away from him, heading to the stairs. "They will be worried."

"Damn it, Mowry. You've got a concussion."

"Eli didn't say that." Harlow went up the stairs surprisingly fast, forcing him to chase after her.

"You puked in his trash can. Pretty sure that's a good indicator."

Harlow knocked on Eva and Brock's door. "I'm fine."

She'd said it to him more times than he could count, and every one of them had been a lie.

Except maybe this one.

The door yanked open and Eva instantly grabbed Harlow in a hug. "Holy shit." Her voice was shaky. "What in the hell happened?"

"I figured out who the mole is." Harlow twisted her lips to one side. "Was."

Eva straightened, keeping her hands on Harlow's arms. "Are you okay?"

"I kicked him in the nuts." She smiled just a little. "And I dug my fingers into his eyeballs." Her lips flattened just a little. "But Mona shot him, so I guess she wins."

"Can I have a gun too?" Heidi peeked in behind where Eva stood. "It seems like they're real handy to have around here."

"No. No guns for you." Dutch started to back away. "We're going to go try to get some rest." He tried to pull Harlow along with him.

He just wanted to be with her. Hold her close and make up for failing her tonight.

She should have been safe, and tomorrow he would have a conversation with Zeke about what the fuck is going on.

But for now he just needed her body against his.

Harlow turned, shooting him an almost-glare. "No. We have shit to do."

"What?" Dutch looked to where Brock sat at the kitchen counter, hoping for some back-up. Brock shook his head.

Dutch dropped his gaze to the tiny woman facing him down. "What shit do you have to do?"

"We need to come up with some sort of plan, Pretty Boy." Harlow stepped into the room, leaving him in the hall.

"Ms. Ayers." Pierce's voice carried down the hall. The owner of Alaskan Security trailed behind Mona as she marched Dutch's way.

Mona stopped, spinning to face Pierce. "Now I'm Ms. Ayers again?" She stepped his way, making Pierce stop in his tracks. "I don't know what your deal is, *Mr. Barrick*, but you hired me to do a job and I plan to do it." She turned away, shoving past Dutch and going into the room where the rest of the women were huddled together.

Pierce stared at the open doorway like he expected Mona might come back.

"She's had a rough night." Dutch tipped his head Pierce's way. "I'd give her some space."

Pierce straightened. "Very well." He turned without another word and went back the way he came.

"You coming?" Harlow's eyes were on Dutch from her spot on the sofa. "I need you."

Three little words he never expected to hear from her lips.

He went into this ready to do whatever helped her get through the trauma of her past. Unfortunately, that now included the trauma of her present.

And working was how Harlow coped. It kept her mind occupied until she was in a spot where she could handle processing what happened. Taking that from her now wasn't something he could make himself do. "I'm coming, Mowry."

EPILOGUE

DUTCH RELAXED BEHIND her, his long body cradling hers in the tub they both barely fit into.

He'd given her what she needed, and now it was time to return the favor.

"This doesn't seem as hot as last time." Harlow eased deeper into the heat of the bath water.

"You're getting used to it."

"Or," she tilted her head to peek up at him, "it's not as hot as last time."

"That doesn't sound right." Dutch's arms wrapped around her as his lips came to rest against her temple. "How's your head?"

"It hurts." She shifted a little, situating the lump against the icepack tucked into the crook of Dutch's shoulder. "But not as bad."

"How about your neck?" His hand moved over her skin, sliding down her arm to catch her hand, lacing their fingers together.

"Irritated." She swallowed to confirm the mild burn was still there.

"I'll have Shawn get some sherbet."

"To go with my salt and vinegar chips?" She smiled.

"Gross." Dutch shifted a little, grabbing the body wash she used and squeezing some out onto a washcloth. "You have terrible taste in chips, Mowry."

"Good taste in men, though." She watched as he worked the soap over the skin of her shoulder and arm. "Now."

"I'm going to agree with that one." He lathered up her other arm and shoulder. "But only because it makes me look good."

"You don't need any help looking good." She leaned as Dutch carefully worked the soapy rag down her leg.

"You're getting awful generous with the compliments, Darling."

Harlow studied his face from under her lashes as he washed her. "I like when you call me that."

"Yeah?" Dutch's fingers trailed along her thigh. "I seem to remember catching hell about it."

She started to apologize, but before she could get the words out, Dutch eased her body forward. "Tip your head back."

"Why?" She twisted to see what he was doing.

"Because I want to wash the throw-up out of your hair." Dutch rubbed his palms together, working the shampoo between them into a lather. "That okay with you, ball-kicker?"

She smiled a little, turning so he could reach her hair. "I think he was wearing a cup."

"Doesn't matter much now." Dutch went quiet as he worked the lather through her hair. "I fucked up, Harlow. I thought Shadow could handle things while we were gone."

"Seems like they might have their own agenda." Harlow closed her eyes and Dutch carefully worked his way around the lump at the back of her head.

"Shadow always has their own agenda. Their relationship with the government offers Alaskan Security opportunities we wouldn't have any other way."

"You mean like body disposal?" She hadn't asked what happened to the men who kidnapped her, Eva, and Mona. Mostly because she was pretty sure she already knew.

"Like that." Dutch picked up the cup he brought in and used it to slowly pour water down her hair.

"Maybe Shadow handed Howard over to the government." Harlow straightened. "Holy shit. That's it, isn't it?" She spun toward Dutch, catching the next cup of water straight down her front.

"I'm never going to get the soap out of all this hair if you don't sit still, Darling."

"I'm right, aren't I?" She and the girls spent an hour going in circles, trying to figure out what Shadow was up to if it wasn't feeding information to the men doing their damndest to ruin her life.

"I would say you're right." Dutch made a spinning motion with one finger. "Come on. Your ass needs to get in bed."

Harlow eased a little closer, rubbing her bottom against Dutch as she did. "Maybe I'm not tired."

"You are most definitely tired." Dutch poured another cup of water down her dark hair, rinsing the last of the suds from her strands. "And the last thing your head needs is to be bounced around."

"You saying you can't do it without bouncing?" She closed her eyes as he continued rinsing her hair.

"I'm saying I'm not willing to try." He leaned in to nuzzle her neck. "But maybe tomorrow I'll be willing to revisit the possibility."

Harlow sighed. "Fine." She stayed put as Dutch stood, water sliding down his naked body.

"You're not bashful at all, are you?" He toweled off, grinning as she watched him.

"You have a nice body. If you didn't want me to look at it then you would keep it covered up."

"Good point." Dutch grabbed the other towel and held his hands out. "Come on. Let's get you out of there."

She reached up, letting him hold her steady as she stepped onto the mat beside him. "Aren't we supposed to get a suite or something?"

Dutch's brows lifted. "You want to share a suite with me?"

Harlow stood still while he dried her off. "Are the tubs bigger?"

"I doubt it." He straightened, reaching around her body to wrap the soft terry in place. "But they've got kitchens and coffee makers."

"I could maybe be persuaded then."

"I thought I was the one being persuaded?" Dutch smiled as his arms came around her.

"Don't even try to pretend you don't want to share a suite with me, Pretty Boy." She reached up to tap him on the end of the nose. "You've been trying to fall in love with me since we met." Harlow wiggled free, walking to the bathroom door with a grin on her lips.

"Mowry." Dutch's tone was sharp enough to make her turn around. "I do love you."

Her grin turned to a smile. One that she never expected to wear again.

Certainly not in Alaska.

"I know."

****

.

Printed in Great Britain
by Amazon